celg

Booking the Crook

Center Point
Large Print

Also by Laurie Cass and available from
Center Point Large Print:

Wrong Side of the Paw

**This Large Print Book carries the
Seal of Approval of N.A.V.H.**

Booking the Crook

A BOOKMOBILE CAT MYSTERY

Laurie Cass

CENTER POINT LARGE PRINT
THORNDIKE, MAINE

For all the restaurants everywhere
that cheerfully allow writers to sit in their
back corners for hours at a stretch.
With a special nod to Touch of Class
in Central Lake, Michigan. Thank you!

Chapter 1

I stood at the kitchen window, staring out into the backyard as January's chill seeped through the glass and into my bones. The cold was making my skin prickle and my teeth chatter, yet I didn't move. If I stayed, maybe time would stand still. Maybe the morning wouldn't happen. Maybe if I went back to bed and pulled the covers over my head, it would all go away.

"Minnie?" my aunt Frances asked. "What, pray tell, do you see? It's pitch dark out there."

She was right. Even though I knew the backyard contained snow-covered maple and beech trees, the only thing I could see was my own self. Whoever had installed the double-hung windows had placed them at a height that forced any five-foot-tall human—in this case, me—to either stand on tiptoes or crouch slightly to see over the top of the lower window. This morning I was standing on my toes and seeing little more than the reflection of a pair of slightly bloodshot brown eyes and too-curly black hair.

"Mrr."

I looked over at my cat. Eddie was sitting in the

kitchen chair he'd claimed as his own and licking his right front paw.

Aunt Frances laughed. "Your fuzzy friend said to sit down and eat your oatmeal." She put two bowls on the round oak table and slid into the chair across from Eddie.

"More likely he's asking about his breakfast." I gave the top of my head one last glance—still a curly mess and likely to stay that way—and sat. "You didn't have to make me breakfast."

"Don't get used to it. However, I thought it only right to commemorate this day." She dipped her spoon into the bowl and held it up in a toast. "To the new director of the Chilson District Library, whatever his name is. May his reign bring joy to all, but especially to the library's assistant director, since she's sitting across the table from me."

"Graydon," I said. "His name is Graydon Cain."

"The poor man. What were his parents thinking? I wonder what his friends call him? Gray?" She raised one eyebrow. "Don?"

"Maybe it's a family name and they call him Junior."

Aunt Frances snorted. "Surely your nimble mind has a better suggestion than that. You're not getting sick, are you?"

"If only," I muttered, but not loud enough for her to hear. When Graydon had interviewed with the library board a few months back, I'd made the event memorable by walking backward into the then-president of the board, falling to the floor, and strewing the contents of my backpack all across the lobby.

Bad as that had been, it had been far worse to have Eddie hack up a hair ball on the Italian shoes of the woman the board chose as the library's director. An early—and heavy—October snowfall had sent Jennifer scuttling back south and the board had gone to Graydon, metaphorical hat in hand, and asked him to consider making northwest lower Michigan his new home.

"Well," my aunt said reasonably, "Graydon can't be any worse than that frightful woman."

I sighed. "You'd think so, but I wouldn't have thought anyone could be worse than Stephen." My former boss, who'd had the personality of a doorstop and a deep reluctance to agree to any change in anything whatsoever, hadn't inspired deep loyalty in his staff.

"It'll be fine," Aunt Frances said comfortably. Of course, she could be comfortable about the whole thing; she hadn't had a new boss in ages. Her fall-to-spring job was as a woodworking instructor at the local community college, and the college president was in fine fettle and likely to stay that way. In summer, she opened up the big house she'd inherited from her long-passed-away husband to eight hand-picked boarders. Or rather, that's what she'd done for years and years. This summer it was all going to be different.

Most of me was thrilled about the upcoming events, but part of me had a kinship with Stephen and his dislike of change. I'd loved the boardinghouse since, starting at age twelve, my busy parents had sent me north from June to August. Every group of boarders was unique and every summer had brought new adventures. I didn't want the evening tradition of cooking marshmallows in the living room's fieldstone fireplace to end. I didn't want the bookshelf full of board games and jigsaw puzzles to be moved. I didn't want the screened porch off the dining room to sprout new furniture, and I certainly didn't want anyone to decide the wide pine-paneled walls needed to be covered with drywall and papered over with some floral print.

"Don't," my aunt said.

I looked up. "Don't what?"

"Think whatever it is you're thinking." Before I could disagree, she added, "And don't bother denying that you're thinking things you shouldn't be thinking about. If it's about that Graydon, quit worrying. If it's about this summer, quit worrying. It'll all work out, one way or another, and worrying doesn't help one bit."

"I know, but—"

"Stop," she said firmly.

Since Aunt Frances was the sanest person

I knew, and since she'd been right the other zillion times in my life when she told me to quit worrying, I said, "You're right. Again." I'd stop. Or at least try to.

"There's a reason you're my favorite niece," she said.

"I'm your only niece."

"Then isn't it wonderful that we found each other?" She grinned. And since my aunt's grins were hard to resist, I grinned back.

"Mrr!"

"Yes, Eddie," I said, patting the top of his head. "It's wonderful that I found you, too."

He glanced up at me, and I got the impression that he was mentally switching the pronouns in that sentence. Almost two years ago, on an unseasonably warm April morning, I'd skipped out on cleaning chores and instead wandered through the local cemetery, enjoying the view of the twenty-mile-long Janay Lake and the horizontal blue line of Lake Michigan just over the hills to the west. My quiet walk had been interrupted by a black-and-gray tabby cat who had materialized next to the gravesite of Alonzo Tillotson, born 1847, died 1926.

I'd assumed the cat had a home and tried to shoo him away, but he'd followed me back to town, much to the amusement of passersby. Since I'd known nothing about cats due to my father's allergies, I'd taken him to the local veterinarian, who said my new friend (a black-and-white tabby once he'd been cleaned up) was about two years old. The "Found Cat" notice I'd run in the newspaper had gone unanswered, and Eddie and I were now pals for life.

"It's going to be different, that's all," I said, letting my hand rest on Eddie's warm back.

"Different isn't necessarily bad." Aunt Frances scraped her spoon against the bottom of her bowl.

"I know. It's just . . ." I sighed.

"Going to be different." My aunt nodded. "I understand, my sweet. I really do. You're getting a new boss. Cousin Celeste is buying the boardinghouse. Otto and I are getting married in Bermuda, I'm moving across the street, and you're—" She stopped. "What *are* you doing? Have you made a decision about the houseboat?"

I shook my head. A few years ago I'd been lucky enough to have been offered the assistant director job at the Chilson District Library. The job paid what you might expect, and since housing in the summer resort town of Chilson was not what you'd call affordable, my living arrangements were, by necessity, creative.

October through April, I lived with my aunt in the rambling boardinghouse, but come May, I moved to a boat slip in Uncle Chip's Marina to spend the summer in the cutest little houseboat imaginable. But this May, someone else other than Aunt Frances was going to open the boardinghouse, and I wouldn't be moving back here in the fall, or ever again.

"I hear," my aunt said, "that Rafe is looking for wide walnut planks to do the entry floor."

"Hmm." A smile spread across my face. A few weeks earlier, I'd come to the shocking realization that Rafe Niswander—who I'd known since I was twelve years old, who infuriated me on a regular basis, who often displayed the sense of humor of a nine-year-old, and who took every opportunity to display stupidity in spite of his multiple college degrees and successful position as a middle school principal—was, in fact, the love of my life. Happily, this realization almost completely coincided with Rafe's confession that he'd been in love with me for years, and that he'd just been waiting for the right time to own up.

Which, as it turned out, was during a critical time. Rafe had spent years fixing up an old shingle-style house and his confession had occurred when he'd said he'd been renovating it for me all along, but that it was time for kitchen design decisions and he'd needed my input.

"I haven't decided," I told Aunt Frances.

"About the walnut?"

I ignored the question, which had to be rhetorical. She knew perfectly well that I had as much interest in the types of wood Rafe bought as I did in kitchen design, which was to say none.

"About selling the houseboat," I said. "If I

13

sell it, I could pay off my last student loan, but once it's gone, it's gone, like oatmeal on a snowy January morning." I reached across the table for her empty bowl. "Thank you for making breakfast. I appreciate the celebration and hope the day deserves it."

Aunt Frances watched as I carried the dishes to the sink. "Celeste sent me an e-mail last night. Shall I read it to you?"

"Yes, please." The e-mails from Celeste Glendennie, the cousin in Nevada buying the boardinghouse, were terse, choppy, informative, and often very funny. My parents claimed I'd met her at a family reunion, but I couldn't summon up a single memory.

My aunt reached out for her cell phone, which was sitting on the kitchen counter. After a few screen taps, she said, "Quoting: *Is boardinghouse one word or two? Inquiring minds want to know. Mine does, too.*" Aunt Frances put down the phone. "She's going to be here the last week of April to get started. Are you planning on being gone by then?"

"Yep."

"If I recall correctly, your houseboat doesn't have central heating. Did you ask Eddie how he feels about living in below-freezing temperatures?"

I glanced at my furry friend, who was now standing with his back feet on the seat of his chair and his front feet on the windowsill, staring at an outside that would be dark for another hour. "Rafe says the house will be done by mid-April."

Aunt Frances hooted with laughter. "And you believed him? Don't look like that, dear heart. I'm sure he thinks he's being realistic, but my money's on October."

"Can't be October," I said. "I ran into Chris the other day and Uncle Chip himself has decided it's time to update the marina. They're going to pull out all the piers and put in new ones right after Labor Day." Though Chris was part owner and manager of the marina, his great uncle was the marina's patriarch, and his wish was Chris's command.

My aunt put a hand on my shoulder. "Poor Minnie. What are you going to do with all this change being foisted upon you? How will you endure?"

"With luck and grace," I told her. "And if that can't happen, with fortitude and a smile. But even without any of that, I'll endure with—"

"Mrr."

As per usual, he was right on cue. "With Eddie."

An hour later, the outgoing library board president, octogenarian Otis Rahn, looked at me over the top of his glasses. "Now, Minnie, I have every confidence in you, but I want you to promise that this year will be a rousing success."

It wasn't easy for me to keep from doing a fidgety squirm, and I tried to forget how much I disliked making promises regarding things that were primarily out of my control and instead focused on how much I loved my job.

"Of course, Otis," I said, smiling and nodding at the two new faces.

Graydon, our new director. Trent, our new board president. Two names out of an East Coast prep school alumni directory and they had the looks to match. Both had thin faces and smooth hair cut to a professional length. Both wore slacks, jacket, and no tie—clothing completely appropriate for a formal Up North meeting in January. Both had greeted me with firm handshakes and friendly smiles.

There was no reason for me to dislike them. None whatsoever. But I would have preferred a hint of awe in their demeanor. Not at me, of course, but at our surroundings. For decades, the Chilson District Library had been stuffed into a concrete block structure that had the aesthetics of a bunker. With the magic of an easily passed millage vote, a historic—and empty—elementary school had been lovingly renovated into a building that was a point of pride for the entire community.

The architects had taken advantage of the

building's Arts and Crafts style and had revitalized its miles of interior wood trim. They'd added large square tile flooring to the lobby and wide hallways. The reading room had a fireplace and window seats. Colored metallic tiles highlighted everything from drinking fountains to directional signs. What had been the school gymnasium now housed the bulk of the library's books, with custom-made oak tables and lamps that invited people to sit and stay. Every time I walked into the building, its beauty almost took my breath away.

Even now, the view from the second-floor boardroom of picturesque downtown Chilson and Janay Lake was gorgeous. Sure, everything was covered with a fresh layer of snow and the lake was frozen, but if you lived in northwest lower Michigan year-round, your mental health depended on finding beauty in winter.

"Looking forward to working with you," Trent Ross said politely.

"Likewise," Graydon said. The only person I'd ever heard use that word in conversation was a long-ago college professor who had tried to teach me statistics, and hearing it from my new boss did not summon happy memories. "And I'm looking forward to having more meetings," he said, nodding.

Otis gazed at him. "My boy, don't make the board regret hiring you."

Graydon laughed. "I was being a bit facetious. It's this room." He nodded at the wood-paneled walls, the long corporate-looking table, and the blotters placed in front of every chair. "It makes me feel that important things are being discussed. It makes me feel dignified."

I smiled, because I felt the same way about the boardroom. Rather, I'd come to feel that way once I'd recovered from being intimidated by its atmosphere. Now that I was a mature thirty-four years old, I was over being intimidated by pretty much anyone or anything. My knee-jerk reaction regarding Graydon started to ease.

"So. Tell me about the bookmobile," Trent said, sitting back and steepling his fingers.

"Do I have a time limit?" I asked, smiling.

Otis laughed. "Minnie Hamilton can talk about the bookmobile for hours. I've heard her."

"That won't be necessary." Trent glanced at a band of electronics strapped to his wrist. "Ten minutes should be plenty."

The man was delusional. That wasn't anywhere near enough to tell the story of the bookmobile. How it got started, why it got started, its many successes, its few failures, and how we were using it to bring more outreach into the county's many rural communities, none of which had a brick-and-mortar library.

And what was his hurry, exactly? We'd been told Mr. Trent Ross was a retired attorney, recently moved up from the Chicago area. What could possibly be more important to him than learning about the bookmobile?

I tried to hitch my thoughts together into a cohesive heap. "Well, the bookmobile came about because—"

"Sorry," Trent interrupted, looking again at his wrist. "My ten o'clock appointment is early." He stood. "Minnie, it was nice meeting you. Graydon, Otis." He nodded at the men and left.

As Otis drifted into regaling Graydon with tales about past library boards and off-color stories about past board members, my thoughts drifted into worry, in spite of my recent commitment to stop doing so. The bookmobile was my pride and joy, and keeping it funded was a constant preoccupation. If the new board president was anti-bookmobile, how long would it take for the full board to start thinking like that? How long would it take them to vote it away?

I wasn't all the way into the break room when my coworkers pounced.

"What's he like?"

"Is he going to be a jerk?"

"Did he say anything about the IT budget? We really need a new server."

"How did it go?"

Ignoring the questions, I pushed through the group to get to the coffeepot. Once I had a mug full of caffeine, I started answering their questions. To Holly Terpening, a full-time clerk a few years older than myself, I said, "Graydon likes the building, so that's a good sign." To Kelsey, a part-time clerk a couple of years younger than me, I said, "He doesn't come across as a jerk," then buried my face in coffee.

Josh, our full-time IT guy, shifted from foot to foot until I came up for air. He looked so anxious that I felt a little guilty that I was about to give him the facts of life. Which at thirty-something he should have known, especially since he was now a homeowner, but perhaps he wasn't raised properly. "We didn't talk about budgets or major purchases. They weren't even mentioned."

I shut my ears to his moan of pain and turned to Donna. I still couldn't decide who I wanted to be most like when I grew up; right now it was a tie between Aunt Frances and Donna, who at seventy-two was working part-time at the library to support her habits of running marathons all over the country and snowshoeing in faraway mountain lands after being dropped off by a helicopter. "You asked how it went. Well . . ." I took a sip of coffee. Then another one.

The previous library director, Jennifer Walker, had been universally disliked. Though I'd tried valiantly to refrain from criticizing her during her short stay, I hadn't always been successful. I wasn't proud of that behavior, and since I was always trying to learn from my mistakes, I framed my response to Donna carefully.

I wasn't about to lie—not only did I think lying was unethical, immoral, and just plain wrong, but quality fibbing required a prodigious memory, a trait that had not yet emerged in my character—so the truth was my only option. However, there was no reason to tell the whole truth.

"Graydon," I said, "seems to be an all-around decent guy. He's from Grand Rapids, and he's spent a lot of time Up North over the years. Not just in the summer," I said, forestalling a typical comment from locals regarding downstaters, "because he and his family like to ski."

Chilson was one of those small towns that was full to bursting from Memorial Day to Labor Day with tourists and summer people up to their lakefront cottages. Old money had come up the Lake Michigan shore on steamers to escape the Chicago heat, and new money was still building houses everywhere else. Tourists included everyone imaginable, and in summer you could see just about anyone on the street, from your third grade teacher to the owner of the biggest tech company in the world.

In winter, though, things were different. Winter was when some restaurants and retail stores closed down completely, because there was no reason to stay open for the two people who might wander in.

On the plus side, winter in Chilson was when you never had to wait in line anywhere for anything. It was when there was never any problem finding a parking space. And when, if your car happened to slide in a ditch, the next car going past would stop and help you get out. Yes, winter was snowy and cold, but it was also full of friends. It was almost a pity that Jennifer hadn't stayed long enough to understand that.

"Good," Donna said. "So Graydon has potential to not be a total disaster. How about Trent?"

I'd felt the question coming, so I'd buried my face in my coffee mug to give me more time. Two swallows later, I was ready. "It seemed like Trent and Graydon have a lot in common." Their commonality might be surficial, but if I kept talking, odds were good that no one would ask for details. "Trent is an Up North newbie, and it seems like he wants to get involved and help make us even better."

Holly and Josh grinned and bumped knuckles, but Donna gave me a searching look, and I remembered that she had years of experience working with boards of various shapes and sizes.

"Good morning!" Lloyd Goodwin shuffled in the door. Mr. Goodwin was in his late seventies, and if we'd been allowed to have favorite patrons, he would have been in everyone's top five. Full of good humor and friendlier than a puppy, Mr. Goodwin had a self-professed medical need for morning coffee, and because of this, we'd opened up the staff break room to library patrons. The only bad thing was that Mr. Goodwin and Kelsey both liked coffee brewed strong enough to burn your stomach lining—some mornings it was a race to the coffee grounds.

Mr. Goodwin received a chorus of return "good mornings." He nodded at everyone and asked, "Do you folks know how to keep Canadian bacon from curling? No?" He smiled. "It's easy. Take their little brooms away."

A half second of silence was followed by multiple laughing groans, and I took the opportunity to sketch a smiling wave and head out. It was bookmobile time.

Fresh-fallen snow blanketed the world. In Chilson there'd been barely an inch of fresh white stuff, but in this part of Tonedagana County at least six inches had come down overnight. I smiled at the sight. New snow transformed the world. Yesterday's line of dark green cedar trees was now a bumpy white row. The dirty rawness of a local gravel pit had been magicked into a soft hole. And that little five-acre lake was now a field of white. If you didn't know there was a lake under there, would you know there was a lake under there?

"Don't tell me you're smiling at the snow," Julia said.

"Mrr," Eddie said in a way that sounded like a Julia echo.

I glanced at the passenger's side of the bookmobile. My part-time bookmobile clerk was, as per usual, resting her feet on Eddie's strapped-down cat carrier. Eddie was flopped against the carrier's door, his black-and-white fur sticking out through the wire in square sections. "The snow likes it when we smile." I'd texted basically the same thing to Rafe when I was working through the bookmobile's preflight checklist, and he'd sent back a tiny, one-second cartoon of a stick figure's head exploding into falling snow. I didn't know exactly what message he'd been trying to send, but I'd decided to assume kindly humor.

Julia snorted, connoting in that one short noise disbelief and a bit of derision that was covered up with humor. It was a lot to convey with a snort, but if needed, she could have troweled on three additional messages.

Though Julia had been born and raised in Chilson, she'd moved to the big lights of New York City before the ink dried on her high school diploma. She'd intended to find fame and fortune as a model, which hadn't worked out, so she'd tried her hand at theater. This had worked out far better—as it turned out, she oozed acting talent and had more than one Tony Award to show for it.

At a certain age, however, offers for leading roles tend to slow to a trickle, even for the best of actors. Just before that happened, Julia and her husband moved back to her hometown, where she had too much time on her hands until the bookmobile came along. Now she and her storytelling abilities were woven into the fabric of the bookmobile as much as Eddie's hairs were.

"Everyone needs a smile now and then," I said. "Even the snow."

"Snow is not a sentient being."

"Maybe. But what if it was? What if it had feelings? Thoughts and dreams for a better future?"

"Mrr."

Julia tucked her long strawberry blond hair behind her ears and gently tapped the top of Eddie's carrier with one heel. "I'm pretty sure he said you're loony tunes and shouldn't be allowed out in public."

"I'm pretty sure he said you should stop pounding on his roof."

When I'd hired Julia, Eddie's presence on the bookmobile had been a deep, dark secret I'd been trying to keep from Stephen, my then-boss. Eddie had been a stowaway on the vehicle's maiden voyage, and I'd intended it to be a one-time deal until Eddie's absence on the following trip had caused the lower lip of Brynn, a young girl with leukemia, to tremble.

There was no way I could deal with her tears, so Eddie had been installed as a permanent passenger. Soon after, the doctors had declared that Brynn's cancer was in remission, something that Brynn's mother tended to give Eddie credit for. Now everyone knew the bookmobile cat, and I was pretty sure more people knew his name than mine.

Julia leaned forward against her seat belt's shoulder strap. "Which of us is right, Mr. Edward? Please indicate with a point of your elegant white-tipped paw."

Eddie yawned and rolled into an Eddie-size ball, tucking all four of his paws underneath him.

I laughed. That Julia played along with my game of talking to Eddie as if he were fluent in the English language was one of the reasons I hoped she'd work with me forever. "Last stop of the day," I said, and took a right turn into a convenience store parking lot, which I was glad to see had been plowed clean of snow.

The day hadn't been a stellar one, as far as the number of patrons went. Though the main roads had all been plowed by the time we were traveling them, many of the side roads were not, and people didn't tend to make optional trips on unplowed roads, even with four-wheel drive. The few people who had come aboard, though, stayed long and borrowed much, which pleased my librarian's soul to the core.

I parked and we quickly went through the preparations. Unlatch Eddie's cage, rotate the driver's seat to face a small desk, turn on the two laptop computers, release the bungee cord that kept the office chair in the back in place, and ensure that no books, DVDs, jigsaw puzzles, or our most recent loan item of ice fishing poles had jostled out of place.

Eddie took part by jumping onto the dashboard, his current favorite spot. This meant I would later be cleaning paw prints off the dash and nose prints off the inside of the windshield and my arms weren't long enough to do it easily, but doing the cleaning was far easier than getting Eddie to change his mind.

"Think we'll have anyone show up?" Julia asked.

"Rowan," I said. "Thanks to her son, she recently discovered that she likes fantasy. I have a stack of Tad Williams and Ursula K. Le Guin books waiting."

Julia made a face at Rowan's name but didn't say anything.

I knew many people found Rowan Bennethum unfriendly and abrasive, but I tended to find her dryly dark comments funny. Rowan had become a dependable bookmobile patron since last summer when she'd started working from home three days a week. She was a loan officer for the local bank and, thanks to computer magic, had convinced the higher-ups that not only would she get more done at home, but it would be even more secure.

Julia, in her early sixties, was about fifteen years older than Rowan, so her animosity couldn't be due to high school rivalries. And as far as I knew, they weren't related. I looked up from the daily chore of picking Eddie hair off the long carpeted riser that served as both sitting area and a step to reach the top shelves. Vertically inflated people, such as Julia, didn't need the step, but vertically efficient people such as myself found it very helpful.

"Why don't you like her?" I asked.

After a moment, Julia said, "Personality conflict."

I was about to drill down and get a real answer out of her when I realized the dashboard was feline-free. "Have you seen Eddie?"

Julia glanced around. "He was here a second ago."

Cats had an amazing ability to compact themselves into half the volume they should reasonably occupy. I'd found Eddie in places a small squirrel shouldn't have been able to fit into, including the thin space underneath my dresser and out a window when the window was open maybe two inches.

There weren't many places he could hide on the bookmobile, but even still, it took us a few minutes to find him tucked behind the 200–400 shelf of nonfiction books.

"What are you doing back there?" I peered at him. His yellow eyes blinked back. "Do you have any intention of ever coming out?" I fully expected to get a "Mrr" in reply, but he was silent. "Are you feeling okay, little buddy?"

"What did he say?" Julia asked.

"Nothing." I reached in and petted him, expecting to feel a purr, and got nothing.

"He's not sick, is he?"

"Probably he's just tired. He only got twelve hours of sleep last night."

Julia laughed. "The poor thing."

"Yes, he needs his beauty rest." I gave him one last pet. "I'm sure he'll be fine with some sleep."

But at the end of the stop, he still hadn't moved. The few bookmobilers who'd shown up couldn't entice him out to say hello, not even the five-year-old boy who jangled Eddie's treat can. "He won't come out," the kid said. "Can you get him for me, Miss Minnie?"

Since Eddie still had his claws, I had no intention of doing anything remotely like that. "Our Eddie is feeling a little sick." I took the can of treats away from the child. "When you're sick, you stay home and sleep, right? Eddie likes to sleep behind books when he's not feeling well."

"He's going to get better, isn't he?"

"You bet." I smiled at the boy. "He has a little kitty cold, that's all."

But I was concerned. This was not Eddie-like behavior. I'd never known him to have anything other than the occasional sneeze. As we closed up the computers, a low guttural whine issued from behind the nonfiction section.

"Something isn't right," I said to myself. But more than one thing wasn't right, I realized. I looked at the stack of fantasy novels I'd specially selected for today. "Rowan never showed up."

"She probably got busy and forgot," Julia said.

Could be. But that wasn't like Rowan. The only time she hadn't shown up for her bookmobile stop was last fall, when she'd been downstate for a conference. She'd told me well in advance, and when she'd mentioned that she needed someone to water her plants, I'd volunteered, and now a tiny part of my brain was permanently stuck with the knowledge of the keyless entry code to her house.

It wasn't like Rowan to order books and then ignore them. Not like her at all.

I looked at Eddie's shelf, looked at Rowan's books, and came to a decision. "Let's go," I said abruptly.

Julia, who'd been securing the rear chair, looked up. "That didn't sound like the normal homeward-bound announcement."

I pulled a suddenly willing Eddie out from behind the books. "We're going to Rowan's house."

"Minnie—"

"It'll only take a few minutes," I said, cutting into her objection before it could get started. "And don't tell her I told you, but Rowan has some sort of heart issue. She takes medication, but still." I'd discovered this by accident, when I'd run into Rowan at the pharmacy a month or two ago, and she'd been discussing side effects of the medication with the pharmacist.

Julia's chin took on an obstinate stance as we buckled up. "Isn't this taking outreach a little far?"

Since I was captain of the ship, I could have ignored the question, but since I liked to have the support of my troops, I said, "Just a quick stop. It's barely out of our way."

This was true and Julia knew it, so she refrained from further comment on the subject. Actually, she refrained from any comment at all, something almost as unusual as Eddie refraining from snoring in the middle of the night. I glanced over a few times on the short drive, but each time Julia was studying the scenery out the passenger window with a concentration that telegraphed a clear message that she didn't want to talk.

I sighed. Julia's dislike of Rowan was deeper than I'd realized. And after dropping off Rowan's books, I'd have to find out why. I did not want to have a mysterious issue hovering in the air between us.

By the time we were approaching Rowan's house, I'd come to the conclusion that Julia was right, that I was going overboard. But with snow piled up on the sides of the road, there was no good spot on this stretch of road to turn the thirty-one-foot bookmobile around, so we were committed.

I was rehearsing both my delivery speech to Rowan ("Ding dong, bookmobile calling") and my apology speech to Julia ("You were right, I was wrong, and I'm sorry") when Julia sucked in a sharp breath.

My mouth opened to ask if she was okay, but what came out instead of a question was my own gasp.

"No, no, no . . ." I stammered, staring wide-eyed at the shape lying in Rowan's driveway. The long, person-size shape.

I'd already started braking, but Julia was flying out the door and into the snow before the wheels stopped turning. Eddie's howls rose as I set the parking brake and took off after my coworker.

We'd both taken multiple first aid courses and the training kicked into gear. Julia turned Rowan onto her back and checked for a pulse. She shook her head, unzipped Rowan's winter coat, and started chest compressions. By the time I was on my knees next to Rowan, I'd already pulled out my phone and dialed 911.

"Emergency dispatch," came the welcome voice. "Where is your emergency?"

I gave the location, then said, "We need an ambulance right away. She fell in the snow. We don't know how long she was here. She doesn't have a pulse. She doesn't have a pulse, she doesn't—" I heard the panic in my voice, stopped, then started again. "She's in her driveway, she has a history of heart problems, and I'm afraid that . . . please . . ." I was holding the phone so hard it hurt, but I didn't want to loosen my grip. If anything, I wanted to grip even harder, so help would arrive faster.

"We're sending an ambulance right now, ma'am," said the dispatcher calmly. "They should be there in less than ten minutes."

"Stay. Alive," Julia gasped out, the words coming out in time with the compressions. "Stay. Alive."

"Are you able to perform CPR?" the dispatcher asked.

"Doing it," I said. "Is there anything else we can do to help?" I looked around wildly, not sure what I was looking for. "There's a snow shovel," I said. "She must have been shoveling her driveway."

"Yes, ma'am," the dispatcher said. She asked about visible cuts and bruises, and I'm sure I answered her, but my attention was on Rowan and Julia.

"Stay. Alive." Julia was still talking. "You turned. Down my. Sister's. Second. Mortgage. She lost. Her house. But don't. Die. Don't. Die."

I stared at Julia. No wonder she didn't like Rowan. But here she was, doing her best to make sure a woman she had good reason to hate survived a heart attack. My throat tightened and I leaned forward, hands flat and ready. "My turn," I said, and started compressions as Julia pulled away and sat back on her heels.

We knelt there, switching back and forth, until the ambulance arrived. The EMTs hurried out and took over. In seconds, Rowan was in a gurney with a uniformed EMT walking alongside doing compressions. Then she was inside, the back door shut, and they were off with lights flashing and siren blaring.

"She's not going to make it, is she?" Julia asked quietly.

I watched the taillights of the ambulance recede into the distance. "No. She's not."

Chapter 2

That night I sat on a stool in Rafe's dining room. Or what would eventually be a dining room. Right now it was partly a room where he was installing crown and floor molding, but mostly it was a storage room for his boxes of stuff. The boxes migrated as he went through renovation phases, and I'd lost count of how many times he'd moved his belongings from one room to another. Why he hadn't rented a storage unit, or at least moved them to a room he'd declared as renovation-free, I had no idea.

And what any of the boxes held, I was pretty sure he had no idea about that, either, because when he'd moved into the house last summer, there hadn't been a concerted labeling effort when he'd packed his apartment. The box at which I was staring was a prime example. The only indication of its insides were two words written in Rafe's distinctive scrawl: "Heavy Stuff." A half hour earlier, when I'd walked in with dinner, I'd seen the box and asked him what might be inside. He'd said, "Not sure. Could be anything from books to free weights. When we open them it's going to be like Christmas." At that point, he'd grinned and slapped his flat stomach. "Hope there's food inside some of them. Nothing like a two-year-old bag of potato chips to take the edge off."

That had been when I'd started crying. His look of shock was quickly replaced with concern. He'd immediately taken me in his arms and hugged me tight. "Minnie. Sweetheart. Holder of my happiness. What's the matter? Just give me the word and I'll do whatever it takes to fix it. Climb mountains. Slay lions. I'll even drive downstate and get you those doughnuts you like so much."

His nonsense made me cry even harder, but my tears eventually dried up and I pulled away. "Sorry about your shirt," I'd said, wiping my eyes with a napkin I'd brought from Fat Boys Pizza and blowing my nose with another one.

He didn't even look at the vast wet splotches. "It'll wash. What's wrong?"

On some deep level, I recognized how much I loved this man, and how lucky I was that he loved me back. The rest of me was filled with sadness for what had happened that afternoon. I'd started texting him about Rowan half a dozen times, but I'd always put the phone away before hitting Send, not knowing what to say, figuring I'd tell him in person. And now that time was here.

By the time Rafe had finished eating, I'd finished the story, which ended with me stopping at the Charlevoix Hospital and getting confirmation that Rowan had indeed died. I'd tracked down an emergency room nurse that I knew and wheedled out a little more information, primarily that Rowan had most likely been dead long before Julia and I had arrived.

"But that doesn't make you feel any better, does it?" Rafe had asked.

I'd shaken my head.

"Eat something," he'd told me. "You probably don't think you're hungry, but just try eating, okay?"

Two pieces of pizza and three breadsticks later, I was feeling better. Part of which could be attributed to the massive amount of carbohydrates I'd just ingested, but a full stomach on top of the comfort Rafe had given me was edging me from shocked grief to a dull sadness that only time would ease.

Rafe was now up on a ladder with a putty knife and a can of wood filler. I spent a few minutes admiring the way his broad shoulders tapered to his waist, but since it wouldn't do to inflate his ego, I asked the obvious question. "Why are you bothering to fill nail holes that are too small to see?"

"Minnie, Minnie, Minnie." His sigh was dramatic and overwrought, nearly Julia quality.

"Haven't you learned the first rule of home improvement?"

Was he kidding? "I know all of those rules. Number one: It'll take forever. Number two: Anything you do will cost half again as much as you think it will. Number three: Nothing is ever delivered on time. Number four is—"

Rafe's voice cut through my recitation. Which was too bad because I could have continued for a long time. "Once again, you have not been paying attention to all that I have been teaching you."

He was partly right, but not completely. "I know that measuring twice and cutting once is more than just an aphorism. And," I said proudly, "I know the difference between flat, Phillips, and offset screwdrivers."

"The first rule of home improvement," Rafe said, ignoring me, "is to hide things."

I frowned. "What exactly are you hiding? There's no room up there to hide anything."

"Mistakes." Rafe peered at his handiwork, added a microscopic amount of putty, and peered again. "You have to cover up your mistakes completely or you'll be staring at them the rest of your life wishing you'd done a better job."

"Better?" I asked in disbelief. "I've lost track of the things you've ripped out and reinstalled because they weren't quite right. How could anything in this place be less than perfect?"

He gave the crown molding one last critical glance and came down the ladder.

That he hadn't replied to my comment was an unusual occurrence, but there was also a suddenly odd feel to the silence in the room.

A silence that was weighted down with . . . something. The back of Rafe's head wasn't giving out any clues, so I started thinking about what I'd said. Started thinking about changes he'd made to the house while my best friend Kristen and I had rolled our eyes about his indecisiveness. Thought about the times he'd asked my opinion about paint colors. Thought about last October, when Rafe told me he'd been renovating the house for me all along. The conclusion was stunningly obvious.

"You kept making changes," I said slowly, "because you wanted me to be part of the renovation."

"For someone who's really smart, you can be pretty stupid sometimes." He grinned sideways at me, his teeth white against skin that was an attractive reddish brown color, thanks to some key Native American Anishinaabe ancestors, the same ancestors that had bestowed upon him thick black hair. "I should write up a change order invoice and send it to you."

"I'd love to see that."

He stopped moving the ladder and turned. "You would?"

"Absolutely. I'll have it framed. We can hang it right over there." I pointed to a blank spot. "It'll look great next to the portrait of Eddie."

"Nice to hear you getting into the spirit of decorating." Rafe slathered more wood putty on the knife. "But I'd rather hear you make a decision about hardware for the kitchen cabinets."

"I don't like to rush these kinds of decisions. What we need is research." I hopped off my stool and pulled a book out of my backpack. Hopping back up, I said, "What I have here, courtesy of your local library, is a history of kitchens that I will be happy to read to you. Shall we start with the preface, or the first chapter?"

"How about we start with the section on cabinet hardware?"

Smiling brightly, I said, "The preface it is and I completely agree with that opinion. The author wrote it for a reason and we need to find out what it is." Disregarding what sounded like a bleat of despair from my beloved, I started to read.

When I got back to the boardinghouse, Aunt Frances was lying on a living room couch, looking very comfortable. The blanket over my aunt's legs was covered with Eddie and Eddie fur. A fire was crackling merrily, and the book she was reading, *Why We Run*, by Bernd Heinrich, was opened at the halfway point. My aunt, who was active throughout the day, had never

40

understood the point of formal exercise. She did, however, have an odd interest in ultraendurance, and had crowed with pleasure when I'd brought the book home from the library.

After my coat and boots were stowed away, I flopped on the opposite couch. "Want to know how he finishes the race?"

Still focused on her reading, she said, "Tell me and you die."

I didn't say anything, and she glanced up and immediately put the book aside. "What's the matter, dear heart?"

The tears that had been absorbed into Rafe's shirt must have been my allotment for the day, so I was able to tell the story of Rowan Bennethum's death with only a couple of sniffles.

"It's so sad," I finished, blowing my nose with a tissue. The nose-blowing was hampered somewhat by Eddie, who'd heaved himself off my aunt's lap and trundled over to mine. His purrs were so loud that I could feel them in my inner ear. "Neil's going to be lost without his wife," I said, "and the twins have lost their mother forever. Yes, they're in college and don't need her like little kids would, but it's still going to be hard."

Aunt Frances eyed me. "You're not blaming yourself, are you?"

"No." I laid my hand on Eddie's back. "She was gone before we got there, so—" I stopped.

"If we'd arrived earlier. If I hadn't waited until the end of the bookmobile stop. If—"

"Stop." My aunt got up and came over to sit next to me. "Don't go there. Don't you dare go there. Your overdeveloped sense of guilt may lead you in that direction, but you are not responsible."

"Mrr," Eddie said, twisting his head around to glare at me.

I smiled faintly. "It seems to be unanimous."

"We can widen the sample if you'd like." Aunt Frances gave me a quick hug. "I can call Rafe. Then I'll call your parents. Your brother and sister-in-law. Kristen and your college room-mates and everyone at the library. They'll all say the same thing. It wasn't your fault. And I'm willing to bet if the tables were turned, you'd say the same thing to me."

"Probably," I murmured. Then, after thinking about it for a moment, I said, "You're right. I would tell you that."

"Then it's settled." She gave me a quick hug, patted Eddie's head, and went back to her couch. "No more guilt. Yes, Rowan's death was a shock, but you did everything you could."

"Yes, ma'am." I saluted her.

"Quit that." She tucked the blanket around her legs. "Now you can ask about my day."

I blinked. It was a very un-Aunt-Frances-like statement. If she had something to tell me, she simply told me. "How was your day?"

"The classroom was fine. There's nothing like the combination of power tools and nineteen-year-olds to get the blood flowing. It's the other stuff that makes me want to pull my hair out."

My aunt's hair looked fine, so whatever it was couldn't be too horrible. "What kind of things?"

She slumped down. "Wedding stuff," she said darkly.

I let out a breath I hadn't known I was holding. Wedding problems were solvable, and my aunt's wedding problems were ones for me, the maid of honor, to deal with. I sat up and put my shoulders back. If I listened carefully, I might be able to hear the *William Tell* Overture, a clear indication that someone was riding in to save the day. "Any particular issue, or just in general?"

Aunt Frances sighed and slid a few inches farther down. If I squinted a little, I saw her as she might have looked forty-five years ago in the throes of teenage angst.

"It's not the wedding so much as the guests." She crossed her arms and dropped her chin to her chest. "Makes me think we should have just walked to the county building and been married by the magistrate."

That ship, however, had sailed months ago. She and Otto, who bore a strong resemblance to Paul Newman, had told oodles of people about their plans for a destination wedding. If they changed their minds at this point, they'd be opening themselves up to the public censure a small town could deal out. Aunt Frances would shrug it off, but she and I both knew that Otto, a newcomer, was still figuring out how to fit into the fabric of Chilson life. A sudden change in wedding plans would not help.

"What's wrong with the guests?" I'd helped my aunt and Otto put together the list and it wasn't very long, which was part of the point of having a destination wedding in the first place. "Is anyone complaining about having to go to Bermuda?"

The hotel they'd chosen was reasonably priced. And Otto, who was retired but had been a very successful accountant, was subsidizing the cost of the airfare for a few people, myself included. (I'd protested, but not very loudly.)

"It's not the guests we invited," Aunt Frances said. "It's the ones we didn't. Two teachers at the college asked when their invitations would show up. When we were in Harbor Springs the other day, getting sandwiches at Gurney's, we ran into my bridge partners from thirty years ago, who wanted to know about their invites. And a few minutes ago, I got an e-mail from an old high school friend who'd heard about the wedding and wanted to know the date so she could make her plans!" she almost wailed.

I slid Eddie off my lap and went over to the other couch. I put an arm around my aunt. "There, there," I said soothingly. My aunt Frances was the most unflappable person I'd ever met. To see her like this was wholly unexpected.

"You think this is funny, don't you?" she asked.

I could not tell a lie. "A little."

"Please don't tell Kristen," Aunt Frances said.

My best friend, Kristen Jurek, was a force of nature and was in the middle of planning her own wedding. I was her maid of honor, too, but Kristen was in Key West for the winter and to date my involvement had been limited to confirming Kristen's choices. "Scout's honor," I promised, making the official salute.

"Excellent." My aunt pushed herself up. "Having her know I've gone all bridezilla is not something I want to live down."

"You're as likely to be a bridezilla as Eddie is to stop shedding hair. This is your wedding and you have every right to make your own guest list. You two wanted a destination wedding and a small group of friends and relatives attending. It's your dream and you need to hold fast to it."

Aunt Frances looked around. "Where's the soundtrack? That speech should have been scored with harps and violins."

I shook my head. "Trombones and trumpets."

"No arguments," she said severely. "I am the bride, remember?"

"Mrr," my cat said.

"See? Eddie agrees with me."

"He would," I muttered, but on the inside I was

smiling, because my aunt's dark mood had lifted. There was no way that I was going to sleep well because I'd keep reliving that afternoon's eternal minutes of kneeling in the snow, but at least Aunt Frances had a good shot at it.

The following week I was in my office, staring bleary-eyed at an article I was writing for the library's newsletter. Or, more accurately, trying to write. Every sentence I wrote looked stupid, boring, or both. Mostly both.

Frustrated, I banged my computer's mouse on the desk.

"Problems?" asked a male voice.

"Only with my brain," I said, looking up in surprise. "To what do I owe the honor?"

The tall man standing in the doorway was none other than Detective Hal Inwood of the Tonedagana County Sheriff's Office. He was the only fully certified detective the sheriff had at the moment, and the number of hours he worked was showing. He'd retired from a job downstate for a large metropolitan police force and moved north, only to find himself with too much time on his hands. Now he had the opposite problem and the sheriff was doing all she could to keep him happy. Deputy Ash Wolverson, my former boyfriend, was training to become the county's second detective, but he had almost a year to go. I hoped Hal made it that long.

"Do you have a few minutes?" Hal asked.

"Um, sure." I stood, picked a towering stack of books and papers up off the guest chair, and dropped them on the floor, where they'd probably stay until spring. "All yours."

Inwood sat, his long arms and legs folding themselves tidily. "What are you working on?" He nodded at my computer.

I stared at him. In my experience, Hal Inwood was not a small talk kind of guy. It was possible that he had a bet with his coworkers regarding who could talk the least during an investigation, but it was also possible he believed that people were allotted only so many words in a lifetime and he was conserving his for the important things, like ordering pizza and yelling at the television when plotlines went stupid.

"It's an article for the library newsletter," I said.

"About what?"

"Why the board made changes to the public computer use policy." I glanced at the two sentences I'd written. Yup. Still boring. "They want to make sure people know the library is considered a limited public forum."

He made a *hmph*-ing sort of noise. "No wonder you're having trouble. Why aren't you writing about what's-his-name, the new director?"

Inwood knew about our new boss? Wonders never ceased. "Graydon's doing that himself."

"And you get stuck with the boring article."

Without his face actually smiling, he gave the impression of having smiled. "Guess that's what happens when you're assistant director and not top dog."

My chin went up. Our relationship, which had started with me accusing him of not doing his job and him telling me to stick to the library, had improved over time, but it could also regress.

Besides, if I'd wanted to be director, I most likely could have been. The sticking point had been if I'd moved up to the director's office on the second floor, there was no way for me to stay on the bookmobile. Though my coworkers had questioned my choice to keep my far lower salary with its heap of routine tasks, I hadn't regretted the decision for a moment. There was no way for Hal Inwood to know that, but it was also none of his business.

I folded my hands on top of my desk. "What can I do for you, Detective?" I asked politely.

His shoulders slumped a bit, and just for a moment, he reminded me of Aunt Frances. About the same age, both tall with long arms and legs, and both, within a twenty-four-hour period, acting out of character. "This morning I got the final report on Rowan Bennethum's autopsy, and considering your involvement with the incident, the sheriff thought I should give you this news in person."

"Okay," I said slowly.

He sighed. "The results were accompanied by a toxicology report. A targeted report. The full report will be another week or two, depending on the labs."

I was starting to get a bad feeling about this. "Just tell me," I said.

"Ms. Bennethum's death wasn't the result of heart issues."

"It . . . wasn't?" The inside of my mouth was dry and the words came out raw and scratchy.

Detective Inwood shook his head. "Her system was full of stimulants, medications that weren't prescribed to her and weren't found in her home. Rowan Bennethum was poisoned."

Poisoned? The word rolled around in the air, waiting for me to catch it and understand, but before my brain got itself under control, Inwood said it flat out.

"She was murdered."

Chapter 3

After Detective Inwood left, I stood and went to my office window. Outside, it was one of those thick cloud cover days, when it felt like the sun had never gotten completely out of bed. Though it was almost noon, the daylight was so meager that the parking lot lights had turned on, which made the dim light seem even worse.

I leaned my forehead against the cool glass. "She was murdered," I whispered.

Someone had intentionally killed the mother of two wonderful young adults. Someone had taken the life of a loving wife. Had destroyed a family, and done who knew what damage to a neighborhood, friends, extended family, and coworkers. The ripple effects could go far. I could almost see them in the falling snow. If one flake was blown north, it would knock into an adjacent flake, which would knock into its adjacent flake. The pattern could be endless.

Well, almost. I hadn't retained much from high school physics, but I did remember that friction played a factor in pretty much everything. Ripple effects, even on a completely flat lake, eventually phased back to a flat surface, as if nothing had ever happened.

But that was physics, and I could easily imagine the ripples of murder going on forever. One or both of the twins could spiral down into—

No.

I stepped back from the window and stood up straight. No good came out of that line of thinking, so I needed to stop. What I needed was a little bit of caffeine and a hefty dose of camaraderie from my fellow staff members.

With my favorite mug in hand, one I'd picked up at an Association of Bookmobile and Outreach Services conference, I made my way to the break room. I'd hoped to talk to either Holly or Donna, but Josh was the only one there.

"Hey," he said. Or at least that's what I assumed he said, because his face was buried in a sandwich and his mouth was full. Holly, if she'd been there, would have pointed out that it was rude to talk with his mouth full, but I just said, "Hey," back, and made a direct line for the coffeepot. "What's lunch today?"

After Josh had bought his first house last year, many of his habits had changed. Formerly a vending machine soda and take-out lunch guy, he'd shifted to using the library's coffee for his caffeine intake and bringing a brown bag lunch. And he'd started spending time with the library's generous selection of cookbooks. It was all very unexpected for a computer guy, and Holly was still wondering who had flipped what switch inside him.

Josh eyed his sandwich. "Not much. Chicken I heated up in the microwave and put on that bread. You know, the one that starts with an F? Plus some baby spinach, a little bit of pesto, and Swiss cheese."

"Did you happen to make an extra one? That sounds really good."

He took another bite. "Bring your own lunch."

I had, but my peanut butter and jelly suddenly didn't sound very appealing. The news about Rowan might have had something to do with my loss of appetite, but usually the will of my stomach was stronger than that of my emotions. Or my brain.

With a longing look at Josh's meal, I took my sad little sandwich out of the refrigerator and sat across from him. I had no desire to discuss Hal Inwood's visit, so just in case Josh had seen him in my office, I preempted the conversation. "What do you think about Graydon?"

Josh shrugged. "Seems okay."

"Really?"

He swallowed. "You sound surprised."

"Well, your disapproval rate of the last two directors was roughly one hundred percent."

"You make it sound like I was the only one," Josh said. "Everybody hated Jennifer, and she doesn't count since she was barely here long enough to do laundry. And Stephen was such a tool. Maybe he kept the library in decent financial shape, but that was the only good thing about him."

"Sure, but two weeks ago you were all doom and gloom about having to break in a new director."

"Yeah, well." He shrugged again. "Graydon could be okay. It seemed like he was really listening when I explained the reasons we needed a new server. It's the new board president, Trent What's-his-name, that's making me wonder."

"Ross," I said. "His last name is Ross. Makes you wonder about what?"

"Oh. Well." He shoved the last of his sandwich in his mouth, then held up a finger.

His sudden concern about etiquette tweaked my radar. "Wonder about what?" I asked again, putting my sandwich down on the table and staring him down.

He got up to rip a sheet of paper towel off the roll and wipe his mouth. "Holly told me not to tell you, but I think you should know."

"Know what?" This time my question came out a little loud. "If you don't tell me now, I'll keep bugging you until you do, so you might as well save us both some serious time and energy and talk."

"Don't tell Holly I told, okay?"

I kept my eye roll internal. Sometimes those two acted more like sister and brother than coworkers. "Promise."

"When you've been out on bookmobile runs, Trent has been in here asking questions. He's been talking to staff, members of the Friends of the Library, people in the reading room. Everybody."

It was a little weird, but maybe he was just trying to learn about the library, about the community, about the wants, needs, and desires of the staff. If you looked at it that way, Trent's actions were commendable, and I told Josh so.

"Yeah? Would you say that if almost all his questions were about the bookmobile?"

"About . . ." I didn't finish the sentence. Couldn't, really.

"You heard me. Our bookmobile." He sounded angry, but I knew he wasn't mad at me. "It doesn't sound good."

"It'll be fine," I said. "Trent's new. He's asking questions to understand, that's all."

But Josh wasn't reassured, and neither was I.

"He said *what?*"

On the computer screen, Kristen's eyes went wide. My best friend spent April through October in Chilson, as owner and manager of Three Seasons, one of the best restaurants in the region, but in November she lit out for Key

West, where she divided her time between lying in a hammock and tending bar. Well, that used to be her schedule. This winter she'd flown up to New York City a few times for the same reason her Key West days had been occasionally interrupted, a reason otherwise known as Scruffy Gronkowski.

The ironic label of Scruffy had been bestowed upon him in his clean-cut childhood by his father, the well-known Manhattan-based television chef Trock Farrand (not his real name). The expansive and larger-than-life Trock owned a summer place near Chilson, and due to an odd set of circumstances, we'd become good friends. A spin-off of this was the engagement of his son and my best friend, and every time Trock and I got together, we congratulated ourselves on the match. Not that we'd really done anything, but that didn't seem to matter when Trock got on a roll.

"Rafe said," I repeated, "that I need to make a decision about kitchen cabinet hardware."

Kristen shook her head in disgust, flipping her long blond ponytail from side to side. "The unmitigated gall! He knows not what he asks. He cannot."

He did actually, and Kristen knew that he knew one of my secrets, which was that I had an abject fear of hardware stores. There were many things in them that I didn't understand, and I always felt small, uncertain, and inadequate when hardware store guys—who always seemed to be judging me—asked if I had everything I needed. Rafe said my parents had woefully neglected to provide me with a basic life skill, and my counterargument that I'd often shopped at home improvement centers carried no weight with him whatsoever. "Apples and oranges, Minnie," he'd said. "Maybe even apples and car tires."

"I can't put him off much longer," I told Kristen now.

"You might enjoy it," she said.

"Not the point." I sighed, and she peered at me through the miles of electronic connectivity.

"What's wrong? And don't say it's the idea of walking into hardware land. You don't really care about that. What's up? Is it your new library director, what's-his-name? Talk, Minnie Hamilton."

Sometimes having a best friend you'd known since childhood and who understood the motivations behind every twitch in your face had its drawbacks. "Can I say I don't want to talk about it?"

"You can, but it won't get you anywhere. Spill."

I made one last effort. "We're supposed to be talking about your wedding. Making plans and . . . stuff. We need to figure out what weekend you're going to come up here, because some decisions need to be made sooner rather than later and—"

Kristen leaned forward, her face filling my screen in an alarming manner. "Talk!" she ordered.

Since I was left with little choice, I talked.

I told her about finding Rowan in the snow, about doing CPR and calling 911, about the ambulance showing up, about the shared glances of the EMTs who took over from Julia and me, and about watching the ambulance's taillights fading from view as they took Rowan away.

"There's something else." Kristen's voice was gentle, but I knew if I didn't tell her everything, she would keep at me until I did. "Yeah." I sighed. "Rowan was murdered."

"She . . . what?"

"Murdered," I repeated. "Hal Inwood told me. She was poisoned. Given something that triggered her heart condition, a medication she hadn't been prescribed and wasn't in her house."

Instead of murmuring a familiar platitude, Kristen said nothing. I was grateful for her non-comfort, which from her was more soothing than an "I'm so sorry, but there was nothing you could have done." I had Aunt Frances for that; what I needed from Kristen was something exceedingly different.

"That stinks," she said.

I almost smiled at the immensity of her understatement, but I knew she was doing her best. There were no appropriate responses to this kind of situation. "Yeah. Big time."

"Do they know who killed her?"

"No." I replayed the conversation with the detective in my head. "They're just starting the investigation."

"What are you doing to help?"

"I told Hal everything I could remember," I said. "Other than that, there's not much I can do."

Kristen scoffed. "Says the woman who's helped the cops more than once. I assume they're still understaffed? I assume they're overworked, even in January when only insane people live in Chilson?"

"Hard as it is for you to believe, some people like winter."

She passed over that comment. "No matter what your aunt Frances or I or anyone else says, you're going to feel guilty about Rowan's death. That if you'd shown up earlier, she might have recovered. Which, from what you've said, is ridiculous, but I know how your brain works. To keep yourself from drowning in guilt and self-loathing, you need to help find the killer. So, like I said, what are you doing?"

"Hal and Ash are professional law enforcement officers," I said. "The last thing they need is for me to butt into an official police investigation."

Before she could launch into a recitation of the times I had, in fact, helped with a police investigation, I firmly turned the conversation to wedding planning.

After a few attempts to circle the conversation back to murder, Kristen rolled her eyes, sighed heavily, and let me talk about photographers. When the last item on my list of wedding plans had been crossed off, I said, "Sorry, I really have to get going. Things to do and places to go," and before she could point out how little there was to do in Chilson during winter, I gave her a cheery wave and closed down the call.

I felt a little bad about cutting her off, but not that bad. Resisting Kristen's will was exhausting even when she was almost two thousand miles away. If I got exhausted, I'd be far more likely to get sick, and getting sick was nowhere in my future plans since I had no alternative driver for the bookmobile.

Every so often I tried to talk Julia into taking a course to get a commercial driver's license, but to date, she'd resisted. Though the state didn't require a CDL to drive a vehicle the size of the bookmobile, the library's policy did require one. I'd added it myself, partly to placate my then-boss, and partly because I thought it was a good idea. Which it was, but the difficulty of finding a backup driver hadn't been one of my considerations, and it probably should have been.

"Soon," I said out loud, then replaced my shoes with boots, put myself into my coat, hauled on my hat, and pulled on my mittens. My technical quitting time had slipped past almost two hours ago—my talk with Kristen had lasted roughly half an hour, so the library had once again made money on me. Not that I kept track, but I also wasn't about to feel any guilt for using the library's computer and high-speed Internet connection for a bit of personal use.

I padded out to the lobby, waved to Donna, who was working until the library's eight o'clock closing, and was about to head into the cold when someone said, "Minnie? Do you have a minute?"

Turning, I saw a young woman toying with her long lovely auburn braid. A young man, with his hand on her shoulder, looked at me with question marks in his eyes.

Stepping forward, I gave first Collier Bennethum, then his sister, Anya, long hugs. "I'm so sorry about your mom." I wanted to apologize for not being able to do anything to help Rowan, but at the last second I held back from blurting out my own guilt. A confession from me wouldn't help the twins deal with their mother's death; I needed to deal with my feelings on my own.

"Thanks." Anya sniffed down a sob. "It's been hard."

Collier put his arm around his sister. "We wanted to thank you for all you did that day."

I murmured something about doing what anyone would have done.

"I don't think so," Collier said. "Most people would have maybe called nine-one-one, but you tried CPR and kept trying, and . . ." He swallowed. "Anyway, we wanted to say thank you. In person."

Anya nodded. "Dad says thanks from him, too."

Responding with, "You're welcome," didn't seem appropriate, so I simply nodded. Then I took a closer look at the twins. Both were, of course, far taller than me, with dark-haired Collier close to the six-foot mark and Anya a few inches less. They were both college seniors, Anya at Central Michigan University and Collier at Northern Michigan. The first year I'd worked in Chilson, I'd had the fun of helping them complete high school term papers, and I'd enjoyed hearing Rowan tell me about their college acceptances and exploits.

I'd seen Collier over Christmas, and he'd still been bursting with happiness over the fact that his girlfriend had said yes to his Thanksgiving marriage proposal. Now his face was pale, his expression bleak, and Anya didn't look much better.

I longed for words that would make things

easier, but I knew no such words existed. Time was the only thing that could soften their pain, and that would likely be a long time coming. Still, I wanted to say something. I opened my mouth to do what people do, which was to offer any kind of help they needed, but Anya started first.

"You've helped others," she said softly.

Collier edged closer. "Leese Lacombe. Over Christmas we heard you helped her find out who killed her dad."

"And Dana Coburn," Anya added. "Dana's parents are summer customers, you know how we run errands for people? Dana told us about your research into the DeKeyser family and how that helped you figure out who killed that lady."

Dana was a twelve-year-old who possessed more brains than three Minnies put together. Leese Lacombe was a good friend and an attorney specializing in elder law. I made a mental note to respectfully ask both of them to keep their mouths shut about my past involvements in murder as it wasn't a reputation I aspired to. And since I could see where this conversation was going, I jumped in ahead of their request.

"The sheriff's office," I said, "is working very hard on your mom's investigation. What I did those other times was more a matter of circumstance." I echoed what I'd been told before by numerous people. "Let the police do their job. They're professionals and they know what they're doing."

"But—"

I shook my head. "Your hearts are in the right place, but there's nothing I can do that the sheriff's office isn't doing already." Plus they actually knew what they were doing, but I didn't say that out loud.

"At least think about it?" Anya begged.

I glanced at Collier, who was staring at the floor, his face vacant of . . . anything. It was an expression I recognized, that of too much pain. Too much sorrow.

"Sure," I said, "maybe I could think about it." Collier lifted his head and a small spark of life flitted across his eyes. I gave them both another hug. "I'll let you know, okay?" And then, coward that I was, I hurried out before either twin could say another word.

"Mrr."

I looked at my cat. "Are you aware that you bear a striking resemblance to a vulture?"

Eddie blinked, but didn't say a word. He was sitting up straight in a new spot—the top of the low bookcase that was jammed full of jigsaw puzzles and board games—and peering down at me in a manner that was a bit unnerving.

"Cat got your tongue?" I asked. This was an old joke between us, and just like all the other times

I'd said it, I laughed and he didn't. "Oh, come on," I said, "it's funny."

A double yellow-eyed gaze drilled a hole in my head.

"Really? Not even a giggle?"

His shoulders heaved as he sighed a little kitty sigh. Back in my pre-Eddie days, I'd had no idea that cats could sigh, sneeze, yawn, or snore. "Thanks to you, my horizons have expanded immensely," I said, getting up off the couch. "And to show my appreciation, I'm going to give you a big snuggle."

I swept him off the bookcase and gave him a gentle squeeze. Most times, Eddie enjoyed a good hug. This was not one of those times. He squirmed out of my grasp and made a Herculean lunge back to the shelf. I watched his wake of cat hair tumble in the air and make its way to the floor.

"Nice," I said. "Do you realize I need to clean up all of that unwanted fur?" Preferably before Aunt Frances got home from her night class. "How does it feel to have someone tidying up after you at every turn?"

"Mrr!"

"I'm right here, pal. No need to yell."

"MRR!"

I winced, hoping my eardrums healed quickly. "Now what did I do wrong? Not enough treats? No, wait, it's too cold outside? Or is there too much snow? Maybe there's not enough snow? I know—you've suddenly decided you like Otto's adorable little gray cat and want me to take you over there to play with her?"

Eddie glared and jumped to the floor. Before reaching the floor, however, he landed on a board game that was a bit too big to fit all the way into the bookcase. This created a spectacular crash of board games and jigsaw puzzles and decks of cards. Dice, cards, puzzle pieces, and poker chips scattered and rolled across the living room floor.

"Someday," I said, "this will be funny."

"Mrr."

It didn't sound like an apology, and the set of his tail as he trotted up the stairs didn't look embarrassed.

Cats.

Sighing, I crouched down and swept together a deck of cards older than I was and started counting to make sure I had all of them. I sorted the cards into suits, counting the hearts, diamonds, clubs, spades, and suddenly there it was.

The ace of spades. What some called the death card.

Fingering the card's corner, I thought about death. About Rowan. About the right thing to do. About the kind of person I wanted to be. About how easy it would be not to do anything.

I slid the deck of cards into its box and stood. My cell phone was on the coffee table, and I reached for it before I changed my mind.

Tomorrow, I texted Anya and Collier. *I'll start doing what I can to find your mom's killer.*

Chapter 4

The next morning, instead of dawdling over breakfast with my aunt, I sucked down a bowl of cold cereal, hurried into boots, coat, hat, and mittens, and scuffed through three inches of new snow to the sheriff's office.

The deputy on front desk duty slid open the glass window. "Hey, Minnie. How you doing?"

"Morning, Carl," I said, stomping my feet on the mat and brushing snow off my sleeves. "Never been this good. And yourself?"

"Wouldn't a better question be how is the sheriff doing?"

I grinned, but only on the inside. "You make an excellent point." A few months of dating a deputy had given me a partial glimpse into the inner workings of the office and how much the staff felt intimidated by the boss. Personally, I'd always found Sheriff Kit Richardson to be smart, funny, and approachable, but then I'd seen her in a ratty bathrobe while cuddling a purring Eddie.

As I shoved my mittens in my coat pockets, I asked, "What did you do to get stuck up front?"

He grimaced. "Wrenched my shoulder a couple

of weeks ago. I'm on light duty until the doctor says I'm fit for active. What can I do for you?"

"Would Ash have a few minutes?"

"Dumping Rafe already?" Carl leaned toward me, batting his eyes. "You know I'm single, right?"

I nodded thoughtfully. "So this is how rumors get started. I always wondered." Carl laughed and I said, "Ash or Hal. To me they're interchangeable."

Carl picked up the phone. "Can't wait to spread that one around." After a short conversation, Carl buzzed open the interior door and I was ushered into a small room, one that I'd visited so many times that, during the long periods when I'd sat alone at the battered table, I'd considered carving my initials into the tabletop. Not a very strong consideration, because vandalism was wrong and the table was metal, but still.

I pulled out a paint-chipped chair and thought about purchasing a plaque instead. Next to the door would be a good spot as it would cover that big gouge in the drywall. Or maybe directly across from where I usually sat; looking at a plaque would entertain me far more than flat beige paint.

As I considered the possibilities, two men came in. Detective Hal Inwood first, followed closely by the man I'd for a short period of time thought might be the guy who would accompany me into old age. Deputy Ash Wolverson was an amazingly good-looking guy and one of the nicest people I'd ever met. But no matter how hard we'd tried, we couldn't get a single romantic spark to flare up. It had been like hanging out with my brother. We'd started as friends, parted as friends, and happily were still friends.

"She hasn't noticed," Hal said.

Ash pulled a bill out of his pants pocket and handed it to his superior officer. "I am deeply disappointed in you, Minnie."

"What are you talking about?" I glanced from one to the other. Hal looked exactly the same as he had the day before. Ash looked the same as he had last time I'd seen him, which was the previous week when Rafe and I had gone bowling with Ash and his mom. "No haircuts, no new clothes." I glanced under the table. "No new shoes." Or even new shoe polishing, but I didn't say that part out loud.

Hal Inwood sat down and spread out what had formerly been Ash's one-dollar bill.

"Do I get a hint?" I asked.

Ash sat across from me and glanced at the ceiling. "Just one."

"Okay. What is it?"

Detective Inwood smiled and fingered his dollar. Ash sighed. Neither said a word.

Time ticked away, but eventually I clued in to Ash's clue and looked up. I stared, wide-eyed.

"You fixed the ceiling!" When I'd been in the room before, I'd often entertained myself by seeing shapes in the water stains on the ceiling tiles. Hal and I disagreed, of course, on the identities of the shapes, but there would be no more debates because there were new tiles, all an even flat white.

"A by-product," Hal said, "of a leak in the fire suppression system. Never would have happened otherwise."

"You didn't replace them for my sake?" I put a hand over my heart. "I'm truly hurt."

Hal did what I figured he'd do, which was ignore my comment. He took a memo pad from his shirt pocket. "To what do we owe the pleasure of your presence this morning?"

The night before, I'd actually thought through how this meeting would go and had continued texting Anya and Collier for some time. "It's about Rowan Bennethum. I have some information that might be helpful."

My former boyfriend looked at me. "I just lost a dollar of my hard-earned cash because I thought your powers of observation were keen. Since that's clearly not the case, do you really think you have some information that will help us?"

"Apples and oranges," I said.

He grinned and took out his own memo pad. "Give us something good and Hal might not remind you of the ceiling thing the rest of your life."

That was incentive, so I led with the second best point I had. "Did you know that Rowan had recently started a strict diet? One that didn't allow her to drink anything except clear liquids?"

Hal looked up from his notebook. "You didn't mention this earlier."

Since I'd learned it from Anya the previous night, I couldn't have. But I wasn't about to blab that Anya—and apparently Neil, Rowan's husband—hadn't thought to mention it, so I shrugged and said, "Well, I'm mentioning it now." I wasn't sure how much difference it made, but as the detective had told me many times in the past, you never knew what was going to be important until you knew what was important. As a circular argument, it was one of the best ever.

"Anything else?" Hal asked.

I shifted. Last night, lying in bed, I'd remembered something about Rowan. At the time it had seemed significant, but suddenly I wasn't sure. "You know the twins are away at college and Neil started working in Lansing last year and is home only on the weekends?" Both Hal and Ash nodded; I nodded back like a delayed bobblehead. "Right. Well, in mid-September, Rowan started a walking routine. She kept to it religiously, never missing a day no matter what the weather conditions."

Ash's pen stopped scribbling. "Is that it?"

Hal glanced over. "Look at her. Does she look like she's done?"

"Well . . ." Ash studied me. "No. She's leaning forward. Her eyes are open wider than normal and her chin's up a little."

Nice to know I gave away so many hints. I made a mental note to work on a poker face. Then again, I'd made that mental note in the past and done nothing to change my behavior, so why burden myself?

"Exactly," Hal said. "So what would have been a better approach to an interviewee than asking, 'Is that it?' "

Ash flushed, which was slightly adorable. "It depends on the situation. I could have said nothing and waited for the interviewee to start talking again. Or I could have asked for clarification. Or I could have asked something like, 'What else can you can remember?' Or restated what I'd just been told, because that often jogs things loose."

"Fit the interview style to the interviewee. Always," Hal said, giving a tiny nod. "Minnie, do you have anything else?"

Hal was writing something on his memo pad, which might mean that his full attention wasn't on me, making this the perfect time to slide in the question I most wanted to have answered. "Who are you considering as possible suspects?"

"Ms. Hamilton," Hal said. "How many times have I said we won't discuss an active investigation?"

I grinned. "Doesn't hurt to try, does it? Besides, I gave you some good information. Can't you give me something? I'm not asking for specifics, just some broad generalities."

Hal put down his memo pad. "Let me guess. So you don't duplicate our efforts while you conduct your own amateur, unofficial, and completely unsanctioned investigation?"

Put like that, it sounded bad. "On the contrary," I said primly. "It's more like making sure law enforcement has all the help it can get. Aren't you always saying the sheriff's office is overworked and understaffed?"

Ash winked at me with the eye farther away from his boss. "She's going to find out anyway," he said. "We might as well tell her."

Hal grunted. "I hate small towns."

Taking that as permission to speak, Ash said, "We're looking into the bank where Ms. Bennethum worked. Coworkers, of course, because you never know, but also loan applicants she might have recently turned down."

I frowned. "How would killing Rowan help anyone get a loan?" It didn't make sense to me. If one loan officer turned down a loan, wasn't the next one likely to do the same thing?

"Money is a critical factor in many murders,"

Hal said. "Add an element of anger and the result can be lethal."

"So you're talking about revenge as motive?" I asked.

"All avenues of investigation, Ms. Hamilton." Hal tucked away his notepad. "Now, unless you have something else, Deputy Wolverson and I have work to do."

Seconds later, I was out on the sidewalk, walking to the library with my head down against the gusting snow. Hal was right, all avenues did need to be investigated, but revenge? For a denied loan? When there were other banks in town, and dozens more not far away?

It didn't make sense to me. Not a single bit.

That night, Rafe and I met up at Fat Boys Pizza to grab a quick dinner. We hadn't seen each other in a few days due to some night meetings he'd needed to attend, and I was surprised at the rush of happiness I felt when I walked into the restaurant.

He was sitting sideways in a booth, back against the wall, long legs up on the bench, talking to the couple at a nearby table. A cold whoosh of air came inside with me and he turned around. When he saw me, he smiled, and my insides turned to happy mush. I'd felt mushy on the inside before and thought it was love, but now I knew better. This mush glowed. It warmed me from dawn to dusk and made me want to give the whole world a hug. This kind of mush was making me a better person and maybe that's what true love was all about.

Rafe slid himself off the bench and stood. He gave me a quick hug, whispered, "Hey," in my ear, and helped me divest myself of hat, mittens, and coat. "What's it like out there?" he asked.

"Like January." I sat and pulled my coat over my lap to keep any drafts out of my bones. "Good thing snow is white. Just think what it would be like if it was brown. Or pea soup green."

I'd made the comment before, but I liked to say it out loud every so often, especially in public where I could be overheard, so other people could get the benefit of a pro-snow point of view. Come April I could get tired of the stuff, too, but no matter what the circumstances, snow had fairy-tale qualities. It hid raw ugliness and added beauty to the most mundane landscape. Toss in the basic gorgeousness of Tonedagana County's lakes and forested hills, and you had sheer magic with every snowfall.

Rafe glanced outside. "A light blue might be okay."

"Nope." I shook my head. "It would clash with the color of the snowplows."

"Huh. Guess it'll have to stay white. I already ordered food, by the way. Hope you're okay with what we've had every week for the last three months, except for the week of Christmas."

"It's not just men whose hearts can be won through their stomachs."

"You mean it wasn't my charm, winning personality, and immense intellect?"

"All on the list." I pulled a pile of napkins out of the holder and split them between us. The sub sandwiches here were exceptionally good, but notoriously messy. "I know you're busy with end-of-the-semester stuff, but there's news about Rowan Bennethum's death. Have you heard?"

Rafe reached out to hold my hands. "I heard it was murder. I should have called you."

"No, it's all right." My response was a reflex, but accurate. Immediate sympathy could have made my reaction worse. Sometimes not talking about things was okay. "Truly."

I lifted his hands, gave them a light kiss, and extracted myself. "Anya and Collier are all torn up. They stopped by the library last night— they're home for a week or so."

Rafe pushed one of the two glasses of water on the table over to me. "Didn't Collie get engaged over Thanksgiving to some hot blonde from college?"

"Don't call him that," I said automatically. "He says it makes him feel like he should be wearing a leash."

"Considering the circumstances, I won't call him Collie until summer." Rafe touched the rim of his glass to mine. "Scout's honor."

I wasn't sure Rafe had ever been any kind of a scout, but I let it go. A vow for a temporary ban on the nickname was win enough. "Ash says hey, by the way."

"When did you see him?"

"Stopped by the sheriff's office this morning to—"

"Heads up, kids, dinner's here." Brendan, the evening manager, deposited our food. "Eating along gender lines, I see. Meatball sub for him, veggie for the lady. A bit boring, don't you think?" he asked me.

"My mom likes it when I eat vegetables," I said. "There are lots in here."

Brendan looked at my sandwich, which I loved mostly because it had as much dairy product as vegetables, thanks to my habitual request for triple cheese. "More than in the fish and chips," he said, after considering.

I beamed. "There you go. Mom will sleep happy tonight."

"You two are the perfect couple," Brendan muttered. "Let me know if you need anything."

"Did you hear that?" Rafe picked up his sandwich. "We're the perfect couple. If anyone knows, Brendan does. He's been married four times."

Though I wasn't sure that was proof of romantic expertise, and in many ways thought it proved the opposite, my mouth was too full of food to discuss the point. When I was swallowing and getting ready to start a good-humored argument, Rafe asked, "Why were you at the sheriff's office? Did they have more questions now they know it was murder?"

Um. "Sort of, but not really."

Rafe gazed at me over his sandwich, clearly waiting for me to expand.

"I remembered a couple of things I figured they should know," I said, "but also Anya and Collier asked me to help figure out who killed their mom."

Dark brown eyes blinked at me. "You're kidding, right?"

"No." I got ready to take another bite of cheesy goodness.

"Don't we have a professionally trained sheriff's office to take care of that kind of thing?"

"Well, sure, but—"

"And wouldn't professionals get annoyed by amateurs trying to do things they aren't equipped for?"

Rafe often annoyed and frustrated me but I couldn't think of a time when he'd elicited the emotion that was creeping up inside me: sheer and unadulterated irritation. "It's not like I'm going to walk around tapping potential killers on the shoulder and asking, 'Gee, did you kill Rowan? If so, let me know so I can tell the police. Thanks, have a nice day.' "

"No? Because that sounds exactly like something you'd do."

I glared at him. "You really think I'm that stupid?"

"I think trying to find a killer could be the definition of stupid." He glared right back. "He killed once, he can kill again, and you're . . . you're little."

My anger blew hot and red, but I kept my voice quiet. "Just because I'm short doesn't mean I'm weak. Just because I'm a woman doesn't mean I can't take care of myself. I'm not stupid enough to think I'd win a physical contest with a man, but all I have to do is be smarter, which most of the time is pretty easy to do!"

By the end, I'd lost my low and controlled volume, but I didn't care. A while back, I had taken self-defense courses, and I was also the new owner of a concealed pistol license and, under Ash's watchful eye and with a handgun I borrowed from him, practiced regularly at a local firing range. Only my aunt and Rafe knew about this, but that was part of the point. The fewer people who knew my capabilities, the safer I'd be because of the surprise factor.

Rafe sat back and crossed his arms. We stared at each other. Then stared at each other some more.

"We're fighting," he finally said. "I don't like it."

My anger seeped away. "I don't, either."

"How about we stop?"

I fiddled with my napkin. "I promised Anya and Collier I'd do what I could and I intend to keep that promise."

"Does it matter that I don't like it?"

"Of course it does. It's just . . ." I looked up at him. The expression on his face was one I couldn't ever remember seeing before. "What's the matter?"

For a second he didn't say anything. Then, "I'm not sure. This must be what I look like when I'm worried about someone."

"Huh." I examined him closely. "You could be right. Let me take a picture so we can immortalize the moment." It was a weak joke, but he smiled anyway.

Our attention went back to the food, and we both allowed the talk to turn to other things, but when I snuggled up with Eddie that night in bed, I thought about what Brendan had said, that Rafe and I were the perfect couple.

"Pretty sure we're not," I murmured into Eddie's fur.

Eddie, in reply, started to snore.

The bookmobile's windshield wipers flicked back and forth on high speed, but they couldn't keep up with the precipitation. "The weather guy didn't mention anything about this," I said.

There was no return comment, which wasn't a huge surprise, since I'd already dropped Julia off at the restaurant where she was meeting her husband for dinner. Dropping Julia off at various locations throughout the county had become a regular practice, but that particular meeting spot seemed questionable.

"Are you sure?" I'd asked, glancing around at the dark storefronts in the teeny tiny town of Chancellor. In summer, the sidewalks teemed with pedestrians and the adjacent lake offered serene vistas with convenient benches for any-one's viewing pleasure. In January, however, ninety percent of the businesses were closed, and it would take some serious snow shoveling to clear off a bench, even if you wanted to sit outside, which seemed unlikely. "It's only four thirty," I said, "and you said he was meeting you around six."

"My dear," Julia said in a very upper-crust English accent. "I have a book. If he's an hour late, it will not matter a whit." She waved a copy of Joanna Cannon's *The Trouble with Goats and Sheep*, put up the hood of her coat, and skipped down the bookmobile's steps.

I'd waited until she was inside the restaurant, then dropped the bookmobile into gear and eased away. Now it was ten minutes later and what had been gently falling snow was turning into . . . something else.

For approximately the millionth time, I wished the bookmobile had an exterior temperature sensor. Newer models came equipped with them, which I liked to think was a direct result of my numerous e-mails to the manufacturer, but that was no help to me now.

"It's not snow," I said. "But it's not rain, either." The technical difference between sleet and freezing rain was not something I kept in my head. "I'm pretty sure this is what Josh calls 'snain.'" The word was a fun one to say, so I said it out loud a few times.

"Mrr!"

"Not quite," I said. "More of the S sound. And try making the M sound more like an N."

"Mrr."

"Nice try, buddy, but without human vocal cords, I'm not sure you'll ever be able to—"

My attention, which had been ninety-five percent on the road and five percent elsewhere, was suddenly one hundred percent on driving.

The bookmobile had slid. The bookmobile never slid, not like that.

"Hang on, Eddie," I whispered. Not that he had anything to hang on to except the soft pink blanket a summer boarder of my aunt's had made to replace the ratty towel that had previously been in his carrier, but the warning was all I could do.

Snow was easy enough for the bookmobile to deal with. The vehicle's weight and its tires made the typical northwest lower Michigan winter a metaphorical walk in the park. Freezing rain, however, was a different matter. "Hate this stuff," I muttered. To me, freezing rain was like mosquitoes—absolutely no redeeming qualities.

One swipe of the windshield wipers and my vision was clear; another swipe and the road ahead was a translucent fuzz. I instantly took my foot off the gas and turned the defroster on high. A few swipes later, the windshield cleared enough for me to see what I least wanted to see. Ice was already coating the world, covering mailboxes, trees, houses, and power lines with a skim coat of freezing rain, a layer that was getting thicker and thicker every second.

"We have to get off the road," I said. The day had never been very bright, and dark was coming down fast. Leaving the bookmobile on the side of the road for someone to slide into was not an option. I had to find a safe place to park until the salt trucks could get out. The only question was where?

My grip on the steering wheel went tight as I considered the possibilities. At this point on the route there were no churches, township halls, gas stations—or any type of commercial establishment—for another ten miles. And none of the public parks in this part of the county were plowed in the winter.

There was no choice left but to slip into the

widest driveway I could find and hope I wasn't inconveniencing the property owner whose driveway I'd just blocked. I scanned the roadside left and right. The few driveways in sight were either unplowed or narrow or both; I wouldn't risk driving the bookmobile into a driveway that might require a tow truck to get us out.

The freezing rain pelted the windshield in a furiously fast tempo, and the windshield started to glaze over. I reached out to the defroster, but it was already as high as it would go.

"This is seriously not good," I murmured. We were driving so slowly the speedometer barely registered. I turned on the four-way flashers in spite of the fact that I hadn't seen a car in miles and wasn't actually sure there was anyone else on the planet. Dark ahead of us, dark behind us, dark all around—

Eddie howled, a low rumbling whine of the sort that made me want to make sure he was on a hard surface, the easier for cleaning up afterward.

"Are you okay, pal?" I wanted to glance over, but didn't dare take my attention off the road. "You haven't sounded like that since . . ."

Since the day we'd found Rowan.

On the same route we were driving that very minute.

I breathed out a soft "Hallelujah," because Rowan's driveway was not only bound to be empty, but was nice and wide and only half a mile away, and one of the twins had mentioned that their dad was hiring the driveway plowed the rest of the winter.

Oh-so-slowly, I steered us in that direction, and in relatively short order, the bookmobile slid to a slippery halt. "How do you feel about breaking into a house?" I undid my seat belt and leaned over to release the strap that kept Eddie's carrier in place.

"Mrr."

"I'm glad you've recovered from whatever was making you make those horrible noises."

"Mrr."

"Really? Well, how about I keep an eye on you. Any more of that and I make an appointment with Dr. Joe." I pulled out my phone, scrolled through the contacts, and sent a group text to Neil, Anya, and Collier: *Caught out by your house in freezing rain with the bookmobile. OK if I use the code to go inside and wait it out?*

Ten seconds later, I got texts from the twins. Anya: *All yours. Heat's down, though.* Collier: *Stay overnight if u need 2—don't use Anya's room it's a mess.* Anya's next text was an image of a sticking-out tongue, which I assumed was to her brother. I decided not to wait for Neil's permission, texted a thank-you, and picked up the cat carrier.

Eddie retreated to silence as I tried to open the bookmobile's door. It didn't open and didn't open and I finally put the carrier on the floor and put all my weight into the effort. With a tinkling crash of ice breaking, the door flew open wide and a blast of wind whooshed in. I climbed down the stairs carefully and reached back in for Eddie's carrier.

"Hold on tight." I closed the bookmobile door and, head down against the wind, shuffled toward the house, knees bent and my free hand out for balance. Every step was a risk, but at least the freezing rain was falling on an inch of fresh snow. Once each footstep broke through the crust of ice, there was something for my boot to grab on to. Even still, twenty feet had never seemed so far.

What felt like an eternity later, I touched the corner of the house and then we were in front of the door that entered into the garage. I tucked my right hand under my left elbow, pulled off my mitten, and entered the five-digit code. Blessedly, the battery was still working. The deadbolt slid open and we were inside, out of the wind and rain.

"Safe," I said, gasping a bit because for a while there I hadn't been completely sure things would work out.

"Mrr."

"It's good to know you weren't worried at all. Nice to know that you have that kind of confidence in me." I opened the door into the house and set Eddie's carrier on the floor. "Promise to be good?"

My cat blinked up at me, but didn't say a thing. Which was just as well because, even if he'd promised, I wouldn't have believed him.

"Here you go." I opened the wire door. Eddie, who had been lying on his pink blanket, leapt to his feet and pranced into Rowan's kitchen.

Oak cabinets with brushed nickel drawer pulls and cabinet knobs. Off-white tile counter-tops with a comfortable clutter of coffeepot, dry goods canisters, and cookbooks. Rowan had been close to fanatic about keeping things clean, but she hadn't minded a little clutter, especially if the clutter was family heirlooms. She'd told me she had a number of them because she was the oldest grandchild. "None of it is worth a penny," she'd said, "so the term 'heirloom' is a bit of a misnomer, but calling the kids to dinner with the cowbell from the last cow my grandparents owned makes me smile every time."

In a sudden rush, the full impact of her death wrapped around me. She was gone forever. No more of her dry humor, a type of humor that many people interpreted not as humor at all, but as being cold and distant. My father had a similar tendency, so I'd found it easy to laugh at her comments. The absence of her wry observations was a hole in my life, and it would never be filled, not completely.

I sat on a handy bench and, after I'd finished crying and wiping my eyes, pulled off my boots and put them on the mat next to boots left behind by other Bennethums. I unzipped my coat, but didn't take it off. When Neil and the twins had left the house, they'd turned the heat down to a level that would have been chilly without an outer layer, even over my bookmobile sweaters, which were long and warm and pocketed, the better for carrying cat treats.

"Eddie?" I called. "Where are you?"

"Mrr!"

Though I didn't see him, I heard the pitter-patter of Eddie paws as they thumped up the stairs.

"Nothing up there for you to see," I called. There was nothing upstairs but bathrooms and bedrooms, including the very empty master bedroom. At some point, Neil would open the closet and have to make decisions about Rowan's shirts, pants, dresses, and shoes. Or would he ask Anya to do the sad task?

I tried to remember Rowan's sibling situation, but couldn't quite. Though she'd talked about brothers and sisters and cousins, she'd also had a tendency to drop the term "in-law" and talk about Neil's blood relatives as if they were hers.

Eddie thundered down the stairs and cantered into the kitchen.

"Why would anyone kill her?" I asked, standing

to look at the collection of magnets on the refrigerator. Hal and Ash's theory about a revenge murder because of a denied loan seemed like a stretch, but I didn't have any better ideas.

My fuzzy friend galloped around the kitchen table and back into the living room.

Of course, why anyone would kill was a mystery to me, unless your life or the life of someone you loved was in danger. And the idea of Rowan being a dangerous threat to anyone seemed beyond unlikely.

"Then again," I said, "what defines a threat might be a relative concept."

"Mrr!" Eddie said as he ran back into the kitchen. He started to take another lap around the table, but he miscalculated his speed. Centrifugal force tipped him over and he slid into the row of boots, knocking footwear everywhere.

Before I could get to my feet, he was up on his, trotting around as if he was proud of his stunt.

"You must have been at the back of the line when the gift of grace was handed out." I went over to, once again, clean up after my cat. "Or maybe you're just getting older. You're four now, if Dr. Joe was right about your age. That's what, college age for a cat? Not that you would have studied enough to get into any college. And if you'd managed to get admitted, I can see you flunking out after . . . huh."

I was down on my hands and knees now, and

had seen a small flat rectangle on the floor, way behind the boots and underneath the bench. Since I was an unexpected guest, it was my duty to do some chores, so I reached out for the whatever-it-was.

My fingers recognized the shape and texture of an empty sugar packet before my brain caught up.

A sugar packet? But that made no sense at all.

I brought the object into the light and put it on the kitchen table.

Sugar. Rowan hated extra sugar in anything. She'd considered it responsible for death, disease, and general disorder in the world. She'd been a bit of a fanatic about it.

I poked at the thing, reading its print. This particular packet was maple flavored, something put out by a local company. Even still, there was no way Rowan would have bought it and no way she would have allowed it in her house. There was absolutely no reason for it to be there.

Except one.

I backed away from the sugar packet, not wanting to touch it, not wanting to even see it any longer.

My fingers fumbled for my phone. "Hey, Ash? There's something you need to see."

Chapter 5

At breakfast the next morning, I held my aunt spellbound while I told the tale. Or at least partially spellbound, because some of her focus was on keeping Eddie off the table.

"But Hal and Ash didn't think the sugar packet was important?" she asked.

"They're reserving judgment until it can be analyzed." My instinctive leap had been to the conclusion that the sugar packet had contained whatever it was that had killed Rowan. There, in her kitchen, I'd seen the scene unfolding. Someone at the front door. Rowan inviting her or him inside. An offer of coffee. Two coffee mugs brought to the kitchen table. Then a request for something not handy. Rowan would have turned away and the killer would surreptitiously have added the poison, with the cover of an innocuous sugar packet if Rowan had happened to see the movement.

I'd envisioned it so clearly that I'd been shocked when Ash and Hal hadn't seen it along with me. Looking back, I realized that I might have been a little sharper with them than I'd needed to be.

I'd been tired, hungry, and worried about getting the bookmobile back home, and during the three hours I'd waited before they showed up—the time it took for the road commission's salt trucks to get to Rowan's road—my confidence that the packet had contained poison had grown to one hundred percent.

Eddie, who had abandoned his efforts to get on top of the table, jumped onto his chair. He sat upright with his chin just level with the tabletop.

I spooned up the last of my oatmeal. "And it's possible I told Detective Inwood and Deputy Wolverson that waiting a week for the lab analysis would be a waste of a week and wasn't time of the essence in a murder investigation?"

Aunt Frances half smiled. "More like you said they were nuts to ignore what was right in front of their faces."

"Well." I grinned. "That sounds more like me, doesn't it?"

My aunt nodded. "Yup."

"Mrr."

The previous day's freezing rain had been covered with a fresh two inches of snow overnight. While the main roads were clear, most of the side roads were still exceedingly slippery. Schools were closed and events were being canceled all over the county, but the library had never closed for weather in the history of the library, so I slipped a set of handy-dandy ice grips over my boots and headed out.

My normal morning walking route took me through the tree-lined residential streets of Chilson, zigged to hit the core downtown blocks, and zagged back up to the library. Today, however, I took the route of safety and made a beeline for the main road.

The city's sidewalk plow had made a pass and dropped a mix of sand and salt, but the footing was still variable, so like a responsible adult, I kept my head down and my attention on my boots. Which was why, when my name was called out, I jumped and almost lost my balance.

"Sorry about that. You okay?" Mitchell Koyne looked down at me. Way down. I understood that my own compact and efficient height was not the norm, and every time I met up with Mitchell, it was very clear that he was on the opposite end of the human height bell curve.

"Fine. And nice work on your sidewalk." I nodded at the stretch in front of the toy store, shoveled and scraped down to the concrete, even though it was almost two hours until the store opened.

Until last year, Mitchell had been one of those guys who bounced from seasonal construction job to seasonal ski resort job, making ends meet in the shoulder seasons of spring and fall by selling firewood and not eating much. He'd worn untucked and raggy flannel shirts over T-shirts of questionable condition, jeans worn to white at the knees, and shoes held together with goo and sometimes duct tape.

He was also very intelligent and insatiably curious, but only in a sporadic sort of way. That, paired with his complete lack of ambition, had created his life of unparalleled laid-back Up North–ness. But everything had changed for Mitchell when he'd started dating Bianca Sims, one of the most successful real estate agents in the region.

The high-powered and energetic Bianca pairing with Mitchell was not a combination anyone ever would have expected, but it was working so well for them that Mitchell was essentially living with her. Which was a relief to Mitchell's sister and brother-in-law, in whose attic bedroom he'd been living.

I'd often wondered what Mitchell might have done with his life if he'd been born into a family that valued education. Looking at him now, though, it was hard to imagine him anywhere else or doing anything else other than managing Chilson's toy store. A more natural fit was hard to imagine, and it was all due to Mitchell wanting to improve himself in order to win Bianca's love.

"Doubt you'll get much business today," I said.

"There's always something to do." Mitchell set down the bag of salt he'd been holding and shoved his bare hands into his coat pockets. "Say, Minnie, can I ask you a question?"

"Sure. Fire away."

He shifted his weight from one foot to the other. "Well, it's a personal question."

Silence reigned. I waited, waited some more, and finally said, "Okay. I can deal with personal." At no point had any of my college professors warned me that librarians could become surrogate therapists, but as a librarian, and especially as a bookmobile librarian, I'd been asked to give career recommendations, about the right time to have children, and what I'd do if I'd been offered a big promotion a thousand miles away. "Go ahead."

"Well." He shifted again. "It's Bianca."

"Okay," I said slowly. "Is there a problem?" Every time I saw the two of them together, they looked happy. Laughing, holding hands, all that.

"Well, it's just . . ." He hung his head. "I want to, you know, take things to the next level, and I'm not sure how to do that."

Alarmed, I started backing away. No way was I going to give Mitchell Koyne advice on the physical aspect of his relationship with his girlfriend. "Um, Mitchell, this isn't something—"

"I mean, how do I know if she wants to make us a permanent thing? What if I'm reading things wrong? Because the last few weeks things have been a little weird. It's like she's impatient with me. And at Christmas she seemed really disappointed with her present." He sighed. "I thought about it a lot and figured she'd really like what I gave her, a set of framed pictures for her office, of historic houses from all around here."

It sounded like a great present, and I said so.

"Yeah, well." He shrugged. "She acted happy and everything, but things haven't been right since then."

I relaxed. This was familiar territory. Every few months Mitchell went through a "What does she see in me?" phase. Oddly, Bianca seemed to occasionally suffer the same internal debate. "You're not reading things wrong," I assured him. "If you want a forever future with Bianca, why don't you talk to her about it?"

He hesitated. "There's this friend of mine. He took his girlfriend downstate to a baseball game last summer, the Tigers, and had them put his proposal on that big screen. Everyone was watching, and she . . ."

"She said no," I said quietly. The video had been all over the Internet for days. I'd felt awful for the poor guy; I just hadn't realized Mitchell knew him.

"Yeah. After, he told me he'd been so sure she'd say yes. So even if everything seems good between me and Bianca, how can I know for sure?"

I wanted to reassure him, but he had a point.

How did anyone ever know for sure how someone else felt? About anything, really?

"Can you help me?" he asked. "Figure out how
she feels? About me, I mean?"

What kind of friend would I be if I didn't help?
Not that Mitchell and I were friends exactly. But
we were more than acquaintances, and if I could
help out, I should.

"Sure," I said. "I'll do what I can."

"Thanks, Minnie!" He grinned a wide Mitchell
smile, and I was suddenly very glad I'd agreed
to help. He slapped me on the shoulder and I
staggered. "Sorry about that," he said. "I forget
sometimes how little you are. One more thing,
don't let Bianca know I talked to you about this,
okay?"

I smiled a bit grimly. "I'll do what I can," I said
again and, all the way to the library, wondered
what on earth that might possibly be.

I spent the morning doing the post-bookmobile
chores I should have done the day before but
hadn't because we hadn't made it back to the
library until long after closing time. At the time,
my priority had been to get Eddie and me back
to the boardinghouse safe and sound. After all,
I was the only one who would care if I didn't
lug all the returned bookmobile books back into
the library and process them, and I was willing
to give myself a pass from having to do it

on nights we didn't get back until ten o'clock.

Bringing books, DVDs, and CDs back home to the library always made me happy. The only thing better than checking them back in was checking them out, sending them on their temporary way to a new loving home. Truly, I had the best job in the world, because I got to help people find what they wanted every day.

I ran all the returned materials through the computer, put them on a rolling rack, and, whistling, started to put them back into their proper places. Some would go straight back onto the bookmobile; others would stay here in the library until someone requested one of them, or until I decided to rotate them into bookmobile circulation. I was gaining more experience with what bookmobilers liked, but what I was mostly learning was that I really needed a magical crystal ball to predict what people wanted.

For instance, just yesterday Mrs. Portz, who had in the past been interested only in reading cookbooks and biographies of U.S. presidents, had asked for "one of those steamy books my granddaughter goes on about," and once I'd realized that she was talking about steampunk, I'd been happy to oblige.

A light knock made me look up. Graydon stood in the doorway.

"How are you this fine morning?" I asked cheerfully.

"Very happy that I didn't have to drive more than three miles to work. And I'm glad you made it back safely last night. That freezing rain must have been frightening, especially in the bookmobile."

My new boss was showing concern for the bookmobile? For me? What was the world coming to? "The weight makes it easier than you'd think," I said. "The worst thing was trying to keep the windshield clear."

He nodded. "Well, I'm glad you texted me. Let's make that standard operating procedure in bad weather."

"Sounds like a good plan." One of these days I was going to finish revising the library policies regarding the bookmobile. Before my former boss had approved the purchase of the bookmobile, I'd been required to put a number of policies in place. There had to be two library staff members on board at all times. That the driver must have a commercial driver's license. And on and on. I'd done the best I could, but now that we'd been on the road for a year and a half, it was time to adjust things. I also wanted to rewrite the job descriptions for the driver and the assistant, adding core competencies. And the pre-run and post-run checklists could stand an update. Now that winter had dug in, I was a little nervous about the rear door's keypad access working in extreme cold. We didn't use the rear door, which was the handicapped entrance, all that much, but when we did need it, there was no substitute. "I'll run the revised policy past you when I get a draft done."

"This week?"

"Um . . ."

Graydon smiled. "Trent is reviewing all of the library's policies. As the new board chair, it makes sense. But if we're going to make changes to the bookmobile policy, it would be best to have it in front of him as soon as possible."

I did the best I could to hide my complete and utter dismay. Policy revision was not my favorite task. In fact, it was near the bottom of my Least Favorite library chores and was another reason I'd decided against applying for the director position. "In that case, I'll move policy revision to the top of my list."

Graydon seemed satisfied and went away, but my happy mood had shifted and I realized that I was going to have to resort to serious measures to get it back. I was going to have to ignore the peanut butter and jelly sandwich I'd brought for lunch and go to Shomin's Deli instead.

No one else wanted to go back out into the weather, so I left the library solo. I carried a book with me wherever I went, just in case I had to spend more than ten seconds waiting for anything ever, but off season I preferred to eat my meals with someone. In winter, Chilson's population dropped by ninety percent, and most of us year-rounders tended to huddle together, especially in January.

"Well, hello there, Miss Librarian!" Pam Fazio, owner of Older Than Dirt, a retail establishment that was partly antiques, partly shoes, partly kitchen wares, and all fun, waved at me from a booth. "Come sit with me."

I didn't even bother looking at the chalkboard menu. "Hey, Mike," I said to the twenty-something behind the counter. "Swiss cheese and olives on sourdough, please, with root beer." After paying, I slid into the booth across from Pam. "I almost didn't recognize you," I said.

Pam looked down at herself. "Same clothes. Same haircut. What do you see as different?"

This was true. Same short black hair, same top-notch fashion sense, even in January. However, there was one massive change. "Might be the only time I've seen you without coffee in your hand."

She glowered. "Stupid doctor. Just because I'm 'of a certain age,' I'm suddenly supposed to start thinking about my caffeine intake? Why now?"

"Because you can only get away with abusing your body for so long before it catches up to you?"

"Wait your turn," she said darkly. "Hit fifty

and you're in a whole new demographic. It's all different."

"Didn't you turn fifty two years ago?"

"Three, but who's counting?" She grinned, but it slipped away as something across the room caught her attention. "That's odd. I thought he was gone."

I turned and saw Neil Bennethum, Rowan's husband, place an order with Mike. "Is it okay if he joins us?" I asked. At Pam's nod, I got up and invited Neil over. After a pause, he nodded. "Thanks."

The three of us settled down, Pam and myself on one side of the booth, Neil on the other. "I thought you'd gone downstate," Pam said. "Back to work."

Neil picked at a hangnail. "I tried, but couldn't concentrate. They gave me a leave of absence so I'm headed down to Chicago to visit my brother and his family. Then . . . we'll see."

"I'm so sorry," Pam said.

"Yes. Well." Neil seemed to shrink. "I can't sleep at the house. I tried, but . . ." He shook his head. "The last couple of nights I stayed with my sister in town." He gave a wan smile and tapped his rounded midsection. "You know what's funny? For years my doctor was on my case to lose fifty pounds. Now I've dropped ten in the last week. Who knew there could be a benefit to something like this?"

I inched forward. "Neil, did you see my text? I was at your house yesterday."

"You were?" He stared at me blankly. "My phone . . . so many people are texting me about Rowan." He looked at the table and muttered, "I haven't been looking at it much lately."

Pam and I exchanged a glance. The man was not doing well. "Your house," I said brightly, "was a port in the storm," and explained about the bookmobile and the freezing rain. Then, after a quick moment, I told him I'd found something odd and called the police.

"What did you find?" he asked.

Of course he asked. How could he not? But I hesitated. "I'm not sure I'm supposed to talk about it. Part of the investigation."

Neil made a rude noise. "What investigation? I told Hal Inwood exactly who killed Rowan, but does he do anything about it? No. All they have to do is arrest him. They tell me it's all under investigation, but I don't see anything happening. Another reason it'll be good for me to leave town—if they don't arrest him soon, I might do something to him myself."

Pam and I exchanged glances. "You know who killed her?" Pam asked.

"The week before Rowan died," Neil said, his face flushing, "she and Land had a huge fight. A big blowup. She fired him and he threatened her. Said she'd regret firing him, and soon."

"Land Aprelle?" I asked. But it had to be. There weren't many men named Land wandering around the world. For decades he'd been a contractor, putting up houses and pole barns and anything else people hired him to build. Now that he was in his sixties and had had a knee and a shoulder replacement, he'd shifted to handyman and caretaking services. He was a longtime library patron and had happily taken advantage of the bookmobile the first week it was on the road. People who used the library and bookmobile weren't guaranteed to be upright and honest citizens, but in my mind the odds were better.

"Rowan hired him to do chores after I started working downstate," Neil said. "She wanted me to have real weekends, not weekends working on the house. She said we could afford it, that it would give us more time together, that—"

He stopped. Swallowed. "If I hadn't taken that job, I would have been home. She never would have hired him. She wouldn't be . . ." His voice trailed off and a vast silence filled the booth.

My heart ached for him. I wanted to give him a hug, or at least hold his hand, but we were barely more than acquaintances and I didn't want to weird him out. "I'm so sorry," I said softly, because there wasn't much else I could do.

"Thanks," he said. "Rowan really liked you. Both of you," he said, finally looking up at us.

"She didn't like everyone, but she liked you two."

"And I liked her. Her sense of humor was just like my dad's." I swung around to face Pam. "And yours, too, come to think of it."

Pam laughed. "So that's why the three of us got along so well. A warped worldview."

"Lots of folks didn't get when she was making a joke," Neil said. "She got on the wrong side of people for that."

The back of my neck tingled. "Anyone in particular?"

"Besides half of her own family?" Neil almost smiled, then stared off into space. "You know," he said thoughtfully, "Hugh Novak couldn't stand her. Hated everything she stood for and believed in, politically speaking." His face hardened. "I wonder where he was that day."

Mike showed up with our food, and as we ate, we talked of other things. As soon as the sandwiches were gone, Neil left and I moved around to the other side of the booth. "I don't see Land Aprelle as a killer," I said.

"Me, either." Pam picked at her potato chips. "Who's Hugh Novak?"

I knew the name, but couldn't summon a memory of what he looked like. "If I remember right, he's from Chilson. An insurance adjuster, but I hear he's getting into developing real estate."

Pam looked in the direction Neil had gone. "It's weird knowing someone who was murdered."

It certainly was. "I don't think Neil has any idea who killed Rowan," I said. "Do you?"

Pam shook her head, but in agreement. "He just wants her killer found."

It was what we all wanted. And I was going to do everything I could to make it happen.

When I got back to the library, I went straight to my office. I sat down, fired up my computer, strong-mindedly avoided looking at my e-mail inbox, and focused completely on updating the bookmobile policy.

After ten years in the workforce, I'd come to the conclusion that there were two types of tasks. The kind that took longer than you expected and the kind that didn't take nearly as long as you expected. Tasks that took exactly as long as you anticipated were as rare as a pair of my pants that didn't have any Eddie hair.

As it turned out, revising the bookmobile policy took only a couple of hours as opposed to the full day I'd anticipated. "Maybe I'm getting better at this," I said happily as I e-mailed it off to Graydon. For half a second, I toyed with the idea of diving straight into checklists and core competencies, but decided after two solid hours of sitting that what I needed was to stand up for a few minutes.

I sent a group text to all the staff who were working that I was about to brew a fresh pot of coffee—half caffeine in light of the fact that it was three in the afternoon—and headed to the break room. Three minutes later, Holly came in, followed by Josh, Kelsey, and two library patrons, Stewart Funston and the elderly Mr. Goodwin, who'd repeatedly told me to call him Lloyd.

Today I cheated and said a blanket hello to everyone. First to the coffeepot was Stewart. "Just so you know," I said, "it's half caffeine and half decaf."

He smiled. "Exactly what I wanted. How did you guess?"

Stewart was one of our library regulars. Just shy of six feet tall and on the edge between sturdy and stocky, and with graying brown hair in dire need of a haircut, he was in his late forties and worked for a local manufacturer designing electronic doohickeys of some sort. He telecommuted from home and from the library on a regular basis. I'd once asked him for details on what, exactly, it was that he designed, but then he'd told me and at the end I was no wiser than I'd been before the explanation started.

"Working today?" Josh asked Stewart.

Feeling like a mother robin putting worms into upturned baby bird beaks, I poured coffee into the mugs held out in front of me.

"The plant isn't open," he said. "But here's the problem when you can telecommute; there's never a time when you can't work."

We all laughed. Stewart was a personable guy, and he'd also been an early supporter of the bookmobile, so I was automatically inclined to like him. I would always remember the people who'd spoken up back when I was trying to convince the library board that a bookmobile was needed in an age of digital everything.

"Thanks for brewing an afternoon pot, Minnie." He set his mug on the table and reached for his wallet. "For the fund," he said, pulling out a five-dollar bill.

I stuffed it into the mug Holly's kids had decorated with stickers and glitter that tended to get on everything within a five-foot radius. "Thanks, Stewart. We really appreciate it."

"Can't have my library staff going without coffee," he said. "It doesn't bear thinking about."

Kelsey made a face at her mug. "You call this stuff coffee?"

"Better than the sludge you make," Josh said. "Do you even care that no one else drinks the pots you make?"

"You can always add water," Kelsey said.

It was an old argument and winning was impossible due to the subjective nature of the topic. In spite of the no-win reality, it felt like both Kelsey and Josh were gearing up for another round.

I tried to think fast for a less divisive topic—politics? religion?—but Holly spoke first.

"Stewart, how is your family doing?" she asked. "It was all so sad. I hear there's going to be a memorial service in summer."

"Late May," he said. "Neil wants to wait until the kids are done with school, but not wait so long that hotel rooms will be expensive for the people who have to travel."

"You're related to the Bennethums?" I asked. Just when I thought I was used to running across connections in a small town, up popped a family tie that surprised me.

Stewart sighed. "Rowan and I were first cousins. Her dad and my mom are siblings. She was the first grandchild, but I was the first grandson, the first one born to carry on the name," he said, sounding proud.

For some reason, I'd never once considered that Rowan's parents would still be alive, but I should have. Rowan was in her late forties, so her parents were likely around seventy, an age that used to sound ancient to me, but I now knew numerous people in their eighties who put my energy and activity level to shame, so I'd revised seventy in my head as nothing to fear.

Stewart picked up his coffee mug, then set it back down. He put his hand into his pants pocket and pulled out a sugar packet. "Has anyone tried this? It's maple-flavored sugar. A company north of town started making it a few months ago. I'm not a huge fan of sugar in coffee, but this stuff is—" He glanced at me. "Minnie, are you okay? You look a little funny."

"Fine," I said vaguely. "I was just . . . thinking." But I'd looked funny because the sugar packet Stewart was holding in his hand was a twin to the one I'd found the night before in Rowan's house. I gestured. "Where did you get that? It sounds like something Kristen should be using at the restaurant."

"Christmas present," he said. "Don't remember who, though. My best present was from my son. He gave me this amazing new kind of hat that no one around here has. It's a wool felt fedora with earflaps I can fold down. What's revolutionary is the design. Four-and-a-half-inch crown height is typical, you see, and it's brilliant to make it lower for winter, when the winds are stiffer."

"Sounds cool," Josh said. "My brother and his wife gave me a set of kitchen storage containers." He rolled his eyes.

Mr. Goodwin asked Josh about purchasing a new tablet, a conversation that Stewart joined in, and Holly and Kelsey started talking about their respective children. I let the voices wash past me and thought about three things.

Cousins.

Sugar packets.

And poison.

Chapter 6

The walk home that night was, physically, far easier than the morning trip. It hadn't snowed all afternoon and the plows had been busy. Mentally, however, I was having a hard time.

Land Aprelle as a killer? Not a chance.

Stewart Funston as a killer? Not a chance.

Hugh Novak? I'd never heard anything against him other than Neil's diatribe, so I inched his name toward the "not a chance" side of my mental spreadsheet.

I wanted to shy away from imagining scenarios in which any of the three might have wanted to kill Rowan, but I took a deep breath of cold air and went at it.

Land. A builder turned handyman/caretaker; had thick gray hair with a streak of white straight down the middle. Years ago, he'd fallen off a ladder, been knocked out, and hadn't woken up for three days. Afterward, he was fine except for that white streak of hair. He also was clean shaven in summer and grew a bushy white beard in winter because, with the addition of pillow stuffing and a costume, he transformed from a

111

guy who hardly talked to the area's best Santa Claus.

Maybe that was why I was having a hard time imagining him as a killer. But I also had a hard time seeing him in a shouting match with Rowan, and that had apparently happened. Could Land have killed Rowan because of an argument? Or should the question be, what kind of argument could have led to murder?

Hal Inwood's favorite motives were money or love gone wrong, with the most powerful motive being a combination of the two. Could Land and Rowan have been having an affair? Could Land have been stealing from the Bennethums?

I had no idea and had no idea how to find out. Hal and Ash knew about Neil's suspicions, though, so they were most likely looking at Land, no matter what Neil thought.

On to Stewart Funston. Who, unbeknownst to me, was a cousin of Rowan's. I made a mental note to ask my aunt about the Funston family tree. No, wait. Stewart had said his mom and Rowan's dad had been siblings and I'd never known Rowan's maiden name. Another note went onto my mental list—*librarian, start your research!*—and I carried on with my cogitating.

What reason could Stewart have to kill his cousin? Using the second of Hal's classic motives, love, was too impossibly icky, but some other kind of love could be at play. Could there be some weird competition for parental love? Was it possible that either Rowan or Stewart had been raised in the other's family and was harboring resentment for not being treated as full family? Possible, but why would that kind of anger come into flower now, so many years later?

The other reason was money. Rowan and Neil seemed comfortable enough, but there was no ostentatious display of wealth. No big boat, no fancy vacations, a house they'd owned for years, and two kids in college.

I blew out a breath, creating a soft ball of steam that disappeared as quickly as it had formed.

Hugh Novak. Since I didn't know the man, I felt myself wanting him to be the best candidate on my very short list. It was intellectually lazy and morally reprehensible, and I was ashamed of myself the moment I realized it. Yet there it was.

I let myself in the front door and called out my normal greeting. "I'm back!" From upstairs came a sleepy "Mrr." Eddie was in serious winter mode, and unless I shook his treat can, it was unlikely he'd venture off my bed anytime soon.

As I began to divest myself of outerwear, I almost hoped that Aunt Frances was out. Though she was the best aunt ever and I loved her dearly, I could feel a mood descending, a mood with a capital M. It would pass, but a night on the couch with Eddie and Netflix might make it pass even quicker.

"Hello, Minnie. How are you this evening?"

"Oh, hey, Otto." I glanced behind my aunt's fiancé. "Where's the beloved relative?"

"Someone called about selling some bird's-eye extremely cheap and she was out of here before I could figure out why she could possibly want bird eyeballs."

I laughed and my mood started to evaporate. Maybe human companionship was what I needed, not a burrowing in. "It's a relatively rare kind of hard maple that looks swirly." I glanced around and found some. "Like this." I pointed at an end table's drawer front. "See? Swirly. And please don't ask me what causes it because I have no idea."

Otto nodded and tapped the end table. "Did you know that your aunt doesn't want to take any of this furniture across the street when we get married?"

"No, but I'm not surprised." I spread my arms wide, gesturing at the room. At the entire house. "This furniture has been here for years. Decades. Taking away even one piece could change the magic recipe."

"You sound like Frances," he said.

I flopped down on a couch. "Well, there are reasons for that. And I'd name some, but you just sounded the teensiest bit grumpy, so I won't."

"Thank you." He sat on the couch across from me. Even in jeans and a zip sweatshirt, he still looked as if he'd stepped out of a magazine advertisement for what the elegant senior gentleman should look like. "I recognize that Celeste will need the bulk of the boardinghouse furniture, but I think not taking anything is a mistake."

"Why's that?"

"I want the house across the street to be our home. Ours together. I don't want her to think of it as my house, a place she just happened to move into."

Smiling at him fondly, I said, "If she changes her mind about marrying you, I wouldn't mind being second choice."

"Dear Minnie. Rafe Niswander would have my guts for garters."

I laughed at the English expression. "Then we'll have to leave things as they are."

"Except for the furniture," he said. "I fully expected to donate half my furniture to the church's resale shop. She needs to bring something from the place she's lived in for so many years."

"Does Eddie hair count?" I picked a few examples off my sleeve.

Otto, sensibly, ignored me. "Could you talk to her? Tell her I'm thinking of our future, that I don't want her to resent living in a house that doesn't feel like hers. Please?"

It sounded as if he'd already made his arguments and that she'd already rejected them. Still, he had a point. "Sure," I said. "I'll talk to her. But I can't promise it'll change her mind."

He smiled, looking satisfied. "I know you'll do your best, and that's all anyone can ask. Thank you, Minnie."

But I knew he was wrong. Doing your best wasn't always enough. Sometimes it wasn't anywhere near enough.

After Otto went home, I ate a dinner of leftovers—hardly any dishes to wash, how handy!—and carried Eddie downstairs to help me watch a couple episodes of *Detectorists*. It was a BBC show that amused me immensely, and now I had a mission, to see if anyone on the show ever said 'guts for garters.'

Though I didn't hear anything about garters, the show made me laugh and distracted me nicely, so it was a surprise when I spent the night tossing and turning so much that Eddie abandoned me. Come morning, I found him on the dining room buffet. "Really?" I asked. "That's where you spent the night? Perched on a hard piece of wood? Sleeping there was better than snuggling with me?"

My cat looked at me and didn't say a thing.

"Love you, too, pal," I said, planting a kiss on the top of his head as I went past.

In the kitchen, Aunt Frances was a whirlwind of activity. Coffee was brewing, her lunch was on the counter only half made, and the microwave was counting down to zero.

"Morning." I went to the silverware drawer for spoons. "How was the bird's-eye?" I'd already been in bed when I'd heard the front door. "You were out late. What did you do, start a project with it already?"

"Good morning," she said. "Could you get the oatmeal? Thanks. The wood is wonderful, but I need to move it right away. Death in the family, house is sold, and if I don't get it out before the closing date, it's the property of the new owners."

"Would they even want it? Maybe they'd be fine giving you an extra week or two." I was no woodworker, but even I knew that moving wood was a laborious process.

"Don't know, and I don't want to ask. It's bird's-eye." She spoke almost reverently.

"Do you have any place to store it?"

She nodded. "There's room in my storage unit. I just have to move a few things."

My aunt's storage unit was on the north side of town and contained nothing but wood. Rough-sawn wood, planed and milled wood, stumps, bits of specialty woods from faraway places, and even some pedestrian two-by-fours. I'd been there only a handful of times, and though the contents changed, the volume always seemed the same. Packed to the gills. I tried not to think about it because there was an inevitability about the fact that someday I would have to deal with the contents.

Trying to be a good niece, I asked, "Do you need any help?" Since I'd scheduled myself for the noon to close shift at the library that day, I could give her a hand. I had other plans, but if she needed me, of course I'd change them.

"You are a kind soul and thank you, but no. I have some students who volunteered to help if they could walk away with some bird's-eye of their own."

It sounded like an excellent plan and I told her so.

"Yes," she agreed. "Or it will be as long as we can get the door to the storage unit open after that freezing rain."

"Hot water," I said promptly. "Take a thermos of hot water and pour it along the door's seal."

My aunt stared at me with frank admiration. "Brilliant. I am proud to be related to you."

"Voice of experience is all. The bookmobile's garage door sticks sometimes in winter and that works fast. Just make sure to dry off that rubber seal."

Aunt Frances laughed. "You are a treasure trove of practical knowledge. Do your parents know this about you?" She got up from the kitchen table, having eaten her oatmeal so fast that pouring it might have been slower.

"No one is a prophet in her own home."

"Is that a quote?"

I thought about it. "Not as far as I know, but then I read a lot."

"Well, I'm off." She bagged up her lunch and grabbed an empty thermos. "I'll get this filled at the school when I'm picking up the kids. See you tonight!"

A few seconds later, the front door shut. "I hope she slowed down enough to put on her boots," I said to Eddie, who had wandered into the kitchen. "A coat would be good, too, since it's only twenty degrees out there."

"Mrr," he said, jumping onto his chair.

"I'm sure you're right. She probably slid right into those nice wool-lined duck boots without breaking stride." I scraped up the last of my oatmeal. "And if you see Otto, could you please tell him this morning wasn't the right time to talk to her about the furniture?"

"Mrr!"

That hadn't sounded like agreement, but I could have been wrong. "Cool. Thanks."

I washed the dishes, patted Eddie on the head, and headed out for my first self-imposed chore of the morning.

The sign at the road was mostly covered with snow, but enough was visible for my brain to fill in the bottom part. Maple Staples. This was the company that sold the sugar packet I'd found at

Rowan's. Well, technically, Eddie had found it, but I wasn't about to tell that to my friends in law enforcement. They barely tolerated my ideas; letting them know some of them came from a cat wasn't going to get Hal or Ash to take the ideas more seriously.

The building was a typical Up North manufacturing facility; large pole barn with metal siding and an office tacked on the front. The parking lot, thankfully, was plowed reasonably well and held half a dozen vehicles. I parked between a four-wheel drive pickup and an all-wheel drive SUV and went in.

"Hello." From behind a wooden desk worn at the corners, a twenty-something man with long hair and an even longer beard smiled at me. "Can I help you?"

Smiling back, I said, "I certainly hope so," and went ahead with the truth-stretching story I'd concocted early that morning. With any luck it would sound just as solid now as it had at 3 a.m. "You're the folks that make that maple-flavored sugar, right? Well, it turns out that stuff is basically addictive and I have this friend who would love me forever if I could track down a case of it. He can't find it anywhere and . . ." I stopped, because his smile had turned rueful and he was shaking his head.

"Sorry. We sold the last box a month ago to a restaurant in Traverse City."

"What restaurant?" I asked. "Maybe they still have some and—"

Again the head shake. "Nope. It's all gone. They called last Friday and asked for more."

Huh. Maybe the stuff really was addictive. "That's too bad." Sort of. I didn't really care if I bought any; I just wanted to know more about the product and how it might have ended up in Rowan's house. "It seems very popular. I'm surprised I haven't seen it before now."

"We've only been in business a couple of years," the guy said. "My boss and her husband are really into beer, but Bob can't stand the smell of wort—that's beer before it ferments—so beer was out when they started thinking about a startup company. But you know how some craft breweries have lots of short runs?"

In a general sort of way. I nodded.

"That's what we're doing with our maple syrup. Lots of different products, smaller production quantities. We make things from that sugar to ice cream to a barbecue glaze." He spread his arms. "And it's all local."

"Really?" I'd known Michigan was a big producer of maple syrup, but I'd never thought about value-added products. Yet another reason I was never going to be an entrepreneur.

"And like some craft breweries," he said, "we've decided to relabel products every year. The contents don't change, but the labeling does.

That's why you might not have seen that sugar packet before—last fall was the only time it was made."

I hesitated. "Doesn't that make brand recognition harder for your customers? I mean, what if they really liked that particular flavor of whatever, and think the new label is something different and get, um, maybe irritated?"

"Yeah, we're getting some of that." He leaned back in his chair. "I think we should do a longitudinal data analysis and figure out the spikes, both up and down, for correlations and see what we can do to maximize the positives. Don't you think that makes sense?"

"More data is often useful," I said, looking for the middle-of-the-road response to what was clearly a very pointed question about a topic. Plus I'd mostly stopped listening when he'd said "longitudinal," so I wasn't completely sure what he was talking about.

"Exactly." He nodded. "That's what I keep telling Robbie and Bob. You know what? I'm just going to do it. Easier to ask forgiveness than permission, right?"

I smiled. "Thanks for your time. I appreciate it."

"No problem. Say, if you're interested in the sugar, I can put you on a waiting list. Bob started a sheet right after Christmas." He rooted through the piles of papers on the desk. "Here you go," he said, handing me a clipboard. "Robbie wants to expand into birch syrup, too. The sky's the limit with this place. Of course, we'd have to change the name."

But for the second time in two minutes, I'd stopped listening. Because at the top of the list of names and e-mail addresses was one I recognized.

Hugh Novak.

Since I'd estimated the driving time out to Maple Staples and back poorly—to the dry road travel time I'd only added twenty-five percent instead of the fifty percent I should have to properly compensate for the snow that was falling from the heavens—I didn't have time to make the other stops I'd planned. I arrived at the library a few minutes early, but I hadn't had lunch, since I'd also planned a return to the boardinghouse to eat.

I stopped in the break room on the way into my office and peeked in the refrigerator. There was always a chance that I'd left something in there and forgotten about it—yogurt? leftovers? anything?—but I came up dry. The offerings in the vending machine were heavy on the sugary side. I made a face at the bag of peanuts I was pretty sure had been there since the machine had been installed and wondered if there was any chance I'd left a can of soup in the bottom drawer of my desk.

"Minnie, you're just the person I was hoping to see." Graydon was in the doorway, buttoning his navy peacoat. "Do you have lunch plans?"

"Nothing that my mother would call a meal." I tapped the vending machine. "College students, yes. Mom? No."

Graydon laughed. "Lunch is my treat, if you have time."

I blinked. Never in the history of my working life had a boss ever taken me out to lunch. There'd been the occasional group outing, but those had been separate checks for all and didn't count. "That would be nice. Thanks."

"I'll defer to your local expertise for a restaurant choice," Graydon said. "I have no allergies and like almost everything except cottage cheese."

Since I'd just eaten at Shomin's and didn't feel Fat Boys Pizza was a suitable place to take Graydon, there wasn't any other affordable place open this time of year except the Round Table.

A short walk later, I led the way past the SEAT YOURSELF sign and paused. Sitting in a booth with my boss, a seating arrangement that implied intimacy, would be too weird. Of course, sitting at a table would be weird, too, since the only time I did that was in summer when all the booths were full. Still, a table it was.

"Hey, sunshine." The diner's forever waitress,

Sabrina, put down glasses of ice water. "Who's your new friend?"

Graydon held out his hand and introduced himself. "I'm the new library director."

"Hmm." Sabrina shook his hand. "Well, you can't be any worse than the last two. Don't know that I ever saw that Jennifer in here, and Stephen?" She rolled her eyes. "Chicken sandwich with mayo, chips, and water, every time. Never tipped more than fifty cents. I'll be right back with a menu."

I hadn't had time to ask how her husband, Bill, was doing, but since she was her normal sparkling self, I was pretty sure he was doing okay. He and Sabrina were in their mid-fifties, but Bill was already suffering from macular degeneration. Special treatments down in Traverse City seemed to be slowing the symptoms and maybe even halting them, and we were all hoping he wouldn't get any worse.

After we ordered—ham and cheese with fries for me, a club sandwich and cup of chicken noodle soup for him—Graydon sat back a little. "Do you mind if I ask a few questions?"

"Fire away," I said, mirroring his movement. "But just so you know, I'm horrible at mental math."

He smiled. "Not that kind of questions. Library questions."

"Way easier. What do you want to know?"

"For one, how long do you think Donna will keep working?"

I laughed. "She works to support her habits. Turns out that traveling to Africa to run marathons and to Norway to snowshoe is expensive. She's in great shape for any age, let alone someone who's in her early seventies. If I had to guess, I'd say she's going to work for another decade." I thought about it for a moment. "And I wouldn't be surprised at two."

It would be a sad day when Donna left her part-time job. She was intelligent, capable, and could be extremely funny. I didn't like to think about the library without her.

Sabrina slid our plates in front of us. "Cookie's rolling them out fast today. Let me know if you need anything else."

"Thank you," Graydon said. "This looks great."

"Absolutely." I took hold of the malt vinegar bottle and shook it lightly over my fries. "And tell Cookie thanks, too."

"The speed isn't for your sake," Sabrina said. "He overcooked Otis's bacon this morning and he's still trying to recover." Smirking, she pulled a pencil out of her graying hair bun and went to take orders from a table of EMTs.

"Otis Rahn?" Graydon asked. "The past library board president?"

Nodding, I sprinkled salt on my fries. Cookie never added enough for my taste. "For years and years." I was about to say how much I missed him, but decided that might not be in my best professional interest.

Graydon took in a few spoonfuls of soup. "What do you think about Kelsey?"

I kept my face blank and wondered what this was all about. "Personally or professionally?" I tacked on a smile at the end of my question because I was afraid it might have come out a little snarky.

"Whatever you feel comfortable telling me."

To delay giving an answer, I picked up my sandwich and took a bite. It was so good that I took another. Graydon, by this time, had started eating his. "This is very good," he said.

"Cookie graduated from the culinary program at Northwestern Michigan College. He worked in Chicago for a while, but came home a few years ago."

"His name isn't really Cookie, is it?"

"I honestly don't know." And I didn't want to know, either. I enjoyed thinking of him as Cookie. My earlier liking for my new boss was turning to something else. I put my sandwich down. "About Kelsey. And anyone else you might ask about. I'm perfectly comfortable giving you professional assessments, that's part of my job. But if you want me to—"

Graydon's cell phone buzzed. "Sorry," he murmured, looking at the screen. "It's Trent. I should take this." He stood and went to the far corner of the room, turning his back to me.

I finished my speech to the back of his head. "But if you want me to spy on my coworkers and report back, that's not going to happen."

"What isn't going to happen?"

I looked up. And smiled at Rafe, who had materialized out of nowhere and was sitting himself at the table. "Curing the common cold in our lifetimes," I said. "What do you think isn't going to happen?"

"Right now, I'm concerned that it's getting hardware for the kitchen cabinets."

Oh. That. "Um . . ."

He sighed so heavily that hyperventilation was a mild concern. "The one thing I ask you to do. One thing."

I pushed my plate toward him. "Have some fries. They'll make you feel better. What are you doing here anyway?"

"Picking up lunch for the admin office."

"Then you don't need any of my fries, do you?"

" 'Need' is such a subjective word. Your fries are hard to resist because you always add the perfect amounts of malt vinegar and salt."

"It's one of my proudest accomplishments. And keep your hands off Graydon's food," I said as I saw him eyeing the potato chips. "He's back there, on the phone."

Rafe turned briefly. "Ah, I could take him."

A forty-ish man who was either bald or regularly shaved his head, I'd never been able to determine which, dropped a bulging plastic bag on the front counter. "Hey, Niswander. Your order's up."

"Thanks, Cookie." Rafe leaned over to give me a kiss and stood. "See you tonight?"

"I have one stop after work, but that's it."

"You're finally going to stop at the hardware store to look at drawer pulls?"

"Aren't you cute." I smiled at him fondly. "See you later."

He sighed again, but there was a grin in there, so I knew the hardware decision could be put off a little longer.

I turned my attention back to my food. Graydon, however, was still on the phone. What could he and the new library board president be talking about? Okay, any number of things, probably, but what could be so critical that Trent needed to interrupt Graydon's lunch? From the expression on Graydon's face, the conversation was not completely positive.

A slightly twitchy feeling started to form in my stomach. I tried to ignore it, or to think it was the result of too much fried food in too short a time. And I almost succeeded until my ears picked up the word "bookmobile." Startled, I glanced up, directly at Graydon, and found that he was looking straight at me. He half smiled and let his gaze drift past, but I was left with some distinctly uncomfortable knowledge.

My boss and the board president were talking about the bookmobile.

And they were talking about me.

After I locked the library down for the evening—Friday was the one winter weeknight we closed at five—I drove the few blocks to meet with Hal and Ash. The late meeting time had suited them both for various reasons, so I'd stopped feeling guilty about canceling our morning appointment and shifted to feeling guilty about driving such a short distance instead of walking. Some days I could pull off being like Aunt Frances and not feel guilty about hardly anything and, even better, not worrying about anything at all, but today wasn't one of them. "Tomorrow is another day," I said as I opened the door to the sheriff's office.

Hal Inwood was in the lobby, tacking an announcement about keeping mailboxes clear of snow to the glass-covered bulletin board. "Yes, unless the world ends in the middle of the night."

"Aren't you a ray of sunshine." I stomped my boots free of snow.

"You should meet my wife." He shut the glass door and locked it. "Unless you two are already

130

good friends. That would, in many ways, explain quite a bit."

But Mrs. Hal and I had never met. Which was both odd and not odd. Chilson was a small town, but for transplants, which the Inwoods and I both were, if your paths didn't cross, you could easily never meet. I grinned. "Tell her to stop by the library. We can exchange all sorts of stories, for hours and hours."

He gave me a pained look as he let me go in front of him into the interview room. "Fortunately, she's downstate with grandchildren, and it's possible that when she returns, I'll forget to mention your kind invitation."

Right then and there I made a silent vow to get to know the detective's wife. "How is the testing going?"

"Of the sugar packet? No results yet, and I believe I mentioned at the time that it would take at least a week."

"You did," I said, "but I was thinking maybe January is a slow time at the lab and they could get it through faster than a week."

"Still the funny one, aren't you," Ash said as he came into the room. "None of the labs in the state have slow seasons. All they have are busy and really busy times."

"The poor things," I murmured, meaning it. How stressful it must be to always be pushing your staff to the limit.

"Job security." Ash pulled out the chair next to Hal and sat. "Sorry I'm late, I was finishing up a report."

"That's what I like best in a detective-in-training," Hal said, nodding. "Finishing my work."

I smiled and didn't say a word, but I was thinking how far the relationship between Detective Hal Inwood and myself had advanced. Not all that long ago he'd barely tolerated my presence and had clearly considered my suggestions an interference. Now he seemed as if he could be almost likable.

"Now, Ms. Hamilton," Hal said, focusing on me. "You said you have information to share. Please go right ahead. I'd like to get home at some point tonight."

"Sure," I said. "Neil Bennethum has already told you some of this, but I have some thoughts, too."

I told them about Rowan's argument with Land, and how Neil was so sure that Land had killed Rowan. The two law enforcement officers across the table had both opened their respective notepads and clicked on their pens, but no notes were taken during my little speech.

"You know all this," I said.

"Looking into it." Hal glanced at his watch. "At this point we're still gathering information."

Well, almost likable. "Right. How silly of me to think I might tell you something useful."

Hal sighed. "Ms. Hamilton, please. It's been a long day. What else do you have?"

I told myself to cut the detective a little slack. He was getting up there in age, and he was serving the people of Tonedagana County for a wage that didn't anywhere near make up for the hassles he had to endure.

"Assuming," I said, "that the sugar packet was a vehicle for the poison, there are at least two people who use that particular type of sugar. Stewart Funston, who I saw with the same kind of packet just yesterday, and Hugh Novak. He's on the waiting list at the place that makes the stuff to get a box as soon as they make any new."

Hal's and Ash's pens scribbled away as I talked. When I stopped, Hal asked, "And their connections to the victim?"

He was taking me seriously—hooray! "Stewart is Rowan's cousin. A first cousin. And though I'm not sure of the details, Hugh couldn't stand Rowan. They were on opposite sides of the political spectrum, and he never missed an opportunity to disagree with her publicly." That's what Neil had implied. I'd confirmed it with Donna, and she was one of my most trusted local sources.

"There's a lot of that going around," Ash said. "If people killed each other because of politics, we'd have a lot more murders at Thanksgiving."

But people did kill each other over politics, and the look Hal gave Ash was one of fatigued reproach. "Thank you, Ms. Hamilton. We'll take this information into account as the investigation moves forward."

It was a statement of dismissal, but I wasn't ready to move an inch. "And what have you found out? Don't say you can't discuss an active investigation. Surely you can tell me who you've talked to at the bank. If you don't tell me, I'll go the bank and any teller will let me know."

Hal gave Ash a nod. "Okay," Ash said. "Technically, this information is public knowledge, but we'd prefer you keep it to yourself." When I murmured agreement, he went on. "We talked to Sunny Scoles."

I frowned. "Isn't she the owner of that new restaurant halfway between here and Charlevoix?" I couldn't remember the name.

"That's the one. She opened up there because it was what she could afford, but it was affordable because it's not a great location. Apparently she's doing okay, but wants to buy a food truck to expand."

"Rowan turned her down?"

Hal stirred. "We can't give out that information."

I squinted at the men across the table. "But you talked to her so—"

"Can neither confirm nor deny."

I turned back to Ash. "Sunny Scoles. Anyone else?"

"The last person we talked to was Baxter Tousely."

"Baxter . . ." The name sounded familiar. Then my mental lightbulb clicked on. "You mean Bax?"

Ash nodded. "That's what everyone calls him."

"Is he about twenty-two?" If I recalled correctly, Bax had been in the same high school class as the Bennethum twins. He hadn't been a fixture in the library, but I remembered Anya and Collier mentioning his name in a way that had made me assume he was one of their friends.

Hal flicked me a glance. "How many men named Baxter do you know, Ms. Hamilton?"

And back to the not-quite-likable side. "Bax is still in Chilson?" If he'd been a friend of Collier and Anya, I would have thought he'd gone off to college.

"Working for the city," Ash said. "Public works department. But his dream is to have a post-production video service. It can be a good business, I guess, putting together short movie-like bits for everything from big companies to nonprofits to weddings, but to do it right, you need some expensive equipment up front."

"And Rowan turned him down for the loan."

Ash smiled. "What I can tell you is that he's

135

still working for the city and hasn't been in the best of moods the last few weeks."

"Is there anything else you can tell me?" I asked.

"No." Hal stood. "And I'm not sure I'm comfortable with how much we've told you already. Good night, Ms. Hamilton. Deputy Wolverson, I'll see you tomorrow." He walked out, leaving me with Ash.

I sat back. "Is he getting enough sleep? Eating properly? I worry about the man, especially now that I know his wife is out of town."

"You're one to talk about eating right." Ash stuffed his notebook into his uniform's shirt pocket. "When was the last time you ate any vegetables?" I opened my mouth, but shut it when he added, "And French fries don't count."

"We're talking about Hal," I said, "not me. Besides, older people are more fragile than people our age. He should be taking care of himself."

"Do you want to tell him that?"

The answer, of course, was, "Not a chance." But since I didn't want to say so to Ash, I went back to the main topic of conversation. "About these two." Sunny, the restauranteur. Bax, the wannabe filmmaker. "Do you really think one of them killed Rowan?"

Ash glanced in the direction Hal had gone. Hesitated. "We're exploring all—"

"Never mind," I said, sighing. Clearly, Ash now belonged heart and soul to the sheriff's office. It made sense, it was appropriate, and I understood, but it was going to make life a little harder for me.

Chapter 7

The next day was Saturday, a half book-mobile day, and the morning was filled with mostly happy people and an exceptionally sleepy Eddie.

"Where is the bookmobile kitty?" one small book-holding homeschooled urchin asked. "I wanted to pet him."

I smiled at the youngster and, after getting the nod from her dad, brought her up front. "Eddie is asleep," I said, gesturing to the cat carrier. "But next time we're here, I think he'll be wide awake and ready for you."

"But I want to pet him now." The urchin's lower lip started to tremble. "Why is he sleepy?"

The correct answer was that he'd been up half the night in the downstairs bathroom, shredding facial tissues and toilet paper and batting around the miniature rubber duckies that lived on the edge of the claw foot tub. Happily, Aunt Frances and I had both slept through the episode, and this morning it had been easy enough to avert my eyes to the mess and mutter that I'd clean it up when I got home.

But I didn't want to spread the word that Eddie could be a Bad Cat, so I said, "He was up late, watching the sky. He likes to see the stars, so when the clouds cleared off last night, he got up to see the Big Dipper." I tried to remember the names of any other constellations I was absolutely sure we saw this time of year. "He really likes the Big Dipper," I said, then pointed outside. "And isn't it nice to have some blue sky?"

The youngster ignored my distracting gesture. Instead, she leaned over and petted the cat carrier. "Sleep tight, Bookmobile Kitty. Don't let the bed bugs bite." She gave the carrier one last pat, and marched back to her father with a satisfied look on her face.

It was adorable, and for the millionth time I thought how lucky I was to have this job.

The happy feeling stayed with me the rest of the day, despite the thick clouds that hid the sky by noon and despite Eddie's snoring, which Julia found immensely amusing. "I had no idea cats could snore. It's the cutest thing."

"You wouldn't think so if it kept you awake at three in the morning." I was pretty sure that Eddie's day-long sleep was going to result in another active night, but how did you keep a cat awake during the day when he wanted to sleep? There was no victory for me here. As per usual, the cat won.

It wasn't until I was stowing Eddie in my car

and we were about to head home that I remembered my promise to Rafe.

"Rats," I said out loud. "Big fat rats."

"Mrr?" Eddie was lying on his side. He rotated his head so his face was upside down and blinked at me. "Mrr?" he asked again.

I buckled his carrier in. "There's this one short errand. Do you want me to take you home first, or are you okay in the carrier for a little longer?"

Hearing nothing, I leaned down to look. My cat was, once again, sleeping.

"Carrier it is." I shut the passenger door and got in on my side. "But I'm sure it won't take long. I mean, how long can choosing cabinet hardware possibly take?"

Ten minutes later, I was finding out. "No wonder Rafe wanted me to do this," I said, stunned by the thickness of the catalog.

Jared laughed. "Niswander said you'd say that."

I knew his name was Jared, because his crisp name tag said so, and that he was the store owner because that's who Rafe had told me to talk to. The owner of the used bookstore in town was also named Jared, but they were not, in fact, the same person, although they were roughly the same age, which was also mine.

I'd assumed the owner of a hardware store would be approaching geezer age, or would at least have lots of gray hair. Instead, he had nary a gray hair in sight, and the moment I set foot in the door, he'd come up to me and said, "You must be Minnie. I've been expecting you."

After blinking at the oddness of his greeting, I'd grasped what was going on—Rafe had stopped by earlier and prepped the poor guy. I laughed. "Did Rafe also mention what I'm supposed to be doing?"

He had, which was why I was sitting in Jared's office, paging through a catalog thick and heavy enough to require weighing in for a commercial flight. It was a nice office, bright with fluorescent lights and cheery with framed posters of abstract art. Through the open office door, I could see out into the store, a pleasant enough space of utilitarian metal shelving filled with items whose uses were a complete mystery to me.

"You see how the different designs are arranged, right?" Jared asked. "By finish and style?"

"Um." I returned my attention to the catalog. "Sure. It's just . . . there are so many." It was overwhelming and reminded me of the sensory overload I felt in a shopping mall. It made me tired and tended me toward crankiness.

"What kind of cabinets is Rafe building? Knowing that will help you choose a style."

Jared's patience seemed extensive, but my own was far more limited. "I don't know," I said, sitting back. "Maple, is all I remember."

"Three panel? Single panel? Beadboard?"

I looked at the man. "Do you seriously think I have any idea what you're talking about?"

He grinned. "Don't want to assume you don't."

"Excellent attitude," I said approvingly, "but in spite of my exposure to woodworkers and woodworking for most of my life, very little has stuck in my brain." This wasn't strictly true, but it was close enough. "What I do know is that Rafe is using a light stain and—" I'd been using my hands to talk and knocked a pile of folders to the floor.

"Sorry about that." I jumped out of the chair and kneeled down.

"No worries," Jared said, rolling his chair around and leaning forward to help. "Just a stack of customer account files I was going through, studying buying habits."

I hadn't thought about purchasing habits for hardware, but I supposed every business had trends. "You have a lot of customer accounts?"

"Wish I had more." Jared piled the folders into a tidy heap. "A few people have them, and a few businesses. The city is our best customer by far, but . . ." His voice drifted off.

"But what?" I asked, because his face looked troubled. "Are they starting to buy stuff from Amazon?"

Jared shook his head. "No. At least I don't think so. It's just that Bax Tousely—you know him? No? Friendly guy, always comes in with some horrible joke he can't wait to tell. He was in first thing a couple of weeks ago and didn't say a word. No joke, no nothing. And he left all of a sudden, without buying a thing. It was weird and I haven't seen him since. I hope nothing's wrong."

I felt a prickle at the back of my neck. "Do you remember what day that was?"

"Sure. It was a Monday. Almost two weeks ago. I remember because it was the first anniversary of when I bought this place. I gave the day's first customer a gift certificate and Bax was the second guy in the door."

And it was also the day Rowan had died.

Had Bax gone to the hardware store, ostensibly looking for a piece of hardware, but instead driven to Rowan's house and killed her? It was possible; surely it was possible. But why?

Jared was looking at me. "I have a suggestion. You've looked at too many possibilities. Why don't you look at some magazines, or watch some home improvement shows. See if any cabinet hardware catches your eye. When you have a couple that you like, come on back."

"That's a great idea," I said vaguely, put on my coat, and headed out to the car, where Eddie was waiting for me.

Monday morning was very January-like: snowy, cold, and blustery. For a short second I thought about driving to the library, but knew that was a slippery slope to start sliding down. "Get it?" I asked Eddie. "You know, because it's the middle of winter and pretty much everything everywhere is slippery anyway?"

Eddie, who was roosting on the back of the couch, opened one eye, then closed it again.

"Huh." I kissed the top of his head. "Since you don't appreciate my very funny jokes, I'm going to take them to the library for the day."

"Mrr."

"I'm going to assume that was shorthand for have a nice walk, do good work, come home to me safe and sound, and I'll miss you like crazy the entire time you're gone."

My cat's response was a whistling snore.

Smiling, I headed outside. And as I knew would happen, my reluctance to venture out disappeared by the time I reached the bottom of the porch steps. Yes it was snowy, yes it was cold, and yes the northwest winds were blasting my face. But the cold was invigorating and the very fact that I was outside made me feel brave and intrepid. There I was, mushing myself through the mean streets of Chilson, intent on ensuring that everyone had access to the wealth of knowledge and wisdom that resided inside the library walls. Valiant Minnie! Strong Minnie! Dedicated . . .

I winced as a particularly strong wind gust blew snow down the back of my neck.

Bleah. Snow down my neck was almost as bad as snow up my sleeves. Both chilled me, giving me shivers that seemed to last for hours.

I looked up from the study I'd been making of the sidewalk. Ah. I was downtown. And even though it was long before any retail stores typically opened, I could see Mitchell inside, dusting the toys on the top shelf. I stopped and knocked on the front door.

He turned and saw me. "Come on in," he said, his words barely making it through the glass. "The door's unlocked."

Silly me. I opened the door and hurried inside, accompanied by a rush of snow and cold.

"Surprised you walked today. It's ten below out there, and that's without the windchill." Mitchell headed toward the back. "Coffee?"

"Yes, please," I said through chattering teeth. Ten below? Seriously? I hadn't looked at the thermometer that morning, something I was suddenly quite sure I would never forget to do again. "Thanks," I said as Mitchell handed me a plain white mug of steaming goodness. I buried my face in the heat, letting its warmth thaw my nose and cheeks. "This is exactly what I needed. You're the best."

Mitchell shuffled. "Well, I remember you like coffee, that's all."

I took a sip and ignored the faint blush that was coloring Mitchell's cheeks. Once upon a time, he'd asked me out on a date and I'd let him down so gently that he'd managed to get the very mistaken impression that I'd been pining for him but couldn't walk away from an existing relationship without doing serious harm to another man's soul.

Since there was no earthly reason to discuss any of that, I said, "You asked me about Bianca, so I've been doing some investigating."

Mitchell stiffened. "You're not talking to her, are you? She's smart, she'll figure out what's going on and—"

"Don't worry," I interrupted soothingly. "Not that kind of investigating. I've been reading journal articles and relationship books"—Okay, technically what I'd done was glance over the abstracts and conclusions, but that's where all the good stuff was, so I didn't feel I was misleading him, not really—"and from what I know of you and Bianca's relationship, what you have going on is positive, healthy, and sustainable."

"Yeah?" Mitchell perked up. "What should I do now?" He could have been a human version of a puppy, albeit a very large one.

"If it was me," I said, "I'd just talk to her."

"Sometimes I think about doing that." Mitchell stared at his mug, a chipped version of the one he'd given me. "But then I wonder what if I got this all wrong? I don't want to be like my buddy at that Tigers game."

I suddenly got a hint of what it might be like to be a guy—or at least a guy like Mitchell—and I got an inkling of how the possibility of humiliation could shape life decisions.

"Well," I said, "hang in there. I'll try to think of something."

I finished my coffee and headed back into the weather, not at all sure I'd be able to help Mitchell solve his problem.

That noon, bowing to the needs of my coworkers—plus their vow that if I went out in the snow to get the food, they wouldn't ever again complain about having to listen to me review the library safety policies, something we did every other month (not that I believed the vow, but it was nice of them to recognize how much whining they did)—I ventured downtown to the Round Table.

Sabrina was at the register when I came in. "How is it you stay so skinny?" she asked, thumping her hip with an elbow. "Me, I'm squishy and soft and I'm doing my darnedest to lose weight."

"Sorry," I said apologetically. "I figure it'll catch up with me in a few years."

"Huh." Sabrina pointed with the top of her head. "How about that one? Is it going to get him, too?"

I turned. Ash had just come inside and was still

stomping the snow off his boots. "Depends," I said. "If he convinces someone to marry him, I bet he puts on thirty pounds the first year. If he stays single?" I shrugged.

Ash came up beside me. "Sabrina, you're looking as lovely as ever." She glowered at him and whirled away. "What? What did I say?"

"It's not you," I said. "Trust me."

"Okay." He glanced around. It being January, ten minutes before noon, there was no one else in the restaurant other than the elderly men at the round table in the back of the room. Today there were only three of them, but at times there could be eight, grousing about the state of the world and what should be done to fix it.

As a general rule, I smiled at them politely and stayed as far away as possible. Rafe, on the other hand, said it was his goal in life to be invited to sit at the round table. Sometimes I believed him and sometimes I didn't. I squinted, trying to envision Rafe next to Bob Dawkins, who I could hear, from thirty feet away, complaining about the crappy way the road commission plowed the county roads, and how much better they did it in Charlevoix County.

"Speaking of trusting you," Ash said, "we're moving on those names and . . ."

His voice trailed off.

"And what?" I asked, then realized he was looking out the front window, studying a hatless young man dressed in the dark red coat worn by city workers. The guy had been clearing a fire hydrant, but had stuffed his shovel in a snowbank to help a woman maneuver her double stroller—laden with an infant and a toddler—across the snowy mess that was currently the street. "Who's that?"

"Bax Tousely," Ash said.

My attention focused. He had hair as curly as mine and almost as dark. He also had a wide smile and was grinning down at the kids. He didn't seem likely as a killer, but who did?

Ash and I watched for a moment, then when the stroller was safely across the street and Bax had gone back to shoveling, I asked, "You're moving on those names? Which ones?"

He got a faraway look. "Well, since I can't give out information about an ongoing investigation, all I can give you is—"

"Ash Wolverson," I said severely, putting my chin up, "you give me everything or I'll tell your mother on you."

Grinning, he continued, "What I can give you is some general information that you could find out easily enough if you wanted to. Like this. Hugh Novak is an insurance adjuster. He looks at cars all over the region. On the day of the murder, what would you guess about his whereabouts?"

Interesting. I thought a minute and said, "I'd guess he had appointments lined up, but there's no one who can confirm where he was at the key time."

Ash grinned. "No need to tattle on me to Mom, right?"

"Not this time," I said, trying—and probably failing—to sound ominous. "Let me know if anything else turns up, okay?"

Sabrina appeared with the bag that held the library's lunch order, and I went to pay. It was only when I was outside and halfway up the sidewalk that I realized Ash hadn't actually answered my question.

The next morning, I got up early. If I was going to make it to the restaurant owned by Sunny Scoles and back to the library to get the bookmobile out on time, I was going to have to scamper.

"What about breakfast?" Aunt Frances asked. "You have to eat something."

"I'll get something at the restaurant," I assured her.

"Who is it you're meeting?"

Sort of meeting, anyway. I zipped up my coat and picked up Eddie's carrier. "Sunny Scoles. Do you know her?"

"Don't know the name at all." She frowned. "You sure she's a good candidate for the catering at Kristen's wedding?"

"Her name came up," I said, which was the absolute truth. "I can't imagine Kristen allowing anyone except her own staff to cook for her wedding, but it doesn't hurt to talk to a few people, right?"

All true, though intentionally misleading. The entire drive to the restaurant, I kept trying not to think that intentionally misleading was perhaps worse than a lie, and not succeeding. Yet another character flaw to improve. "Add it to the list," I muttered to Eddie, who didn't comment.

I parked the car near the front door of the Red House Café. "Be back in a flash," I told my furry friend. "All I'm going to get is oatmeal, so the car will barely even cool down before I'm back."

"Mrr," Eddie said, then yawned and flopped on his side.

The restaurant's exterior matched its name and was solid red with white trim. It was a jumble of multiple additions, and when I went inside, I was clued in to what the original building had been, and why it was red.

"Oh," I said softly, smiling at nothing in particular and everything in general. "It was a one-room schoolhouse." All around me was the evidence. Wooden school chairs served as dining chairs, and penmanship instructions were wall art. An entire gallery of lunch buckets rested on a shallow shelf that circled the room, and a school bell hung from the ceiling, right above the front counter.

"Hasn't been a school for sixty years." A

woman about my age approached from the back, drying her hands on a towel as she went. "It was a house longer than it was a school, but all it took was a little demolition and there were the bones of the original room."

Her dark blond hair was pulled back into a ponytail, and she wore a chef's outfit of black cotton pants and the nifty white jacket that chefs wear, with the name "Sunny" embroidered on the upper left side.

"This place is great," I said. "I've been driving past it for years, but I didn't know the history."

She smiled. "I'm hearing that a lot. You can sit anywhere you'd like. Let me get you a menu."

"Sorry." I shook my head. "This morning I don't have time to sit down. But if I could get a carry-out container of oatmeal, I'd really appreciate it."

"Walnuts?" she asked. "Pecans? Blueberries? Dried cherries?"

Life was full of decisions, some harder than others, and this was one of them. "I like them all. Pick whatever you like best."

"A little bit of each it is," she said cheerfully. "I'll be back in a jiffy. Do you want some coffee, too?" She bustled away, laughing at my heartfelt answer of "Yes" to the coffee question.

When I heard food-related rattling in the back, I put my elbows on the front counter and sighed. What had I been hoping to learn this morning?

That Sunny was a nasty person of the type who looked like a killer, meaning she must be one? When I'd decided to drive down here, it had seemed so sensible. Then again, how many one-thirty-in-the-morning decisions were good ones?

Well, at least I now had a new restaurant to try. Oatmeal was great for a workday breakfast, but it didn't really count as food.

I wandered to the nearest table, looked for a menu, and stopped short. Right there, in a wire rack right next to the salt and pepper shakers, was a stack of sugar packets. The same kind of sugar packet that Maple Staples had sold out of and that I'd recently added my name to a list to buy when available. The same kind that had been at Rowan's house.

All my theories about limited access to this very special type of sugar vaporized in a second. Everyone had access to them. Everyone.

I was back to the beginning, and I had no idea what to do next.

Chapter 8

hat do you think I should do next?" I asked.

Eddie, comfortable on my lap, which was covered with a fleece blanket, closed his eyes and purred.

"Give me a hint, please? Even a little one would help."

"Help what?" My aunt plopped herself down at the end of the couch. The movement disturbed Eddie enough that he opened his eyes and picked his head up half an inch. "Now look what you did," I said. "You disturbed his sleep for almost a second."

Aunt Frances rubbed the fur on Eddie's back leg. "Sorry, Mr. Ed. Next time you get up, I'll treat you to a treat." She turned her head, listening. "He's purring. I think he forgives me."

"Cats aren't big on forgiveness," I said, "but they can be bought. At least this one can." I scratched Eddie alongside his chin and the purrs grew even louder.

My aunt smiled. "Tell you what. I'll bring cat treats and make popcorn if you tell me why you're asking the fuzzy one for advice instead of your wise old aunt."

"That's easy." I kept scratching Eddie's chin. "It's because I don't want to tell anyone what I've been doing."

"And that is what exactly?"

I gave her a mock-exasperated look. "If I tell you, I'll have told someone what I'm doing, and that's what I'm trying to avoid, see?"

"Why?"

Another easy question. "Because I'll get scolded for doing things I shouldn't be doing."

She laughed. "Dearest niece, I know full well that you're trying to figure out who killed poor Rowan Bennethum."

"You . . . do?"

"Please." She snorted. "How long have we lived together? And how long have I known you? Wait, I remember. All your life."

"Okay, so maybe I'm more transparent than I thought." I rested my hand on Eddie's back. "Do you think Rafe knows?"

"You haven't told him, either?" Aunt Frances's gaze zeroed in on my face. "Minnie, are you sure that's wise?"

Right now I wasn't sure about anything, and I said so.

"Part of being an adult," my aunt said, nodding. "Which I recognize isn't reassuring, but at least it's honest."

"Wonderful," I said. "But I don't see why not telling Rafe about this is a big deal. All I'm doing is a little extracurricular research, that's all. Just an extension of being a librarian, is how I see it. Why does he need to know?"

"Mrr!"

"Sorry." I released Eddie's fur, which apparently I'd started to clutch a little too hard. "You get double treats for that."

"He wasn't objecting to your petting methods," Aunt Frances said. "He was objecting to what could be pending doom for your relationship with Rafe."

Stung, I said, "Just because I don't tell him everything I do every second of the day? I don't need to know that much about him, and he doesn't need to know that much about me."

"Not every daily detail, no. But don't you think the man who is renovating that house with your every need, want, and desire in mind deserves to know, at least in general, what you're doing, and why?" When I didn't answer, she said, "How would you feel if he was keeping something like this from you?"

I tried the idea on for size and didn't like how I was feeling. At all. For a long minute, I sat there and didn't say anything. "You're right. I need to talk to him about this."

"Excellent." My aunt smiled, and that alone made me feel a teensy bit better. "Time for popcorn and treats, not necessarily in that order." She stood, and before I could get any further in my thoughts than a repeated, *But how do I tell him I'm trying to figure out who killed Rowan? He's not going to like it,* she was back.

"Three treats for you, since you're such a good cat." Aunt Frances dropped the bits on the blanket just underneath Eddie's chin. "And here's yours." She handed over a comfortable-size bowl of buttered and salted popcorn, keeping a twin bowl for herself.

"Now," she said, settling back down. "Ask me what you should do next. I'll tell you exactly what to do without even knowing what the topic is." She stuffed a handful of popcorn into her mouth.

"One size fits all advice?" I laughed. "How about some insider information instead?"

She grinned. "Oh, goody. You have suspects and you need me to dish the dirt again, don't you?"

"Exactly. First is Sunny Scoles. About my age, runs that new Red House Café I went to this morning."

Aunt Frances shook her head. "Don't know her."

"How about Baxter Tousely? Bax, he goes by. He graduated from Chilson High School four years ago and works for the city."

"Don't know him, either."

I scowled. "You're not being much help. How about Stewart Funston?"

"Him I know." She tossed a piece of popcorn into the air and caught it in her mouth. "How far back do you want? As far as I know, for the last thirty years he's been a model citizen."

"All information has the possibility to be useful."

"That has the possibility of being true." Another popcorn piece went in with a perfect arc. Sometimes it was hard to believe we were blood relations. "Back when Stewart was in high school—he was a string bean of a lad, if you can believe it—the principal suspended him from the football team because he got a ticket for Driving Under the Influence. The weekend after he was kicked off the team, someone broke into the principal's office and destroyed everything in it. And by destroyed, I mean books ripped to shreds and furniture reduced to kindling."

"That's . . . awful. And Stewart did it?"

She shrugged. "They couldn't prove it, but everyone in town assumed so."

I shifted, suddenly uncomfortable. "Anger management issues, sounds like. But he grew out of that, right? I've never heard of him blowing up at anyone."

Aunt Frances picked up another handful of popcorn. "It was a long time ago. But it was also a lot of damage."

"Maybe it wasn't him at all," I said. "Besides, like you said, it was a long time ago." And even though I'd seen Stewart with the Maple Staples sugar packet, that didn't mean anything since they were apparently all over the place. "How about Hugh Novak?" I asked.

My aunt squished up her face. "He's one of Those People."

She'd clearly put capitals on Those People. "Which ones are those?"

"Every once in a while you run into someone you just can't stand, can't work with, don't even want to be in the same room with because their personality is like fingernails on the chalkboard of your life. That's what Hugh Novak is to me. He's an arrogant jerk who thinks he's the smartest person in the room, but half the time he's dumber than a rock."

I was laughing. "Don't beat around the bush. Tell me what you really think."

She held up a piece of popcorn and squeezed it flat. "Years ago, during a talk I was giving at a Rotary meeting about the benefits of vocational training, he said the only people who went into the trades were ones who couldn't get into college."

"Oh, geez." Them were fighting words. "What did you—"

There was a knock on the front door, followed by the squeak of it opening. "Hello!" Otto

159

called. "Does anyone want to share a bottle of wine?"

"Is there anything better," Aunt Frances asked me, "than a man who brings wine without being asked?"

I nodded. "A man who brings advance reading copies of Tana French's latest books." My response was lost on her, though, because Otto had already shed his boots and was giving her a kiss.

So the evening ended happily, with laughter and a glass of what I was told was very good wine. It was only as I was drifting off to sleep that I realized I hadn't asked her about my other suspect, the handyman Land Aprelle.

The next morning, Kelsey knocked firmly on the doorjamb of my office. "I hear you're holding out on us," she said.

I held up my index finger, finished typing an e-mail to the chair of the local arts committee about rotating out the current artwork displayed in the hallway, clicked the Send button, and looked up.

By this time, the number of staff in my doorway had gone from one to four, as Holly, Josh, and Donna all crowded into the space.

"Who's up front?" I asked, frowning.

"Gareth stopped by," Holly said. "He's holding down the fort for a few minutes."

My eyebrows went up. "Our maintenance guy is at the front desk?"

"No one's in the building except us." Josh folded his arms across his chest. "We need to know what's going on with Graydon."

Our boss was downstate for a couple of days, getting some training on the library's software, a system he hadn't been familiar with. I thought it was a good sign that he was willing to suffer through a two-day session when he could have claimed executive privilege and said he didn't need to learn the system's details. "What, you afraid he's going to know more than you do about the system when he gets back?"

Josh gave me a look. "Funny."

I'd thought so. I grinned and said, "You guys need to be a little more specific. What's going on with Graydon in what way? Seems to me it's going pretty well. He's not making any drastic changes right off the bat, and he's taking the time to learn about the culture of Chilson and the library. And he likes malt vinegar on his French fries."

"That's what we're talking about," Kelsey said. "The lunch. What was that all about?"

I suddenly felt the need for coffee. "Let's adjourn to the break room. We shouldn't leave Gareth out there by himself. At least from the break room we can keep an eye on the lobby."

By the time we relocated down the hall, I'd

collected my thoughts and figured out what to say. Sort of. "I've never had a boss ask me out to lunch," I said. "That he feels the need to get to know us on a personal basis seems like a good thing."

"What 'us,'" Holly went on, "is involved with him taking just you to lunch?"

Clearly I hadn't thought this all the way through.

"There's potential for a lot of change," Donna said. "And we're not hearing anything about how things might fall out."

"Exactly." Kelsey nodded. "New boss, new board president, who knows what they might decide behind our backs."

"Graydon seems okay," Josh said, "but he's going to do whatever the board tells him. He doesn't have enough history here to stick up for any of us, or any of our programs."

The front door opened and shut, and in spite of the vestibule that was intended to trap the coldest of the cold air, a chill whooshed in, whirled around the lobby, and slid into the break room.

Donna murmured, "I'll go," and she headed up front to take over for Gareth, who, though he was a very capable and intelligent man, didn't know the Dewey decimal system from the metric system.

"We need you to tell us what's going on," Josh said. "If the board is looking to cut jobs, or hours, or programs, or whatever."

Holly gripped her upper arms. "We're completely in the dark. It's bad enough that Graydon is poking around everywhere, but now Trent is, too. Otis never did that. He came in, ran the meetings, came out, borrowed a book on World War II, and didn't come back until the next month. Trent's been in here almost every day!"

"Otis didn't have to spend time in the library," I said. "He's lived in Chilson all his life. He didn't have to learn about the library programs because he was here when they started. He didn't have to meet the library staff because he was on the board when each of us was hired. Trent is trying to be a good board president. He's trying to learn as much as he can as fast as he can, and we should be grateful he's taking the time."

Kelsey sighed. "I suppose you're right."

"Yeah, I guess," Josh said. "It's just so different, that's all."

Holly sniffed. "Trent has an agenda. He's up to something, I can just feel it."

I knew I had to say something, but I couldn't say that it would be okay, because I had the same feeling about Trent that Holly had. "We'll just have to wait and see."

Late that afternoon, my cell phone started buzzing with my best friend's ringtone.

"Hey, Kristen," I said. "What's up?"

She snorted. "Nothing's wrong, except this cold

is insane. Why on earth does anyone live up here in the winter?"

My mouth moved up and down but nothing came out.

"Hey," Kristen said. "Are you still there? Hellooo!"

"You don't need to shout. I'm right here."

"Well, in a couple of hours, I will be, too, so if you don't want me to freeze my heinie off, I would appreciate you finding me something warm to wear."

I felt my brow furrowing. "Where are you?"

"Detroit."

"Michigan?" I asked.

"Great chef in the sky, of course Michigan! What other Detroit is there? Don't you remember? This is the weekend we agreed that I'd make a trip up to finalize wedding stuff. We talked about this."

Kristen was actually coming home? "I figured you'd cancel and we'd do it all on Skype."

"Would I do something like that?" Before I could answer, she said, "Okay, yes, I would, because I canceled a Christmas visit a couple of years ago. But this is different."

"Four years ago, when you closed down Three Seasons and fled for Key West, you vowed you wouldn't set foot above the Mason-Dixon Line ever again between Halloween and Ides of April."

"Yeah, and I need to shift that October date. We got six inches of snow before I left last fall."

"Yet you're coming home in January."

"Exception proves the rule," she said. "And believe me, it won't happen again. Are you going to bring me something to wear, or not?"

I smiled a slightly evil smile. "See you in two hours."

Kristen sauntered into the airport lobby, towing her purse and small suitcase with one hand and carrying a sign that said, WILL WORK FOR WARM CLOTHES, in the other.

We hugged, then stepped back and took stock of each other. "You look great," I said. And she did. Tan and fit and rested, she looked far better than she had last fall, when she'd been tired and worn and pale. She always looked like that at the end of the restaurant season, and I worried for her health every year.

"You look like you've been in a cave for three months," Kristen said.

"Lowering my risk of skin cancer, day by day."

She looked at my empty hands. "No luck with finding something in my size? Hang on, that's your evil smile," she said, narrowing her eyes. "What did you do?"

I pointed to a massive tote bag I'd parked on a nearby bench. "All for you."

An hour later, I was sitting next to Kristen and

telling the airport story to Leese Lacombe, a mutual friend. "And then," I said, "she proceeded to put on every stitch of it."

Leese, who was almost as tall as Kristen's six feet, but had unruly brown hair and a broad build, laughed uproariously. Kristen and Leese had played on opposing high school softball teams, and I'd gotten to know Leese through the bookmobile. The three of us together were a force to be reckoned with, and I was pretty sure that if we decided to put our time and energy into the effort, we could solve one of the biggest problems ever: how to get rid of a song that's stuck in your head.

"All of it?" Leese asked, still laughing.

We were in one of Chilson's drinking establishments, one of the two open all year. It was early evening, and we were by far the noisiest group in the place. Of course, other than Pete, the bartender, and two men of indeterminate age who were sitting at opposite ends of the bar, we were the only humans in the place.

It would liven up later, after the dinner hour, but since it was January, the term "liven up" was relative. During the height of the summer season, you could wait half an hour for a seat, which to me had never seemed worth it for a place with floors that had a tendency to be slightly sticky, but then I lived here. It was different for summer folks. Worn-down establishments where you were on vacation were charming; at home they were places in need of a good cleaning and a coat of paint.

"All of it," I said, and showed her the picture I'd taken with my phone. There was Kristen, wearing the brown Carhartt overalls I'd borrowed from Rafe, the long maroon parka I'd borrowed from Aunt Frances, a bright pink wool hat and a pair of gray mittens I'd found in the hall closet, and a pair of circa 1980 Moon Boots I'd found at a local consignment shop, with orange and navy blue striping that went with absolutely nothing. They were perfect.

"I'm pretty sure I've never looked better," Kristen said. "Send it to my future husband, will you? He should know what awaits."

Smirking, I texted the photo to Scruffy. "Where is he these days?"

"This week it's New Mexico," she said. "He and Trock are out there filming an episode about foods influenced by the region's indigenous peoples."

Leese tipped her mug of beer in Kristen's direction. "Sounds like the show might be getting some influence from the producer's bride-to-be."

She was probably right, but I'd never thought about it. Rafe influenced me and I him, so it only followed that every other couple in the world, including Scruffy and Kristen, might have that same dynamic. I'd just never dreamed, when I'd walked onto the *Trock's Troubles* set a year and a half ago when Trock had been filming at his Chilson summer home, that one result would be that Kristen could wind up shifting the show's direction.

"It's a weird, weird world," I murmured.

Kristen eyed me. "Is that the start of a joke?"

"No, but it could be." I squinted at the ceiling. "It's a weird world. How weird? Three women walked into a bar: a restauranteur, an attorney, and a librarian. They—"

"Did you hear about our latest murder?" Leese asked Kristen, cutting into my joke. I feigned hurt, but since I hadn't known where the story was going, I got over my fake emotional pain quickly.

Kristen nodded. "Rowan Bennethum? Minnie told me."

"Did she tell you she's helping the sheriff's office?"

My best friend's gaze swung around. "Oh, really?" she asked, her voice laden with something that didn't bode well for Minnie. "And what trouble is she going to get herself into this time?"

Leese glanced at me, sending a visual apology.

"None that I know of," I said. "All I'm doing is—"

"Don't want to hear about it." Kristen put her hands over her ears. "Especially if I'm not around to put the pieces back together. Even if I beg, you're not going to walk away from this, are you?"

"Well, no." I sat up straight and glared right back at her. "Anya and Collier asked me to help. They're just kids and they need to know what happened to their mother. If I can do anything to help them, I'm going to do it, and everyone else should, too."

Kristen stared at me a moment longer, then picked up her beer mug and swallowed the last of it. Her silence was acknowledgment that I was right, that she understood I was right, but that she didn't like what was going on and wasn't going to make any pretense that she did.

Which was all fine and I was glad we'd reached this point so soon in the weekend and didn't have to dance around it for another day or two.

"So what are the detectives saying?" Leese asked. Her father, though she'd had little contact with him for years, had been murdered just a few months earlier and she was familiar with the process. "Anything they're releasing yet?"

"No." I hesitated, trying to remember precisely what they'd said about the names of the possible suspects. Could I talk about them? Should I? "There are a few names that have come up," I said.

Leese leaned forward, and even Kristen looked interested. "Can you say who they are?" Leese asked. "I don't live far from the Bennethums. I can keep an eye out, if you want."

"Just keep it quiet, please," I said, and named the names. Sunny Scoles, of the Red House Café. Bax Tousely, the city worker wannabe post-production video maker. Hugh Novak, insurance adjuster. Stewart Funston, Rowan's cousin. Land Aprelle, handyman.

Kristen, of course, zeroed in on the important thing. "How is Sunny's restaurant doing? If I did breakfast, I'd want to be like her. She makes this amazing maple glaze with walnuts and puts it on French toast."

Leese, however, had an odd expression on her face. "Bax Tousely. He drives a pickup, doesn't he? Chevy Silverado, maybe ten years old?"

"No idea." I was lucky if I remembered what I drove, let alone someone I'd never met. "Why?"

"Because I'm pretty sure I saw him driving past Rowan's house almost every day, right before she was killed."

Chapter 9

I told Leese I'd pass on the information about Bax Tousely to the sheriff's office, and added the task to my mental to-do list. The rest of the evening passed with the mild hilarity that so often accompanies any time that good friends gather together, and I stayed out far later than I normally would have on a night when I had to work the next day.

On the plus side, there was no real reason for me to show up at the library two hours before it opened, so I didn't even bother setting an alarm when I crawled into bed.

Eddie, however, either hadn't heard me or hadn't listened when I'd told him I was going to sleep in. He woke me with a paw pat to the face and a loud "Mrr!" all of ten minutes past my usual get-out-of-bed time.

I looked at his furry face. "When I get up early, you give me a look that could kill. But when I want to sleep in, I get this?"

"Mrr." He sat on my chest and stared at me. "Mrr."

Clearly, he wasn't going to let me sleep, so I

tossed back the covers, pulled on a bathrobe, stuffed my feet into slippers, and stumbled downstairs to the kitchen, yawning all the way.

"Top of the morning to you!" Otto toasted me with a steaming mug of coffee. "Would you like a cup? Or would you rather have tea?"

"Morning." I dropped into a chair. Eddie jumped up onto the chair next to me and immediately curled up into an Eddie-size ball. Still yawning, I put my elbows on the table and my chin in my hands. "Coffee would be wonderful, thanks." In the last couple of months I'd grown used to finding Otto in the boardinghouse at any time of the day or night. Almost, anyway. "Where's Aunt Frances?"

"Off to the college half an hour ago. She had prep work to do for a class." He slid a mug of nirvana in front of me and I gratefully wrapped my hands around it. "Frances made me a delightful breakfast of scrambled eggs and smoked salmon and I stayed behind to clean up. There are some leftovers I could heat, if you'd like."

I consulted my stomach, and it told me to stay away. "Thanks, but I'll pass."

"Ah. Yes. You were out late with Kristen and Leese." His smile was tinted with understanding. "How about a piece of dry toast?"

Another consultation. This time my stomach

gave a thumbs-up. "That would be wonderful. But you don't have to wait on me." I started to stand, but he waved me down.

"Sit, sit. I have an ulterior motive for feeding you."

"Excellent." I sipped my coffee. "Nothing better than ulterior motives with dry toast."

"That's what I've always said." The toaster popped up two slices of multigrain. He put them both on a plate and put it in front of me. Sitting, he said, "There's a bit of a problem with the wedding."

I froze, a piece of toast halfway to my mouth. "Don't tell me you want to back out."

"What?" His gentle blue eyes flew open. "Of course not. I said a problem with the wedding, not the marriage."

"Oh. Right." I relaxed. "Sorry. It's just . . . well, never mind." The night before, after Leese had abandoned us, Kristen confessed she'd been getting wedding jitters. We'd talked it through, and though I was pretty sure she was nervous about the menu and not the man she'd chosen to marry, since I'd never been married myself, how would I know for sure? "What's the problem?" I asked.

Otto slumped, his shoulders sagging. This was troubling, because he rarely had anything but perfect posture. Whatever he was about to tell me was going to be bad. I pushed toast and coffee aside. "Tell me," I said. "Whatever it is, we'll figure it out."

He shook his head. "Remember the hotel in Bermuda? The one Frances had her heart set on for our wedding?"

The use of past tense made me clutch. My aunt and Otto had studied dozens of websites and written numerous e-mails before choosing this particular hotel. " 'Had'?" I repeated cautiously. "What do you mean?"

"They had a fire." He sighed. "An electrical fire that damaged the building extensively. They called me yesterday morning and I spent most of the day looking for another location on that date and within our budget. There's nothing available." His shoulders heaved as he sighed again. "Absolutely nothing."

Out in the dining room, the clock on the buffet ticked and tocked. "You haven't told her, have you?" I asked.

"Tonight. She's going to be . . . disappointed. I just wanted you to be prepared."

Prepared for what, exactly? Still, his heart was in the right place. "Thanks for telling me. If there's anything I can do to help, let me know."

He nodded glumly. "Thanks, Minnie. I appreciate that."

I wolfed down the rest of my toast, put our dishes in the dishwasher, touched his shoulder, and went back upstairs to shower and start the wintry day.

Julia gasped. "The hotel burned down?"

"Don't know about down," I said, "but burned enough so they can't have the wedding there."

"Oh, poor Frances."

I wasn't so sure. Yes, of course she'd be a little disappointed, but in all the years I'd known my aunt—which was all of my life—she'd never let anything truly upset her. She was the person I wanted to be; she stayed calm, never panicked, and always kept a sense of perspective. I was pretty sure she'd spend a moment being shocked and surprised, and would then roll up her sleeves and figure out another way to reach the goal. It was my aunt's fiancé I was more worried about. "Poor Otto, too," I said.

Julia glanced at me across the bookmobile console. "I've only met him a couple of times. Frances and I keep trying to set up dinner dates, but you know how those things can go. What's he like?"

Though I knew my aunt and Julia had known each other for decades, I sometimes forgot how time had shifted their relationship. Back in the day, when she was still getting leading roles on the New York stage, Julia had spent her spare time in Chilson. She and Aunt Frances had developed a solid friendship, but things were different

175

now. I lived with Frances, Otto was in the picture, and Julia and her husband lived here year-round, which you'd think would let you see your friends more often, but the reality of life's busyness has a way of interfering with good intentions.

"What's Otto like?" I repeated. "Well, what do *you* think?"

"Charming," she said immediately. "Smart, but not the kind of smart that has to show off. He can listen. And I think he has a very clever sense of humor, but I haven't seen it come out yet. Maybe he's hiding it until he gets to know us better."

I smiled. "All that. Plus, he loves Aunt Frances very, very much."

"Ah." Julia tapped the top of Eddie's carrier with a booted foot. "Did you hear that, Sir Edward? Otto loves Frances. Do you agree, and think that he will take care of her in the manner she deserves? Will he love, honor, and cherish her as long as they both shall live?"

"Mrr!"

Julia nodded and settled down in her seat. "Okay then. If Otto gets the Eddie stamp of approval, who am I to disagree?"

I rolled my eyes. Sometimes Julia took our so-called conversations with my cat a little too seriously. "You do realize he was just complaining about you thumping the top of his carrier."

"Your interpretation is yours and yours alone. I prefer mine. Right, Eddie?"

"Mrr."

If she'd tapped the carrier that time, I couldn't detect it. I shook my head and said, "If we're running on schedule this afternoon, I'd like to make a short detour on the way back to town."

Julia clapped her hands and smiled like a small child being offered ice cream. "Ooo, a detour. Anywhere fun? Please, please, let it be fun!"

I smiled. "You'll just have to wait and see, little one."

The final bookmobile stop of the day had wrapped up exactly on time, an anomaly for that particular stop because Lisa and Mort Neely, a downstate couple who had retired Up North the previous summer, tended to linger.

They were very nice people, but Julia and I agreed they were still getting acclimated to winter. People who only spent summer and perhaps early fall up here didn't tend to recognize how sparse humans were for eight months at a stretch, and it was a harsh reality for many.

More than one retired couple, whose original intentions had been to live up here the rest of their lives, ended up finding a place to live in Florida or Arizona in the dark months and came north only when all chance of snow was gone. Julia was betting that the Neelys would turn into snowbirds, but I'd caught a calm look from Lisa as she'd gazed out the bookmobile window at the snowy landscape and was sure they'd be staying.

That afternoon, Mort had come to the book-mobile alone. "Lisa's in a cleaning frenzy," he said. "Our youngest is coming up with her boy-friend for a skiing week. Apparently a house that's clean enough for us isn't anywhere near clean for them."

"Well, of course not," Julia said.

I nodded agreement. "Especially when there's a boyfriend involved. He might turn into a hus-band, and then you'll have his family members up to stay. Standards must be established early."

Mort gave us a pained look. "Then I truly hope she doesn't marry this one. He has seven siblings."

We laughed and a few minutes later he checked out the small stack of mysteries and thrillers they'd reserved online, stuffed them into his backpack, and went out into the cold for his short walk home.

Julia turned to me. "Is it detour time?" she asked, her face bright and shiny.

"You got it," I said, closing the door on Eddie's carrier and buckling myself in. "Let's roll."

Twenty minutes later I steered the bookmobile into the parking lot of the Wicklow Township Hall, a fieldstone building I'd never set foot inside. Julia scrunched up her face. "This is the detour? Seriously?"

I laughed. "Did I say it was going to be fun?"

"Well, no, but detours should be entertaining, at the very least. This isn't a detour, it's . . ." She frowned. "What is this?"

"Work," I said. "You know the church lot where we normally park? I got a phone call the other day that their guy who plows the lot for free broke his shoulder blade skiing. He can't plow the rest of the winter. The church has a snowblower, but the whole lot is too much for it, so they're not clearing the back part."

Julia nodded, following along with the saga. "And if they don't blow the snow back there, the bookmobile doesn't have room to turn around, so we need a new stop spot."

"You are just as smart as you look," I said. "This shouldn't take long. I'll leave the engine running and you and Eddie can stay here."

The suggestion was unnecessary, as Julia had already unbuckled her seat belt and was wriggling around to get comfortable. "Hand me that new book by Kent Kruger, will you, please?"

Inside, the township hall felt a lot like it looked, as if it had been here for a hundred years without many changes since construction. Wood floor, wood paneling, wood ceiling, all had been put in place during the boom years of lumber, when the cheapest possible building material was whatever they were hauling out of the closest woodlot.

A bulletin board next to the front door was posted with agendas of upcoming meetings and minutes of past ones. In a place of prominence was a memo noting the day property taxes were due. To the right of the small lobby were the double doors of a meeting room; to the left was a hallway leading toward offices where I could hear a rumble of male voices.

"Hello there, dear."

And at my immediate left was an office separated from the lobby by a counter with a sliding glass window above. A generously sized sixty-ish woman with thoroughly blond hair was smiling. "Can I help you?"

"If you're Charlotte, you can. I'm Minnie Hamilton. I called the other day about using your parking lot for a bookmobile stop." With my thumb, I gestured over my shoulder. "If you want to see it, it's out there."

Charlotte leaned over to look, but didn't get up. "You drive that big thing?" she asked. "And you're such a little scrap of a girl!"

I smiled. This was a familiar conversation. "Power steering and an automatic transmission make life easier for everyone."

"Isn't that the absolute truth?" she said, laughing. "I talked to the supervisor and the other board members, and no one sees any problem with you stopping here, so let's figure out schedules. Come in and have a seat."

Ten minutes later, we were wrapping up dates through the end of the year. I could have shifted the stop back to the church when all danger of snow had passed, but I didn't want to move the location twice in one year. Just as we were making sure the December dates worked for both of us, the male voices I'd heard before grew louder, to the point where I could make out what they were saying.

"We'll have to see what happens at the meeting, Hugh. I'm only one vote."

"But you're supervisor."

"And I cast all of one vote," the supervisor said mildly. "There are four others. Democracy and all that."

"Yeah, I suppose. See you at the meeting."

"Will do. Say, don't forget your hat."

Footsteps came toward us down the hall, then whooshed past without slowing down. I got a glimpse of a dark winter coat worn by a tallish man with brown hair just starting to go gray. In one hand he carried a hat, a fedora with an oddly low profile and with earflaps down. I smiled. Apparently Stewart wasn't the only one around with that new hat.

Then something clicked in my head. "Was that Hugh Novak?" I asked.

Charlotte glanced in the direction of the front door, paused until it shut, then said, "He's been pushing for us to build a new township hall for years, and with the board we have now, he just might get what he wants."

"A new building?" I looked around. "How old is this place?"

"About ninety years, so our maintenance expenses are creeping up. Nothing we can't deal with, though."

"Do you need more space?"

"Just like everything else up here, in the winter no and in the summer yes." She shrugged. "I figure we can muddle through for the three or four busy months. It's not worth it to build something big that'll go mostly empty most of the year."

There was something I wasn't grasping. "Then why does . . . I mean, why would Hugh . . ." I stopped, not sure how to phrase the question.

Charlotte helped me out. "Why on earth would anyone want to spend taxpayer money on a building we don't need, even if we happen to have the money right now? If you're some board members, you want to leave a legacy. If you're some other board members, you feel the need to spend money on something reasonable to keep a stupid future board from wasting it on something stupid. And if you're Hugh Novak . . ." She glared in the direction he'd gone. "If you're Hugh Novak, you want the township to build on the property you own on the state highway, which happens to be property right next to a parcel you bought. If you're Hugh Novak, you think a new township hall out there will increase traffic, creating the perfect climate for the business you want to start."

"What business is that?" Hadn't Neil Bennethum, Rowan's husband, mentioned that Hugh and Rowan had been arguing about township politics? Could this be the topic?

Charlotte made a *hmph*-ing noise. "With Hugh, it changes every time you talk to him."

I thanked her and, as I walked out, pulled out my cell and called Neil. It went to voice mail, of course, so I left him a message.

Back on the bookmobile, Julia looked up from her book. "How did that go? All set?"

I blinked. All set about what? Oh. Right. "Good to go," I said, sliding into my seat and buckling in. Yes, we were all set. With the bookmobile stop and with another clue that might lead to tracking down Rowan's killer.

I'd unscheduled myself from the library for a couple of days in order to help Kristen with wedding plans, but when I texted her the next morning, she texted back that she was doing restaurant work instead.

Me: *Decisions need to be made.*

Kristen: *no kidding . . . need a new strawberry supplier and someone who can grow black carrots . . . plus have lined up two chefs to interview.*

Me: *Don't you have a wedding to plan?*

Kristen: *priorities missy priorities.*

Me: *What I'm saying.*

Kristen: *wedding will be fine . . . you have the day off . . . go play!!!*

Me: *But*

I paused with my thumbs over the phone's tiny keyboard. But what? If Kristen preferred to procrastinate on her wedding plans, there wasn't much I could do about it short of dragging her around by her hair, and since she was taller, stronger, and far more fit than I was, I didn't see how that strategy could possibly succeed.

So I deleted the *But,* and instead sent, *Let me know when you have time to do wedding stuff,* and clicked off the phone. "What do you think?" I asked Eddie.

My feline friend didn't say anything. This wasn't a surprise since he was curled up into a tight ball half the size of a regular Eddie. What was a surprise was the location—the precise middle of the doorway between the living and the dining room.

He was directly on top of a low threshold—Aunt Frances said she removed the physical door years ago to open up the space—so how he could find that particular spot a relaxing location, I did not know, yet I could hear the dulcet tones of Eddie snores.

Which somehow reminded me of one thing I could do.

"Sleep tight," I said, reaching down to pat Eddie's head. Fifteen minutes later, I was knocking on the toy store's front door. Mitchell appeared and let me in. "Hey, Minnie. What's up?"

I came in, stomping my boots on the mat. Six or so inches of snow had fallen in the night, and though the main roads were clear, the side streets and sidewalks were still waiting for plows and shovels. "Could you make me a list? When you and Bianca started seeing each other, when you met her family, when she met yours, that kind of thing. Approximate dates are fine."

"A list of . . ." He frowned. "Yeah. How is that—"

"Great." I wasn't sure how a list would help me figure out anything, but it couldn't hurt. Data was always good, especially if it kept Mitchell busy for a few days. I edged toward the door. "E-mail it to me when it's done, okay?"

"When do you want it?" Mitchell glanced at his watch. "I have a couple of things I need to do first, but I bet I can write that up before noon."

I blinked. The slacker Mitchell, the Mitchell I'd known for years, the one who'd dragged any task out for days if not weeks, the Mitchell I still kept expecting to turn up, was gone forever. "Whenever you have time."

"This is something I'll make time for," he said.

For some reason, his grim tone made me want

to cry. I didn't, of course, because I hated to cry in front of anyone, let alone Mitchell Koyne, but I did sniff once or twice and was pleased to be distracted by an incoming text message. "Sorry," I muttered, fishing my phone out of my coat pocket. "I should check this . . ."

Rafe: *Snow day. You busy with Kristen's wedding?*

Frowning, I looked outside. The snow didn't look any worse today than it had on days when the superintendent hadn't canceled school, but the ways of school administrators were mysterious. My image of a superintendent calling a snow day involved charts, radar, satellite images, and phone calls to secret phone numbers, and I'd firmly told Rafe not to disillusion me.

Me: *Nope.*

Rafe: *Cool. Want to drive to Traverse with me?*

Fifteen minutes later, we were in Rafe's SUV, southbound on US 31. "Isn't it a little wrong to head out of town on a snow day?" I asked.

"How?"

"Well, doesn't a snow day mean the roads aren't safe to drive? Shouldn't you be staying home, staring out the window, and worrying about your students?"

He made a rude noise in the back of his throat. "When I was a kid, a snow day meant I'd call whoever had access to a car. I'd make a pile of peanut butter and jelly sandwiches, stuff them back into the bread bag, and we'd head to Nub's to ski. And before any of us could drive, we'd walk that trail north of town and go sledding."

"Um, doesn't that hill drop right into Lake Michigan?"

He grinned, his white teeth gleaming in the morning light. "My parents still don't know. But even if they found out now, the statute of limitations for childhood punishments is long over."

Though he spoke confidently, I wasn't so sure his mom and dad would agree. Over dinner someday, the subject would come up and we would all see what happened.

"What are you smiling about?" Rafe reached over and squeezed my hand briefly.

"Oh, just happy to spend the day with you." And I was. It had been weeks since we'd done anything other than work on the house or grab a quick meal somewhere. "But if I'm going to be completely honest—"

"Yes, please."

"I'm also happy to get some time in Traverse City. I haven't been down there in months, and even then I didn't have a chance to stop at the bookstores."

"Bookstores?" His eyebrows went up. "What makes you think we're going anywhere near downtown?"

Cold stole into me, all the way down to the marrow of my bones. "You said . . . I mean . . .

I thought . . ." Just like that, my happiness vanished. No browsing at Horizon? No seeing what Brilliant Books was recommending? No checking to see what treasures the used book-store, Bookie Joint, might happen to have?

Rafe grinned. "Breathe deep. I was just messing with you. We can spend all afternoon downtown if you want."

I squiggled around and readjusted myself in my seat. "You are a horrible person," I said comfortably, "and remember what they say about paybacks."

"That's what the school sends me twice a month, right?"

"I'm glad you're not really as dumb as you sound."

"You ain't seen nothing yet."

I laughed, happy inside and out. An unexpected day with my boyfriend—what could be better?

Two hours later, I knew exactly what could be better. That the unexpected day would have included only ten minutes in a specialty wood store, not the hour it was starting to become. Ten minutes had been interesting; the different woods were pretty and learning what countries the exotics had traveled from was fascinating, but my mind started to wander when Rafe and the sales guy—Rafe's new best friend—started talking about wood density and humidity factors.

When I murmured that I wouldn't go far, Rafe nodded and continued the conversation.

The store was located on the south side of Traverse City, past the car dealerships, past the big box stores, and even past the flooring stores. It was in a small strip mall, sharing its parking lot with a Chinese takeout and a nail salon. Since the nail salon interested me as much as the wood store did, I ambled over to the restaurant in hopes of seeing a menu stuck up somewhere.

Wind blew and snow swirled, but I was in the mood to be fearless, so braving the cold for nearly fifty feet didn't faze me a bit. There was indeed a menu taped to the door. I peered at the selections, wondering if eleven o'clock was too early to be thinking about lunch, when a truck door slammed shut.

I turned and saw Land Aprelle, handyman to Rowan, kicking the snow out of his truck's wheel wells. With that streak of white hair, he was easy to spot in a crowd.

"Good morning, Land," I called.

He spun around. "Minnie. What are you doing here?"

"No idea, to tell you the truth. I'm waiting for Rafe." I paused, suddenly unsure. "You know Rafe Niswander, don't you?"

"Yeah. Yeah, I do." Land glanced at the store, then back at me. "I, uh, just stopped to clear the snow out of my truck. It was jamming up the suspension and making a vibration to beat the band, and I know this parking lot is usually empty, so I stopped. Just for a second. I'm going now. See you around, okay?"

As Land's truck sped back out onto the highway, Rafe came outside. "Wasn't that Land Aprelle? Why didn't he come in?"

"I have no idea," I said slowly. "He was acting very strange."

"How can you tell?" Rafe clicked his SUV unlocked and we climbed in. "Land can be a pretty strange guy at the best of times."

"Sure, but he was talking."

Rafe, who was buckling his seat belt, paused mid-buckle. "Talking?"

I nodded. "A lot."

Rafe looked over his shoulder, but Land's truck was long gone. "Maybe it was his long-lost identical twin brother, who dyed his hair just like . . . okay, maybe not." He looked at my expression and grinned. "Okay, almost certainly not. But really? A loquacious Land makes you wonder about the end of the world."

I wondered, too. But I was wondering if Land's odd behavior had something to do with Rowan's death, and even the heady odor of books in the bookstores that Rafe and I, hand in hand, happily traipsed through that afternoon didn't quite dispel my questions.

Chapter 10

Sunday morning I looked at my best friend, who was sitting to my immediate left. "This was an excellent idea."

"Told you," Kristen said. "Why don't you ever listen to me?"

"Because sometimes your ideas are horrible."

"Like when?" she challenged.

I snorted. "Do you really want to talk about the jumping-off-the-roof-of-your-house-onto-the-leaf-pile idea?"

"And I still say it would have been fine. My mom overreacts."

The two of us were sitting side by side on a Nub's Nob chairlift with our feet, boots, and skis dangling, on our way to the top of the ski hill. It was the kind of winter day skiers dreamed of—blue skies, no wind, twenty degrees—and having to spend this day inside working on wedding details would have been painful.

Not that I was a Real Skier. I was happy to ski on the blue runs, the ones marked for inter-mediate skiers, and I didn't care if I ever got good enough to do the steepest hills.

Kristen was a much better skier than I was, having grown up in a family of downhillers, and she'd been on the high school ski team. But that had been years ago, and now she wiggled her mittens, eyeing them critically. "My fingers are getting cold."

"Not possible," I said. "You have three sets of hand warmers in there. And you're wearing those incredibly expensive heated electric socks I borrowed from Donna." This was in addition to the multiple layers underneath the warmest coat we'd found in my aunt's closet.

"Getting cold," she said again as we off-loaded at the top. "We need to go in."

I wanted to protest, but a cold Kristen was a cranky Kristen, and besides, we really needed to work on wedding stuff. Saturday had been marginally productive, but there was a lot more to do and the weight of it was starting to make me a tiny bit nervous. We swooshed our way down, Kristen fast and elegant, me trailing behind slow and choppy.

When I reached the bottom, Kristen had already taken off her equipment and was slinging her skis up onto her shoulder. I took a final turn to get around a man and a woman walking toward the ski lift. Though they were carrying rental skis—usually an indication of novice ability—they looked comfortable with the equipment.

Something about them was familiar, but it

wasn't until the woman said, "New series. Snow scenes without any shades of blue," that I realized who it was. And why I didn't recognize them in ski clothes.

"Barb!" I called. "Cade! What are you two doing in Michigan?"

Russell McCade whirled and grinned. "Why, if it isn't our favorite bookmobile librarian!"

As I was the only bookmobile librarian they knew, I ignored the comment as I gracelessly ski-skated over to the couple. "I didn't know you two were skiers. And why didn't you tell me you were in town?"

Barb and Cade, both on the far side of fifty and neither one looking it, summered on Five Mile Lake and wintered in Arizona. Cade made a mint of money through his paintings, works that his fans loved and that the critics called sentimental schlock.

I'd always loved his work and had been thrilled to learn that he and his wife had a summer place Up North, but we hadn't crossed paths until he'd needed a quick ride to the hospital and the bookmobile had been handy.

"The snowbirds are flocking together," I said, smiling. "Kristen's up for the weekend to do wedding planning." I looked back at the ski rack. "She was here a minute ago. I'm sure she'll want to say hello. Where on—"

A short and sharp shriek startled all of us.

But I was on the move instantly, because it was Kristen's voice, and she was calling my name.

With the points of my poles I jabbed at my bindings, unlocking them, and left my skis lying in the snow. "Kristen!" I shouted, running as well as anyone could in boots with soles that were stiff as boards. "Where are you?" Reaching the parking lot, I looked left and right. Since it was a Sunday, there were dozens of people wandering around, and they were all starting to gather around the back of my car.

"Are you okay?" I hurried over. "What happened?"

Her groan was audible. "Fell. My wrist . . ."

I pushed my way through the small murmuring crowd. Kristen was on her knees, cradling her right wrist with her left forearm. I knelt beside her. Since the only visible part of her skin was her face, it was impossible to see what the damage might be, and I didn't want to make things worse. Kristen was a chef and permanent damage to her wrist . . . I didn't want to think about it. She would be fine.

"She should go to the hospital," a woman said. "But I don't know where the closest one is. Petoskey? Does Charlevoix have a hospital? Maybe Traverse City would be better."

"There's a hospital in Gaylord," offered a young man. "At least that's what my friend said. You want me to Google which one is closest?"

Cade and Barb, their boots thumping fast on the asphalt, hurried over. I knew I could depend on them to do what needed to be done, so I thanked the strangers, telling them we were all set. They wandered off and I said to Kristen, "We're going to McLaren in Petoskey, okay?"

She nodded and the McCades and I helped her to her feet. "I'll help her into the car," Barb said. "Cade will get your equipment and drop it at your aunt's house later." She said the last while looking at her husband, and he nodded and headed off.

Barb talked as she guided Kristen to the passenger side of my car. "He's painting a snow series and two days ago he got it in his head that he had to see Michigan snow. We're here for a few days, so we have plenty of time to help out. No, don't thank me. Minnie has done far more for us than we can ever repay. There you go, Kristen, let me get that seat belt . . . and you're set." Barb gently shut the door, slapped the window, and we were on our way.

Three hours later, we were still in the emergency room, waiting for the results of the CT scan. "Just to be sure," the doctor said. "We don't want a misdiagnosis."

"No, we do not." Kristen used her chin to point at her wrapped-up wrist. "If this doesn't heal properly, there will be no bo ssäm at Three

Seasons. No beef Wellington. And certainly no crème brûlée."

The thought of no crème brûlée sent a chill down my back, but I took a deep breath. Once again, Kristen was exaggerating. Even if she was incapacitated, she had an excellent staff, which included Harvey, the sous-chef, who was aching for a chance to lay down his life for his boss. But Kristen's passion was developing new recipes, and if her wrist was permanently damaged . . . I shook my head. She was going to be fine.

"Odds are extremely good," the doctor said, "that you'll be fine. The X-ray didn't show any breaks. At this point it's likely a sprain. A few weeks, a little bit of therapy, and you'll be back to normal. But we're going to do a CT scan, just to be sure."

And an hour later, the results were in. The orthopedic surgeon was consulted, and she agreed. No broken bones. "I'll get the nurse in to show you how to wrap it," the emergency room doctor said. "We'll get you a prescription for pain and for therapy. Check with your doctor in Florida for recommended physical therapists." He smiled. "Glad you'll be okay. Three Seasons is my favorite restaurant. I'll be in for that crème brûlée."

As the doctor walked out, Kristen flopped back on the hospital bed and stared at the ceiling. "Well, this sucks. But I suppose it could be worse."

"It can always be worse," I said.

"You always say that."

"Because it's always true."

She lay there for a moment, looking almost relaxed, then sat bolt upright. "Okay. Enough of feeling sorry for myself. Time to get to work."

I eyed her warily. "On what?"

"Wedding plans, my dear. That is the reason I came to this land of snow and ice, remember?"

"Hard to tell from your actions the last twenty-four hours."

She grinned. "All in the past, Miss Minnie. All in the past. Sharpen your pencils!"

Rolling my eyes, I pulled my cell phone from my coat pocket and opened the notes file I'd titled *Wedding of the Century*. "Virtual pencil all set, ma'am."

"What's the first thing I need to decide?"

"Venue."

"Ceremony at the Congregational church, reception at Three Seasons. Done!" She used her left hand to draw an imaginary check mark in the air.

I did not move on to the next item. "You talked to the church secretary and got your name set in stone for the correct date and time?"

Kristen's eyebrows went up. "You don't trust me?"

"With my life, absolutely. With following up on this kind of detail, absolutely not."

She huffed, but not for very long. We'd been

friends a long time and we knew each other's weaknesses and strong suits inside and out. "Yes, I talked to Lois and the date is set. And the restaurant will be dark the entire day. Lots of time to decorate."

As we ticked through the big items, I added a few notes about things I needed to do, a big one being addressing the invitations, which we'd planned on doing that evening. "I'll lick every one," she said. "Promise."

"Then the last big item is the food." I put my phone down. "Are we going to have this conversation again? Because I still think it's nuts for you to cook your own wedding dinner."

Kristen started to get the look I knew very well—her stubborn look. "I'm a chef. How can I possibly let someone else cook for my wedding?"

"There are other cooks in the land. Even other cooks in northwest lower Michigan."

"Not like me."

"True enough. But is it worth your time?" I winced inwardly, because I'd said the exact wrong thing. "Let me rephrase that—"

"Worth my time?" Kristen flushed. "This is the most important meal of my life! It's my wedding, for crying out loud! I know you don't understand the importance of fine food, but I do. This isn't a meal I'm handing over to some schmuck who doesn't know the difference between a whisk and a waffle iron."

"Fine," I said, trying not to snap at her because she was undoubtedly in pain. "Then at least get some help. You can't possibly cook for two hundred people all by yourself."

"Of course not." Kristen rolled her eyes. "That would be nuts. Harvey and the rest of the regular staff are donating their time as wedding presents, and I'm talking to a friend in Detroit about coming up to help out. She used to be in advertising, but chucked it all to buy a food truck. I was serving her a drink in Key West when we got to talking, and it turns out she and her husband drive all over the country, following the weather they like best. I saw their setup, and they've developed this really interesting method of—"

Hard-heartedly, I cut her off. "They'll come all the way up here?"

"She got their permit from city council last week."

"That sounds good," I said vaguely, because my mind was wandering backward. Hadn't the loan Sunny Scoles applied for—which had been turned down by Rowan—been for a food truck?

"How much do those cost?" I asked. "Food trucks, I mean."

Kristen laughed. "If you're thinking about ditching the bookmobile for a food truck business, I'd advise against it. Because if you run a food truck, you have to cook. Every day."

I scrunched my face. "No, this is about Rowan's murder." I didn't want to blab Sunny's name around, so I said, "One of the latest loans Rowan turned down was for a food truck. So I was just wondering, how much do they cost?"

"Depends." Kristen shrugged. "How big? What kind of food will be served? How cool do you want it to be? I know one guy who found a used truck, hunted down used equipment, and fitted it out himself. Cost under twenty thousand. But I've also heard about high-end rigs costing more than two hundred grand. I know, right? But I'd say the average for a used vehicle and a little retrofitting is in the sixty to eighty thousand range."

Hmm. I texted Ash, asking if he knew the amount of the loan Sunny had requested. Almost immediately, he texted back: *300 grand. Why?*

Kristen's here, I wrote back. *She said they usually cost about $70,000.*

Well, Ash wrote back, *that's probably why Rowan denied the loan.*

As I turned off the phone, I wondered why on earth Sunny would have inflated her loan request by so much. When I'd met her, she'd seemed capable and sensible. Why would she have done something so dumb?

I stayed up late into the night to finish addressing the wedding invitations. Kristen apologized so many times that I was forced to threaten her with replacing all the good wine she was ordering for the wedding with cheap stuff from the grocery store.

"You wouldn't," she said.

"Do you want to risk it?" I asked, eyebrows raised.

She did not, so she subsided and accepted her role of envelope licker. I'd pointed out that she could use the sponge that I'd dampened, but she said licking so many envelopes was penance for going out to ski when she should have been working on wedding stuff.

What we both knew, but were never going to say out loud, was that essentially all of the planning and preparations could have been done remotely. But it was more fun this way, and since we could spend a few days planning the wedding Kristen had never dreamed of having, we'd done so.

The next day, though, I was dead tired. I yawned all the way through showering, dressing, and breakfast, and even the blasts of cold air in my face walking out of the house and before boarding the bookmobile didn't do much to wake me up.

"Coffee," I murmured to Julia as we headed out of Chilson. "Where's the closest place to get coffee?" The single cup I'd poured down my throat at breakfast wasn't doing the job I'd asked it to do.

Wordlessly, Julia pointed at an upcoming gas

station, which was even on the right side of the road. I drove into the parking lot, parked, and stood. "Anyone want anything? No, Eddie, you don't get coffee." It didn't do to think about the damage a caffeinated Eddie could do to the world.

I brought back a cup of coffee roughly the size of my head, a cup of tea for Julia, and a wadded-up piece of paper for Eddie. Fifteen minutes later, at our first stop, I was feeling almost awake. Eddie, however, had been batting around the paper nonstop and was sound asleep when Julia opened the door of his carrier.

"Isn't he sweet," she cooed. "Look at him, resting his head on his little white paws."

"You wouldn't think he was so sweet if he'd woken you up at three in the morning trying to pull your hair out of your head."

She laughed. "Isn't it adorable that he tries to fix your hair?"

"Adorable" hadn't been the word I'd used, but since we had people coming aboard, I declined to share what I had actually said.

"Good morning," I said, smiling at the young woman who'd just climbed the stairs. With her were two small children, one girl walking mostly steadily, one boy being carried. All three had bright blond hair and round, open faces.

"Morning," the woman said, a little breathlessly. "We're looking for picture books."

"Kitty," pronounced the toddler. "Kitty!"

The woman deposited the child she'd carried on her hip onto the carpeted step and unzipped both of her children's coats. "Emily, what did I tell you? Books first, then we'll ask about the bookmobile cat."

"Kitty!"

She looked up at me apologetically, and I suddenly knew who she was. "You work at the bank," I said, and searched my memory for her name. Something unusual and pretty. Started with an M, two syllables . . . "Mara."

"And you're Minnie." She smiled. "It's nice to finally get on the bookmobile. I usually work Saturdays, but the bank's closed today for software maintenance."

Julia took Emily in hand and guided her toward the picture books, murmuring about cat stories and cat adventures. The smaller child seemed content to sit on the step and look about, wide-eyed.

"Eddie's up front," I said. "He's sleeping in his carrier, but we can haul him out in a little bit. He won't mind." And maybe if he stayed awake all day, he'd sleep through the night. I eyed the small child and wondered if there were parallels between cat and kid sleeping habits.

"I wanted to thank you," Mara said.

"Uh." I stared at her blankly. We'd had a few interactions at the bank, but most of my financial activities were online.

"For what you did at Rowan's. I hear you tried really hard to save her life, and I wanted to say thanks. She was fun to work with, once you got used to her, and I was sad when she started working from home so much."

"Oh. Well." I shifted from one foot to the other. "It was what anyone would have done. I'm just sorry it didn't help."

Mara watched her toddler and Julia stack a pile of books. "They're saying she was murdered," Mara said softly. "That's so hard to think about."

I nodded, but didn't say anything because it seemed as if something was hanging in the back of her mind, waiting to come out, and I didn't want to break her focus.

"You know," she said, "I wonder if the police know about that day at the bank."

More specifics were needed. A lot more. "What day was that?"

She glanced at her smaller child, who was happily stuffing both of his hands into his mouth, and inched closer to me. "It was Bax Tousely."

For a moment there was no sound, no movement, no nothing. Then my heart restarted its beats. "What happened?"

Mara took her son's hands out of his mouth and inserted a pacifier she'd deftly pulled from her pocket. "He came in a while back when everybody else was at lunch and asked about a commercial loan. I told him to talk to Rowan, and a couple of weeks later, on one of the days she was in the office, he marched in and slammed her office door shut so hard all the windows in the building rattled."

"She turned down his loan?"

Mara nodded. "Even with the door shut, you could hear him yelling. Not what either one of them said exactly, but enough to get the idea. Her office is mostly glass, so I could see it all. It was scary, to tell you the truth, and I was thinking about calling the police when Bax threw the loan application across the desk at Rowan—papers went everywhere—and he stormed out of her office."

"Did he threaten her?" I asked.

She looked troubled. "Bax is such a nice guy, I've never seen him be anything but considerate and thoughtful. But he was really upset, and that's when people say things they don't mean, right?"

Sometimes. Other times people said exactly what they meant but under normal circumstances kept buttoned up inside, safe from view. "What did he say?"

Mara looked troubled. "He said . . . he said, 'I won't take this lying down. You'll pay for this if it's the last thing I do.' "

"Earth to Minnie. Hello, Minnie."

"What? Oh. Hey, Josh. How are you doing?" It

was Tuesday morning, I'd just dropped Kristen off at the airport, and I was standing in front of the coffeepot watching the dark liquid dribble down.

"It would be better if I had some of that stuff." He leaned around me and, in one deft movement, pulled the pot aside and shoved his mug underneath the flow. Four seconds later, he reversed the move, saying, "You're a coffee freak. Don't you do it this way when you're in a hurry?"

"Tried it the other day. It didn't go well." Which was an understatement. Coffee had gone everywhere—all over the burner, the counter, and the floor. Even coffee grounds had somehow gotten into the mix. "I'm a bit gun-shy to try it again so soon."

"What were you daydreaming about just now?" he asked. "You looked a million miles away."

"Oh, this and that," I said vaguely. "You know how I get." What I'd been thinking about was Bax Tousely's bank tirade. After Mara had finished telling the story, I'd gently asked her why, once she'd learned that Rowan had been murdered, she hadn't told the police. "I didn't want to get anyone into trouble," she'd said. "I mean, he was just venting, right? After his loan had been turned down. People do that all the time and nothing happens."

I'd wanted to point out that something had, in

fact, happened this time, but I'd smiled instead. Later that day, when I'd called Ash, he'd been very interested indeed and said he'd look into it. Whether or not he'd let me know what he found out was the big question.

Holly came into the break room and asked, "Have you done it yet?"

"Done what?"

"Not you. Him." Holly pointed at Josh, who was leaning against the counter, sipping his coffee. "Time is ticking away. If he doesn't act soon, all will be lost."

I was the one who was lost. I'd once had my finger on the pulse of library gossip, but now that I was out on the bookmobile a third of the time, it was hard to keep up. "What are you talking about?"

"Valentine's Day," she said, huffing. "He needs to start making plans if he wants to impress his new girlfriend."

"She's not my—"

Holly didn't let him keep talking. "Maybe not officially, but tell me this. Don't you want her to be your girlfriend? Don't you think she could be The One? Do you really think you will ever find anyone that suits you better than Mia Lacombe?"

"Well . . ." Josh looked at the floor, and dark red stained his ruddy cheeks.

On the inside, I was cheering wildly. Mia was Leese's half sister and was adorable in every way.

Sure, she had a few problems, but didn't we all? A solid and nonvolatile relationship could easily be the best thing for her. And Josh could certainly use some social companionship that wasn't on the other end of a computer. Of course, Mia herself was in IT and maybe all their romance would be in bits and bytes, but if it worked for them, did it matter?

Kelsey stopped in the doorway. "Well, rats," she said, looking at the coffeepot. "Who made it? Minnie?" She sighed, but came forward anyway.

"Just the person we needed," Holly said. "Minnie isn't being any help. We need to help Josh plan his first Valentine's Day with Mia."

As Josh made a gagging noise, Kelsey nodded. "This is a critical event. It will set the tone for the rest of the relationship. Think carefully, Josh."

"What I'm saying." Holly pointed at Josh again. "Figure out where you want to set the bar. Low or high. Too low and you might lose her because she'll think you don't care enough. Too high and you could scare her into thinking you're an over-the-top freak. Don't be a Bax."

I'd been edging out of the room but stopped dead. "Bax Tousely? What did he do?"

"You haven't heard the story?" Holly squinted at me. "Hang on, I think it happened the February before you started here."

"Everybody was talking about it," Kelsey said. "Half the town thought it was the most romantic gesture ever. The other half thought he was a nutcase."

Josh shot me a glance. "The halves were divided by gender. You can guess which went with the nutcase side."

"What did he do?" I asked again. "Who was his girlfriend?"

"Anya Bennethum," Holly said, and it was possible that my mouth dropped open. "She and Bax were a couple for years. It was the Valentine's Day of their junior year and the entire town of Chilson woke up to a huge banner hung from the top of the steeple of the Catholic church, the tallest thing in town, a banner saying, HAPPY V D, ANYA. LOVE, BAX."

"V D?" I asked, wincing. Even on Valentine's Day, to me V D could only mean venereal disease.

"Yeah." Kelsey grinned. "It was a vertical banner. There wasn't room to spell out "Valentine's," so he used initials instead. They'd broken up by the end of the day."

Poor Anya. How mortifying. And poor Bax, who'd shown a spectacular lack of . . . something.

"Moron," Josh said, not unkindly. "I hear he won't talk about it now."

But I wasn't talking, either, because I was suddenly thinking furiously. Leese said she'd seen Bax driving past the Bennethums' house a number of times before Rowan died. And Jared, the hardware store guy, had told me Bax had been in the store the morning of Rowan's murder, but had been acting oddly.

Was it possible that Bax had heard about an engagement of a Bennethum twin and assumed it was Anya? Had his love for her turned into obsession? Had he meant to kill Anya but killed Rowan instead?

Chapter 11

The next day was a bookmobile day. I got out of bed with a smile on my face and a song in my heart. "Good thing it was just in my heart," I told Julia as we drove across the frozen tundra of Tonedagana County, "because otherwise you'd find out how horrible my singing is."

"Can't be any worse than mine," she said. "There's a reason I never did musicals. Like they say, you can make an actor out of a singer but you can't make a singer out of an actor."

I had no idea anyone had ever said that, but it made sense. Sort of.

Julia leaned forward to peer into the cat carrier. "Eddie, what do you think of your mom's singing?"

"Mrr."

She sat back. "He said he thinks it's wonderful."

"I'm pretty sure he said he wants treats and why haven't we given him any this—" I came to a full stop.

"What's that?" Julia asked, looking up at me sideways.

"Um." I continued to stare out the windshield.

First thing that morning, I'd called the sheriff's office to ask about road conditions, and after listening to the deputies' comments about drifting snow blocking some back roads, I was taking a different route to the first stop of the day, a route that was taking us past Rowan's house. "There's a car at the Bennethums'."

"There is?" Julia sat up. "You're right, there is. Isn't Neil gone?"

"Far as I know. And he drives an SUV."

The two of us studied the small sedan as we drove past. "That's weird," I said.

"Maybe a neighbor has guests and is using the drive for overflow parking," Julia suggested.

I nodded slowly. Possible, but now that it was almost February, a need for extra guest parking seemed unlikely. Also unlikely were any of the other scenarios I was running in my head. "This afternoon," I said, "we'll loop around and come back this way. If you're okay with getting home a few minutes late."

She was, we did, and when we did, the car was still there.

After a moment's hesitation, I turned the bookmobile into the driveway and parked behind the dark gray sedan. "You can stay here," I told Julia, "but I'm going up to the house."

"If you're in, I'm in." Julia looked down at the carrier. "We'll be back in a few minutes, Mr. Ed, okay?"

"Mrr," Eddie replied, and I was pretty sure I heard a little kitty snore by the time the door shut behind us.

As we approached the front porch, we saw that someone had shoveled it clear of snow. This was not normally a part of the service provided by plow guys, and a few seconds after I rang the bell, the front door was opened by Anya Bennethum.

"Wow, hello, Minnie, Ms. Beaton." She looked over my shoulder. "And the bookmobile! Is something wrong?"

"No, no," I said quickly. "We were driving past in the bookmobile and saw a car in the driveway. I just wanted to be sure everything was okay since I didn't think anyone was here."

She smiled. Not a huge one, but it was unmistakably a smile. "It's nice that you cared enough to stop. Do you want to come in?"

I glanced at Julia and she nodded. Since the outside temperature was maybe fifteen degrees and the wind was kicking up, I was in full agreement. "Thanks. Just for a minute, though. I like to get back to Chilson before dark." In theory, the days were getting longer, but on thick cloud cover days like this, it was hard to believe in the sun at all.

Inside, we stood in the front hallway. "I had a couple of days off from school," Anya said, "so I decided to come home." She sighed. "It's just so weird, with Mom gone. They say I'll get used to it, but I can't even park inside the garage. It's where her car is . . ."

I reached out and gave her a long, hard hug. Whoever was giving her advice was an idiot. You never got used to losing someone you loved. You learned to live with it, is all.

Julia snorted as only an award-winning actor can snort. "Get used to it? Utter nonsense. You will adjust, but it takes time. Lots of time. Be patient with yourself. And even years from now, you might have crying jags that come out of nowhere. Grief is triggered by the oddest things. Two years after my dad died, I bawled my eyes out over a hammer."

I looked at her and mouthed, *A hammer?* She shrugged.

"Thanks." Anya sniffed. "I'm kind of a mess, but I'm dealing. It's Collier I'm worried about."

"What's the matter?" I asked.

"He's skipping a lot of classes. Not even showing up to take tests." She wrapped her arms around herself. "He says he's fine, but I know he's not. His roommate and his fiancée say all he does is play video games and sleep. The only thing he talks about is how whoever killed Mom should be in jail."

Anya took a deep breath and looked at me. "Are you any closer to figuring that out? I'm sure Collier would get better if that guy was in jail. It's eating him alive that her killer is walking around free while Mom is . . . while Mom isn't."

"The police are working on narrowing down the suspects," I said, hating how that sounded. "And I just passed on some information they're looking into."

"Really?" Her face brightened. "When do you think they'll make an arrest?"

Her obvious excitement startled me. "I really don't know. As soon as they can, I'm sure."

"That's great," she said. "I'll tell Collier right away. This has been so hard for him. He and Mom were really close, and it's hard that he's going to get married this summer. Mom won't be at his wedding, see?"

I did. But it didn't do to have unrealistic expectations, either. "You should hold off on telling Collier anything about the investigation," I cautioned. "Say the police are working hard. Say I'm helping. But I don't think they have enough of a case yet to arrest anyone."

Anya deflated. "Oh. Okay," she said, and the tremble of her lower lip nearly broke my heart. Right then and there I renewed my vow to do whatever I could to track down her mom's killer.

I gave her a quick hug and said we needed to get going. Then, remembering what I'd learned yesterday, I asked, "I saw Bax Tousely the other day. Didn't the two of you used to date?"

Anya's face turned the faintest shade of pink. "I don't . . . we don't . . ." She took a breath. "I haven't seen him since high school graduation."

Hmm, I thought.

Julia must have had the same thought, because once we were back on the bookmobile, she said, "Looks like Anya still has a thing for Bax, in spite of that unfortunate Valentine's Day episode."

"Looks like it," I said, and hoped for Anya's sake that he wasn't also a killer. Because if making an arrest for Rowan's murder would help Collier, if the killer was Bax, it might crush Anya.

Julia and I lugged the crates of returned books into the room dedicated to the bookmobile's separate book collection. The work was by far the worst part of running outreach, but it didn't take all that long, especially with Julia's ability to distract me with stories of her theater days.

"You do realize," I said, double-checking the computer to make sure the small stack of books checked out of main circulation and returned to the bookmobile matched the list on the screen, "that if you ever run out of theater stories, I'll have to fire you."

She smiled. "I ran out a long time ago. I've been making them up for the last six months." And with that, she waved and left, leaving me to wonder whether or not she'd been joking.

As I finished up the last of the day's tasks, I

finally decided. "She was joking," I said out loud to Eddie, but he was in his carrier and fast asleep.

I squatted down and peered in. He looked as if he could sleep for hours. "I'll be back in a few minutes," I whispered. Eddie didn't move, so I felt hardly any guilt at all for what I was about to do. Hurrying a bit, I headed to my office. All I wanted to do was make a single phone call, and the cell phone reception in the bookmobile collection room was horrible. I had only a few minutes to make the call so what I really needed to do was sneak into my office without anyone noticing I was in the building and—

"Minnie, you are just the person I wanted to see."

And I was toast. Dry burned toast.

I pasted a smile on my face and turned to my accoster. "Hey, Denise. What's up?"

Denise Slade was president of the Friends of the Library. It was a wonderful organization and running the library would be far more difficult without their efforts, but Denise could be a trial. She'd been widowed not that long ago, and I kept reminding myself of that sad fact, over and over, to help me be more understanding.

"What are you going to do about that new boss of yours?" she asked, standing with her hands on her wide hips. Energetic and confident, Denise had a take-charge kind of personality. Which

217

was fine, of course, but since she also had the sense of humor of a rusty metal bucket, she had a tendency to irritate people.

"Help him in every way possible," I said.

"Oh, *pfft.*" Denise flicked away my comment. "Don't give me that politically correct crap. What I want to know is why he and that new guy, Trent What's-His-Name, are running around asking such weird questions."

"Weird in what way?"

"Oh, you know. Just weird."

A deep urge to be scathingly sarcastic bubbled up, but I shoved it down. "Do you remember any of their questions?"

"It was a couple of days ago, so I don't remember word for word, but one of the things Graydon was asking about was the importance of the Friends of the Library. I mean, what kind of question is that!" She flung her hands out. "We're critical! Without us, you couldn't do half what you do."

Although I didn't agree with her math, I smiled and nodded encouragingly. "What else?"

"That Trent character—and aren't those names just the last straw? Graydon and Trent. They sound like the name of an attorney's office—anyway, Trent asked if we'd ever done a survey of library patrons on what they think of the Friends, if we should be doing more, if we should be doing less."

It was an interesting question. "Have you?"

"Of course not." Denise sounded disgusted. "We don't have time to do that kind of crap. Besides, surveys are for organizations that aren't in touch with the people they serve. We don't need to do that."

Again, I didn't agree with her, but disagreeing with Denise was something you did only if you had a spare hour, because she'd do her best to sway you to her side, even if you were disagreeing with her on the merits of the variety of cheese that best accompanied a hamburger.

"I'll talk to Graydon," I said. True enough. "But they're both new. I'd say they're both just asking questions to learn about the library and how we integrate with the community."

She didn't look convinced, but I said I had to make a phone call before six and headed off, not sure I'd convinced myself, either.

After closing my office door behind me, I pulled out my cell phone and did a search for the specialty wood store I'd visited with Rafe. "Darden Hardwoods," a male voice answered.

I blew out a sigh of relief. It was a few minutes shy of six and their posted hours said they were open until then, but it was also the dead of winter and I wouldn't have been surprised if no human had answered. After introducing myself, I brought out the question I'd formulated on the drive back to Chilson. I needed to do more to help find Rowan's killer, needed to help Collier and Anya and Neil, and this was one thing I could do.

"When Rafe and I were at your store the other day," I said, "I could have sworn I saw Land Aprelle pull into your parking lot. A friend of mine knows him, but she hasn't seen him in ages and was wondering if he was okay." Though the story was plausible, it was weak, and I expected an abrupt answer and a dial tone.

"Land?" The guy laughed. "Sure, I've known Land for years. Quite a character, isn't he?"

"I didn't know he was into woodworking."

"Well, I wouldn't call what he's doing woodworking. Furniture, yeah, but his stuff is more like sculpture. You know the Eames chair? Fancy like that, only hardwood instead of plywood. And not steamed. He's doing a lot of carving."

"Sounds interesting."

"Yeah, I'm not explaining it very well. And I've never seen any of his pieces. Land's quiet about it. He wants to get accepted into the juried show up there in Chilson, but the first time he said that, his buddies laughed at him. Now he keeps his lip zipped and he's just doing it."

"Good to know he's okay," I said, and thanked him for his time.

So Land was a closet fine woodworker. Was that enough to explain why he'd acted so oddly at the store? Was Rowan one of the people who'd laughed at him? Could he have possibly killed her to punish her for that?

Though it seemed outside the realm of possibility, killing anyone at all was hard to believe, but it happened on a regular basis.

After dropping Eddie at home, I headed straight to Rafe's house, where his wide smile and huge hug lifted my spirits and made me forget about the sad possibilities that were all around.

Only one other table in the Red House Café was occupied the next morning when Aunt Frances and I came in, stomping our boots free of snow. We'd started the day with a simultaneous realization that neither one of us had remembered to buy milk.

"Hmm." My aunt had eyed the contents of the refrigerator. "There are eggs. All the bacon is frozen, though."

"Is it possible to have eggs without bacon?"

Aunt Frances frowned mightily. "Possible, I suppose. But it sounds sad and dreary."

It did indeed. "If I were a good niece," I'd said, "I'd volunteer to run out for milk. But since you don't have to be to school until ten today, and I don't have to be at the library until nine, how about going out for breakfast?"

And so, twenty minutes later, we arrived at the restaurant owned by Sunny Scoles. The other occupant of the dining area was an elderly man, who was sipping coffee and reading a newspaper. He looked as if he'd been there for a while and as if he intended to stay for quite some time. It also didn't look as if he'd ordered anything except coffee. I hoped, for Sunny's sake, that the restaurant was busier on weekends.

Unless she'd killed Rowan. Then the number of people who came to her restaurant wouldn't matter a bit.

"What's the matter?" Aunt Frances asked. "You look a little sad."

I shook off the feeling. "Hungry," I said. "Where would you like to sit?"

As my aunt aimed us toward a table for two directly underneath a light fixture crafted out of an old hand lantern, Sunny hurried in from the back.

"Sorry I took so long," she said. "Let me get you some menus. Here you go. Would you like some . . ." She peered at me. "Weren't you in here a week or two ago? Oatmeal with all the fixings."

"That's me. My aunt and I are looking for real food today, though."

Sunny laughed. "Eggs, bacon, hash browns, toast?"

"That sounds heavenly," Aunt Frances said. "I can't think of the last time I had a full breakfast in a real restaurant."

"Coffee first, though, please," I said. At this

point my morning had been caffeine-free and it wasn't a condition I wished to continue.

"You got it."

Sunny headed back to the kitchen and my aunt looked around, admiring the room. "This is fun," she said. "How was the oatmeal you had?"

"Good. But, you know."

"Still oatmeal."

Aunt Frances made some comments about the location and how she hoped the food was good enough to make it a destination for folks. I nodded, but a large part of my brain was engaged in wondering why I didn't want Sunny Scoles to be the one who'd killed Rowan.

Was it because I enjoyed the way she'd decorated her restaurant? Because my instinctive response to her was one of friendship? Because I didn't want anyone who rejoiced in the name of Sunny to be a killer?

None of those were good reasons, but I had no others.

"And here you go, ladies!" Sunny poured coffee into our upturned mugs. "Do you need more time or are you ready to order?"

"Full breakfast for me," Aunt Frances said. "Bacon, scrambled, sourdough, and hash browns a little crispy on the edges."

"The only way to cook them." Sunny turned to me. "What can I get you?"

But I was staring at the table's small wire rack.

"The last time I was here, you had another kind of sugar. It was maple flavored, wasn't it?"

"It was," Sunny said. "And really, really good." She started to smile, but the happy expression hadn't fully crossed her face before it faded. "It was expensive, though, so I only ordered a small batch. I put it out once a week on different days to track sugar use. Geeky, right?"

Yes, and it also sounded like something Kristen would do. I had high hopes for Sunny and her restaurant, and I didn't in the least want her to be the killer. On the plus side, I had information on the sugar packets that Hal and Ash might find interesting. The availability of the sugar wasn't as wide open as I'd thought, which had to narrow down something.

But there was still a big question: Why had Sunny inflated the numbers on her loan application? And with it came the even bigger question: Had Rowan's denial of the loan incited Sunny to murder?

Aunt Frances and I went our separate ways after eating, both of our stomachs contentedly stuffed full of breakfasty yumminess. On our way out, my aunt took a stack of the business cards at the cash register and waggled them at Sunny.

"Old-school advertising," she said, "in an old school. I love it. And I love your restaurant, so I will be spreading the news far and wide. Expect great things, young lady, because I'm sure they're about to happen."

Sunny's smile looked a bit forced. "Thanks," she said. "I appreciate that. Very, very much."

Outside, my aunt looked back at the old red schoolhouse. "I meant what I said. Sunny has a great place there and I will spread the news and—*oooff!* What was that for?"

I released her from the hug I'd enveloped her in. "Because you're a nice lady and I love you."

She patted me on the head, which made me feel a little like Eddie. "Keep it up, favorite niece, and I might remember you in my will."

"I'm your only niece, and you'll probably outlive me." At least I hoped she would. I didn't want to think about a world that didn't include Aunt Frances.

"We can only hope!" She waved, climbed into her ancient Jeep Cherokee, and headed off to the college.

I got into my sedate sedan and drove back to Chilson, strong-mindedly parking at the boardinghouse instead of the library. Walking was good for me, if I didn't get frostbite. I popped inside to grab my backpack, which I'd already loaded with a lunch of potato chips and a peanut butter and jelly sandwich, and hunted around for Eddie.

"There you are." I found him on the floor in my bedroom, between the bed and the outside wall.

225

He was rolled mostly, but not all the way, onto his back and looked up at me with eyes barely open.

"Mrr," he said, then yawned, showing me the unattractive roof of his mouth.

"Nice." I reached down to rub his tummy. "See you later, pal, okay?"

"Mrr," he said sleepily, and before I was out of the room, his purrs had turned into a snore.

I tried to shake away the nappy contagion of his yawns as I slid into my boots, then stepped outside. "Well, that did the trick," I gasped as the cold hit me once again. Five minutes inside had let me forget how freaking cold it was. I cast one look at my still-warm car. So tempting. I girded myself to be brave and strong and marched myself in the direction of downtown.

Wind and winter and white swirled about me. I thought about Arctic expeditions and the White Witch and Jon Snow and was startled, just before I reached the main shopping blocks, when a voice called out. "Minnie! Do you have a minute?"

I blinked out of my book-induced reverie and found myself directly in front of the sheriff's office staring at Detective Hal Inwood, who was standing half in and half out of the door. "Good morning!" I said. "You're the exact person I wanted to talk to."

"Not out here," he said, looking down at his

coatless arms and boot-free feet. "Please not out here."

Laughing, I followed him inside and into the interview room. "This morning," I said, unzipping my coat, "Aunt Frances and I had breakfast at the Red House Café, the place Sunny Scoles owns—it's outstanding, by the way, you should try it—and she had those maple sugar packets. But she only has them out on certain days, to help track sugar usage, so maybe that's a . . ." I stopped talking, because though Hal seemed to be listening to me, he hadn't pulled out his memo pad and he wasn't taking any notes.

"You don't think this is important?" I asked, trying to keep my expression neutral. "Maybe it won't turn out to be, but shouldn't you at least check it out?" I glanced into the hallway. Where was Ash? He was usually more sympathetic to my point of view than his staid and rule-bound superior.

"This is why I pulled you in out of the cold," Hal said. "The test results on the sugar packet you found in Rowan Bennethum's house have come back."

"And what?" I asked. "Don't keep me hanging. The suspense is . . . is making my blood pressure go up."

"He doesn't want to tell you," Ash said, sitting in the chair next to his supervisor. "Morning, Minnie."

"Tell me what?" I looked from one to the other. In the past, I'd been able to gauge what Ash was thinking, or at least what he was feeling, but not today.

Hal sighed. "There was nothing in that packet other than what should have been there. Not a single trace."

I stared at him. Listened to my heart thud a few times. Heard my breaths go in and out. "They're sure?" I whispered.

Ash nodded. "Double runs are standard," he said. "They're very sure."

"Like *sure* sure?"

He flashed a short grin. "Lots of sure. There's no room for doubt."

I slumped down in the chair. How could that be? I'd been so sure. It was the only thing that made sense. What other reason was there for the packet to be in the kitchen at all? Hang on . . .

"Okay," I said, sitting up straight. "Maybe it didn't have poison, but someone brought that sugar packet into the house." My words tumbled over each other as I tried to explain. "It couldn't have been Rowan, because she didn't touch the stuff. And it couldn't have been a family member, because Rowan was the only one in the house, and she would have picked up an empty sugar packet left by the kids or Neil. Where else could it have come from if not the killer?"

Ash glanced at Hal, then said, "It could have

come from lots of people. The mail carrier, if he'd dropped off a package and she'd invited him in. Or a neighbor."

I opened my mouth, about to point out that those things could be checked, when Hal put in his two cents.

"It could have been dropped by a friend. Or caught on the bottom of a boot and brought into the house by Ms. Bennethum herself."

"That's ridiculous," I said flatly. "All those scenarios are. You didn't know Rowan. She wouldn't have missed seeing something like that sugar packet. She just wouldn't have."

But no matter how much I argued, they wouldn't budge from their opinion, and five minutes later I was out on the street, face to the wind and fuming.

How could they not understand the importance of that stupid packet, poison or no?

And more important, how was I going to *make* them see?

Chapter 12

The only noise at our table was the light *tink* of two knives and two forks against plates. Rafe and I were at City Park Grill in Petoskey, enjoying a quiet dinner. A very quiet dinner. We'd been mostly silent on the drive, silent while ordering and waiting for our food, and now we were being quiet while eating. This needed to stop, so I said the first thing that popped into my head.

"Remember Giuseppe's?" I asked, naming an Italian restaurant in Charlevoix that had been closed for years. "I still miss their pasta."

"What?" Rafe looked up. "Oh. Yeah. Me, too. But I hear the new place there is good."

I nodded, but since there didn't seem to be anything else to add, I turned my attention back to my food. Sort of. Part of me was wondering why Rafe was being so quiet—I hadn't honestly known he could be—but most of my focus was on something else altogether, as it had been since that morning.

How could Hal and Ash not understand? How could it be that something so obviously important was scoffed at as unworthy by those two? Was it because they were men and not accustomed to proper cleaning procedures?

I didn't want to think so. After all, Ash had lived on his own for years and his apartment had always seemed, if not cozy and welcoming, at least tidy. And Hal was a detective with thirty-odd years of experience. Surely he'd come across cases that were solved on evidence weirder than a sugar packet.

And it's important! I thought, sawing at my meat fiercely. What would I have to do to make them understand?

"Keep that up and you'll need a spoon to eat," Rafe said.

"What?" I looked down at my plate and recognized that the pork was already in pieces small enough to feed a toddler. "Oh. Sorry. I was thinking about something else." Then, since I didn't want him to ask what the something was, I said, "You've been quiet tonight. Did you do something stupid that you're now regretting?"

Since Rafe and I had known each other for years, our new and wonderfully more intimate relationship was starting with the behavioral patterns we'd established when we'd first met as kids, which was to say whatever we felt like without thinking too much about consequences.

"One of the kids has been diagnosed with cancer," he said.

All my breath rushed out in an instant, as if I'd been punched in the solar plexus. "I'm so sorry," I said, wishing there was something better to say. But what else was there? Guilt surged through me. One of the middle school students had cancer, and I'd been making fun of Rafe for being quiet. "And I'm sorry I called you stupid."

He frowned. "You did?"

"I suggested the possibility."

"Oh. Well. That's okay. I am pretty stupid sometimes." He took a bite of steak, then pushed away his plate, on which remained half his sweet potato and most of the squash and carrot mix. "The prognosis for this little guy is good, but . . ." He left the sentence dangling, so I finished it for him.

"It still sucks."

"You know it." He formed his right hand into a pistol and shot the air near my head. "And now's the time to explain why you've been so abnormally quiet. Are there more wedding problems for your aunt?"

"Not that I've heard. We still haven't fixed the last round." Aunt Frances and Otto had been e-mailing daily with people in Bermuda, but at this point there was no solution. If there wasn't an alternative found within the next week or so, they'd have to abandon the island idea altogether.

"So what's up?" He reached out for my hands. "Put that knife and fork down a second and talk to me. You haven't eaten a bite in five minutes anyway. All you've done is cut that poor slice of meat to tiny ribbons."

His hands, warm and strong, were dinged with scratches from working on the house. I traced a short reddish line, remembering how he'd picked that one up from trying to hold too many screws in one hand.

"Talk," he said. "Tell me whatever it is that's bothering you. I want to know."

I looked up. "Truly?"

"Absolutely." He lifted up one of my hands and kissed it. "If it's something ridiculous, I reserve the right to make fun, but I promise not to laugh out loud."

It was as much as anyone could expect. I remember my aunt's words of wisdom, that I should be honest with Rafe about working with the sheriff's department, that I needed to be open with the things that were important to me, that if I hid things now, what would I hide later? And if I wanted him to be honest with me, I should do the same in return.

So I told him. About how I'd been in regular contact with Hal and Ash. How we were exchanging information on suspects. About the stupid sugar packet. About why I wanted so much to help Anya and Collier. When I got all the way to the end, he just looked at me.

"What?" I asked.

He suddenly grinned, and his expression lightened the dim room. Lightened my life. "I knew most of that already."

"What?" I asked again, far more stupidly this time. "How?"

"How not?" He tapped the back of my hands with his thumbs. "Remember where we live? People talk."

"Um." There were numerous benefits to small-town life, but this wasn't one of them. "Are you mad?"

He shook his head. "It was obvious after the First Argument that you weren't going to stop. And I understand why you're doing it. So mostly I was just wondering when you were going to tell me."

"You're not mad about that, either?" I asked, my voice soft. "Because you have a right to be. I should have told you earlier."

"No, I'm not," he said a bit wonderingly. "I'm really not. Weird, isn't it?"

"Nope. It's great," I said quickly. "Thanks. You're the best ever."

"Naturally. But there's one thing."

I knew there'd be a catch. "What's that?" I asked warily.

"Let me help."

The next day was a library day, and I spent most of the morning doing my best to come to grips with the fact that Rafe wanted to help find Rowan's killer.

"It's happened before," he'd said during dessert. "Couples chasing down bad guys."

"Nick and Nora," I said, nodding.

"Who?" He frowned. "Do I know them?"

Clearly not. Though Rafe did, in fact, read books, he preferred nonfiction, and I should have known the reference to the Dashiell Hammett books would be lost on him. "Who are you talking about?" I asked.

"Almost every movie ever produced has a couple figuring something out, whether it's how to save the world, like in *War Games*. Or tracking down precious objects, like in *Raiders of the Lost Ark*. Or finally recognizing how much they love each other, like in *When Harry Met Sally . . .*"

He had a point, and since he'd ended with a movie that bore some similarities to our relationship, I'd given him a kiss. "It's nice that you're so familiar with old movies, and I appreciate your offer. If I can think of anything you can do to help, I'll let you know."

Now I was doing my regular late-morning walk-through of the library. This not only got me out and about and let me chat with library patrons, but also kept my body from freezing into a desk-bound position. I could almost see my mother nodding in approval, so I nodded back to her across the miles.

"Good morning, Minnie."

I blinked out of my parental-induced daydream and focused on the young woman in front of me. "Morning, Anya. I didn't know you were still in town. Doing some research at the famed Chilson District Library that you can't possibly get done at your silly old university library?"

She smiled. "Sort of."

"Anything I can help you with?"

"That's why I'm here." She looked around, saw no one, and moved closer. "Collier told me not to bother you, he said it doesn't mean anything, but I think I have to."

"Okay," I said. "Is this about your mom?"

She nodded. "And Land Aprelle, do you know him? After Dad started working downstate, Mom hired Land to do some of the bigger chores around the house."

I had a feeling I knew where this was going, but I let her keep talking.

Anya took hold of a small lock of her auburn hair and started twisting the daylights out of it. "A few days before Mom died, she and Land had this really big argument, and—"

I nodded. "I'm glad you are telling me, but your dad already talked to me about it. You don't need to relive it again if you don't want to."

"Oh." Anya sighed. "Good. I don't, really. Just so long as you know everything."

There wasn't much to know, as far as I could

tell. I was about to ask what else there might be, but the creaking of the back door distracted me, and when Graydon walked through it, my attention was good and diverted. He'd been downstate attending an undoubtedly fun-filled training session on the library's software, and I'd thought he was due back the next day, not today. Odd.

I swung back to face Anya. "I'll call you later, okay?" She hesitated, then nodded, and I hurried after Graydon. His legs, however, were far longer than mine and I had to jog to catch up to him.

"Good morning," I said, just before he opened the stairway door that led up to his lair. "I didn't think you'd be back until tomorrow."

"Morning, Minnie." Graydon set down his briefcase and pulled off his gloves. "I'd scheduled an extra day to meet with the state library folks, but there was a mix-up with the dates. I'll have to meet up with them next time I'm in Lansing."

State library? Next time? None of that made any sense to me. I mean, it might be useful that Graydon had contacts down there, but I couldn't come up with a reasonable scenario. But determined not to get sidetracked, I ignored that shiny distraction. "Do you have a minute? We can talk in my office."

He looked at his heavy boots, which were dripping snow and ice onto the tile. "Right now?"

Yes, because if he went upstairs to take off his

winter wear, he'd ask me to go with him. Which meant I'd be forced to have this conversation on his turf and I wanted every advantage I could get, teeny tiny though it was.

"This will only take a minute," I said.

"Okay, but if Gareth comes after me, I'm going to confess that you forced me."

I laughed and ushered him into my small office. That he was sparing a second of concern for our maintenance guy made me think, once again, that Graydon was a good and decent guy and had the potential to be a fantastic boss. And yet . . .

Graydon sat in the spare chair and I sat at my desk. A little role reversal never hurt anything, right? Then, before there was any awkward delay, I jumped right into the big question.

"Why are you and Trent asking so many questions about the library staff?"

"Um." Graydon looked at the floor. At the walls. At my desk. Finally, he looked back at me. "I'm not sure what you mean."

My invisible antennae, the ones that everyone has, the ones that detect lies and evasions and off-kilter situations, twanged something fierce. If everything was kosher, if they'd just been asking questions because they were new to town and the library, then he would have said so.

"At lunch the other day," I said. "You asked me about personnel." I ticked off the comments I'd heard from others, finishing with Denise. "I'm your assistant director," I said, trying to keep my shoulders back and chin up instead of my natural inclination, which was to curl up in a ball and howl that the library was changing and I didn't like it. "If you and Trent are thinking about changes in staffing, I hope that you'll include me in the conversation."

"Um," Graydon said again. Silence descended upon us, a silence so complete that the sound of my breathing was almost embarrassing.

After about a million years, he said, "You're absolutely right." He glanced at his watch. "Wow, look at the time. I have to get going. After being downstate I have a lot of e-mail and . . . things . . . to wade through."

Graydon practically bolted out of the room. I stared after him, and realized that I'd learned two things. One: Something weird was indeed going on. Two: My boss was a horrible liar.

When noon rolled around, the sun decided to make an appearance. It felt like months since we'd seen blue sky, and despite the sandwich I'd packed, I decided what my psyche really needed was a walk, and since in winter the best-cleaned sidewalks were downtown, clearly it was best to walk those sidewalks, and if I was going to be downtown at lunchtime, it was only reasonable to eat down there, too.

Having thus convinced myself that I was doing the right thing, I kicked my shoes off into their winter home underneath my desk, pulled on my boots and other outerwear, and headed out to the big white and blue world.

Just as I leaned on the front door's release bar, the door from the lobby to the vestibule clicked open behind me. "Minnie. Headed out for lunch?"

I turned, seeing first only a dark winter coat, then seeing who it was. "Hey, Stewart. That's right. You?"

Stewart Funston, designer of electronic manufacturing thingies who sometimes telecommuted from the library, possessor of a Maple Staples sugar packet, cousin to Rowan, wearer of a fedora, and on the list of murder suspects, nodded as we walked together.

"Hard to stay inside on a day like this, isn't it?" He looked up at the sky and pulled in a long, deep breath. "Ahh. I just love winter."

Smiling, I said, "Days in winter that are sunny and calm, right?"

He chuckled. "Well, these days are a definite bonus. But I'm one of those freaks who actually likes winter. It helps that I don't have to drive much." He glanced at me. "How's the bookmobile in the snow?"

"Not so bad." I actually thought it was outstanding. Though its weight and long wheelbase made the acceleration sluggish and braking distance long, it handled predictably, which was more than I could say about any other vehicle I'd ever driven in winter.

But I also didn't want to tempt fate. I had the sneaking suspicion that as soon as I bragged about the bookmobile's fantastic winter driving capabilities, I'd slide into a great big ditch, a great big tow truck would have to be summoned to haul us out, everyone in town would hear about it, and I'd hear bad jokes for months, if not years. This was a situation to be avoided if at all possible, so I said again, "Not so bad," and shrugged. "So what's new with you? Designed anything interesting lately?"

"Yes, and it's so boring even my coworkers' eyes glaze over when I talk about it. I'll spare you the description. Think of it as a gift from me to you."

"I appreciate that." Smiling, I really hoped that Stewart had not killed Rowan. Surely someone with that kind of self-awareness couldn't possibly have ended a life.

"The big news," he said, "is that my divorce is final."

Divorce? I hadn't even realized he and his wife had separated. "Um, should I offer my congratulations or my sympathies?"

"Both." His voice was light, but something about his diction gave me an uneasy feeling.

"Congratulations for the final result," he said, "and sympathy for having lived with someone almost twenty-five years who was continually lying to me."

The harshness in his voice now made sense. "I'm sorry. That must be hard." And I was sorry, even though at bottom I didn't know Stewart all that well. I'd never met his wife and didn't even know if they'd had children. Still, I was sorry for any human pain, whether physical or emotional.

He nodded. "Thanks, I appreciate that. Our friends are all taking sides, and it's turning out I don't have as many friends as I thought I did."

"Your real friends will stick with you."

"That's what I hear," he said grimly. "But what else could I do, other than divorce? She'd been stashing all this money away in a secret bank account and never said a word. Who knows what else she was hiding? It could be anything!"

He waved his arms about, and I ducked a little to avoid being thumped.

"Oh, sorry." He gave a little laugh. "I get carried away. I'll get over this in time, I'm sure, but I just couldn't live with someone who lies to me. I just couldn't."

I made noises of sympathy and understanding. And I was also very glad I'd come clean to Rafe the night before about my involvement in Rowan's murder investigation, because hearing

Stewart's anger made me realize, way deep down inside, how Rafe could have interpreted my not telling him as a lie. Which was what Aunt Frances had said.

"She's smart," I murmured to myself, and was once again glad I was related to her. And that I should take her advice far more often than I did. Except for any cooking advice. That just wasn't going to happen.

"What's that?" Stewart asked.

"Nothing," I said. "I hope things get better for you soon, that's all." I pushed away the fleeting thought that I might be walking down the street with a killer and concentrated on the clear blue sky.

"Tell me one more time?" I asked.

"Mrr!"

"Okay, you're absolutely right. You're more than right. And I agree one hundred percent."

"Mrr," Eddie said more quietly.

The two of us had been enjoying a cozy evening in front of the fireplace with popcorn and Netflix when, during an episode of *Gilmore Girls*, my furry friend had, for no apparent reason, stood on my lap and started yelling at me.

My agreement seemed to appease him, although I had no idea what he was trying to tell me. But he didn't need to know that. Or . . . did he? Did I need to be completely honest with my cat? There was no way that he understood ninety-nine point nine nine percent of what I was saying, but if I didn't tell Eddie everything, was I establishing a habit that would transfer to Rafe?

I paused the television and looked deep into my cat's yellow eyes. "Confession time. I have no idea what you were talking about, but whatever it was, I'm sure you're right."

Eddie put his front paws on my chest. "Mrr!!" he yowled, his cat food breath hitting my face. "MRR!!" He gave me a disgusted look, stalked to the other end of the couch, and flopped down.

"Sorry I'm so stupid." One of his ears twitched back, so I knew he was listening. "And going on the assumption that I should be telling all the important beings in my life the important things that are going on in my life, I need to tell you that Rafe now knows I'm looking into Rowan's murder."

Both his ears swiveled.

"I hope that's good news for you. But now things are going to get more complicated because Rafe says he wants in. That he wants to help."

Eddie started purring.

"Really? You're purring?" I sighed. "Is this a guy thing? Because I have to say I'm not looking forward to being tag teamed once we move into the house."

The purrs continued.

Cats.

"The next question is, how do I involve Rafe? It's not like I have a task list I could split in two. It's more of a winging-it thing for me."

Eddie continued to purr, which was comforting but no real help. I picked up the remote, then laid it down. "Out of all the suspects—"

"Mrr?"

"Right." I nodded. "Let's review. We have Sunny Scoles, restaurant owner, but not an owner of a food truck due to Rowan's loan denial, which could be because of an inflated dollar request."

I waited, but Eddie didn't say anything. "Moving on. We have Land Aprelle, handyman and woodworker, who had a huge fight with Rowan soon before she died." I suddenly remembered that Anya had more to say about that. And I would have texted her about it, but my phone was out of reach. Later. I'd text her later.

"Then there's Stewart Funston, cousin with the sugar packets, and Hugh Novak, who wanted sugar packets and who is moving heaven and earth to get the township to build a new hall, something that Rowan was committed to preventing."

"Mrr."

"No idea what you're saying. And at the bottom of the list there's the lovelorn and wannabe film guy, Bax Tousely. Which brings up the question, how do I find out more about him? And not the surface stuff. I need the deep-secret-sometimes-scary stuff."

"Mrr!"

Ding!

Eddie yelped at the exact moment my phone dinged with an incoming text. "Nice timing." I inched forward, almost falling off the couch in the process, and with one finger pulled my phone close enough to pick it up.

Rafe: *Whatcha doing*

Me: *Sending you a text in a complete sentence.*

Rafe: *Time waste*

Me: *And what have you done with all that time you've saved?*

Rafe: *Renovated house*

Me: *Point to you.*

Rafe: *Thx*

Me (after a short pause): *Who do I know that would talk to me about Bax Tousely and keep quiet about it?*

Rafe: *Rgessie*

Me (after staring at the screen for a moment): *Who?*

Rafe: *Fat fingers meant Thessie*

Me: *Thessie Dyer?*

Rafe: *Friend w Bs little sister*

Me: *Thanks! You just helped with Rowan's murder investigation.*

Rafe: *Cool gotta go glue setting*

"And if that's how easily it's done," I said to Eddie as I scrolled through my phone's contacts list, "maybe this working together thing should have started a long time ago."

"Mrr," Eddie said, and rotated around so that his back faced me.

Thessie was my former bookmobile assistant, Thessie Dyer, now off at college. My thumbs hovered over the phone. If I texted her, she'd probably reply quickly, but texting would be an awkward way to do this. I hesitated, then pushed her phone number.

After three rings, Thessie actually picked up the phone. "Minnie! What's up?"

"Checking that you're still sure about majoring in library and information science." Though I loved my job, it wasn't for everyone, and I wanted to make sure my young friend knew the bad side as well as the good before making a major life decision.

"Absolutely," Thessie said. I could almost see her, nodding so hard that her long straight black hair bounced up and down. "Can't think of anything I'd rather do. But . . ." She hesitated. "Would you mind if I didn't come home to work in Chilson? I mean, it's home and all, but have you ever been to the library in Grand Rapids? The main one, downtown? It's amazing. And a friend and I are going to the East Coast for spring break—we want to see the Library of Congress.

Wouldn't it be the coolest thing in the world to work there?"

I laughed. "It would be wonderful." If you liked big cities, which I didn't. "Go where life takes you and don't look back. Except every once in a while in the summer, because it's nice here."

"You got it," Thessie said. "Now tell me why you really called."

"Can't put anything past you, can I?"

"That's what happens when you're trained by the best."

My smile slipped. "Rafe tells me you're good friends with Bax Tousely's younger sister."

"Caitlin? In middle and high school, we were pretty close. Not so much now that we're at different colleges."

"Okay, but how well do you know Bax?"

"As much as you'd know the older brother of your high school friend. Why?"

I scrambled for a response. "A friend's daughter might be interested in dating him, and she's had some bad experiences. Did you ever see him lose his temper?"

"Bax?" She sounded astonished. "I don't think he has a temper. He never lost it, not even when Caitlin and I were messing around on his computer and accidentally ruined a video he was doing for the school's theater group. I mean, he was mad for a second, but then he just said he'd be able to do it better and faster the second time."

248

I thanked Thessie for the information, but just as I was about to hang up, she said, "You know, I kind of forget this, but he changed after that Valentine's thing with Anya Bennethum. He was always quiet, but that's when he got even more quiet. Didn't come out of his room hardly at all, except to eat."

Hmm. That didn't sound good. Not at all. Thessie and I chatted a bit more, and when the call ended, I asked Eddie, "Well, what do you think?"

All I got was a blinking stare, but I mentally moved Bax Tousely up toward the top of the suspect list.

The crate of books I carried from my car into the Lakeview Medical Care Facility was heavy enough that I probably should have split it into two trips. But snow was blowing horizontally and night was coming fast, so I chose speed over being smart and staggered across the parking lot, hoping like crazy that I didn't drop the thing and spill library books all over creation.

Step by step, I labored my way to the front entrance. The automatic double doors swooshed open as I approached, and I heaved a huge sigh of relief as I escaped the frigid, howling wind.

"Thought about coming to help you," Max Compton said. "But it was more fun to watch."

I thumped the crate down on a handy table.

"Glad I could brighten your day." My words came out in puffs, as I was still out of breath.

Max rolled his wheelchair a little closer. "My dearest librarian, you brighten my days with your very presence. It's your visits that keep me alive. Without you, I would languish. I would fail to thrive. I would—"

He stopped talking as I held out a large-print book. It was the latest from John Sandford, Max's absolute favorite author.

"Are you lending that to me or taunting me with it?" he asked, squinting up at me.

"Reach out and see."

He grinned. "A touch of surprise to spice up the day. How delightful. But hark! Unless my ears are failing me, which wouldn't be a surprise because the rest of my body has done that already, I hear the footsteps of our Heather."

It was indeed Heather, one of Lakeview's certified nursing assistants, and one of the CNAs who'd cared for my artist friend Cade when he'd stayed there after a stroke. Having the bookmobile stop by Lakeview had been the brainchild of the three of us, and it was a rousing success. I stopped by once a month to read out loud to a group, and also stopped every couple of weeks with a crate packed full of items I'd come to learn would be popular with residents.

"Hey there, Miss Minnie." Heather flashed a smile. "Your timing is awesome. Mrs. Albright was just talking about that picture book she'd read to her kids. Any chance you found a copy?"

I dug through the crate, found what I wanted, and brandished a copy of *Make Way for Ducklings*. "Ta-dah!"

"You are the best," Heather breathed, taking the slim volume. "No matter what Max says, you're my favorite librarian ever."

"For crying out loud," Max protested. "You weren't supposed to tell her!"

I sighed heavily. "All those other librarians who bring you books are taller, smarter, and funnier than I am, aren't they? It's something I should have accepted a long time ago."

Heather lightly bopped Max on the head with the book. "Now see what you've done? Fix that before she leaves. See you later, Minnie. And thanks!" She hustled away, heading off to do one of the zillions of chores that CNAs are tasked with doing.

"We don't have any other librarians," Max said in a stage whisper. "So you kind of have to be our favorite."

I grinned. "It's nice to be the favorite, even if I'm the only one."

"Excellent attitude." Max winked. "Then again, if you'd really like a competition, we could put you into a bigger pool. Say, all the volunteers."

Though I did have a small streak of competitiveness, trying to be the favorite unpaid help at Lakeview wasn't part of it. But to keep Max happy, as I unloaded the rest of the books, I asked, "Who would be my competition?"

He stopped paging through the Sandford book and started counting on his knobby fingers. "There's Lisa, Denise, Molly, and Emily. We have Toni, Theresa, and Tracey. And there's Esther, Rosalind, and Maureen."

"I don't know, Max," I said, tidying the stacks of books into neat piles, because I couldn't just plop them there all caddywampus. "That's a lot of people. How can I possibly win?"

Max kept naming names. "There's Dan, Bonnie, and Bax. And on Fridays we have Rob, Callie—"

"Hang on." I aligned the books with the edge of the table—perfect!—and turned around. "You said Bax. Is that Baxter Tousely?"

"Rob, Callie, Tom, Chris the girl, and Chris the boy." He squinted at the ceiling. "Yes, I think that's it and I have no idea what any of their last names might be. Eighty-six years old and that's how you want me to use up what's left of my short-term memory?"

As if. All terms of his memory were better than mine. "How old is Bax?"

"Younger than me."

Not helpful. "What does he look like?"

Max's attention started drifting back to the book, so I put my hand out and covered up the

252

page. "What does he look like?" I could have asked someone at the front office, but this would be faster and easier and less likely to be spread around. If Max cooperated, that was.

He heaved a dramatic sigh. "A little wide. Not short, not tall. Dark curly hair almost always in need of a cut. Wears one of those silly little beards so many young men have these days."

"Anything else?"

Max squinted at me, and I suddenly realized I needed to justify my questions. "A friend of mine might be thinking about hiring him to do a video thing, so I thought I'd see what he'd be like to work with." As an impromptu explanation, it had to be one of my best ever.

"Huh." Max's squint didn't go away, but it lessened in intensity. "He started showing up here a couple of years ago when his grandmother was recovering from hip surgery. Says he likes hanging out with us old folks. He's a decent kid, but a little off. Vegetarian. Shovels his neighbor's driveway. Finds homes for stray cats. No, I'm not making that up." Max held up his hand. "Swear on a stack of Bibles. The kid's the closest thing to a freaking saint I've ever met. I should hate him. Hasn't happened yet, though. Maybe next week." He sounded hopeful.

"Anything else?" I asked.

Max studied me. "I keep telling him he needs a girlfriend, but he says that never seems to work out. You know, he'll probably be here in a few minutes. How about you ditch that Rafe and I set you up with Bax?"

"Only if you want me to set you up with Lillian," I said.

"Nooo!" Max clutched his heart. "Cruel librarian, to threaten me with that woman. Go away and don't come back until you have another Sandford book."

Laughing, I popped into the front office, collected the returns box, and headed back out into the cold.

So Bax was the kind of guy who volunteered. Rescued cats. Helped his neighbors. He sounded like a kind and gentle soul, the kind of person who would never, ever kill someone.

I tossed the crate into my trunk and slid into the driver's seat.

But as Detective Hal Inwood had told me many times, and as I'd come to learn firsthand, given the perfect storm of circumstances, pretty much everyone had the potential to be a killer.

I started the car and sat there for a moment, letting the engine warm up enough to defrost the window. After a few shivering minutes, the last of the window fog vanished and I saw, walking toward the facility's entrance, a man with his head down and his hands in his pockets, and even from ten feet away, I could see the sadness etched into his face. Just as I was wishing I could make him smile, I realized I was looking at Bax Tousely.

Huh.

A lot of things could cause that level of emotion. The death of a loved one. A bad breakup. But the paper had been free of obituaries for almost a week and his breakup with Anya had been years ago. So what was causing his melancholy? Had he been fired from his job? Did he hate winter? Was he giving up on his dream of post-video production?

I tapped the steering wheel with my mittened fingers, feeling sympathy for a man I didn't even know, but also wondering if what I'd first taken as sadness had instead been guilt over murder.

Chapter 13

I have a confession to make."

Aunt Frances had spoken in a tone that was quiet, shy, and would have been called reluctant if it had come from anyone other than my confident and self-assured aunt.

"Okay," I said, trying to match her tone. "Can I ask what this is about? Because if the police need to get involved, I have contacts with both the sheriff's office and the city police." She had the same contacts, of course, but I was trying to be funny. Instead of laughing, she sighed. Not a good sign.

"It's a civil matter, not a criminal one," she said. A few moments ticked past, then it all came out in a rush.

"I hate Otto's kitchen. Can't stand it. The design is ridiculous, those fancy cabinets with all their trim are expensive dust collectors, and I've always hated side-by-side refrigerators. I know some people love them, but not me, and I cringe when I think of having to use that thing the rest of my life."

I started to say something, but she wasn't done.

"And that kitchen island." Her voice grew louder and more Aunt-Frances-like. "At best it's a complete waste of space and a safety hazard at worst. That room isn't big enough to have an island and I don't know what the designer was thinking."

Probably that the person paying the bills wanted an island, but I didn't say so out loud.

"I can't tell Otto now," she said. "The first time I was over there, I told him I loved his house. He even asked about the kitchen specifically, and I said something like if I ever stop cooking for a full boardinghouse that I wouldn't mind a kitchen like his."

"Ah." I now understood her problem, although it was really Otto she should be confessing to and not me. But even though I understood the problem, I didn't truly think it was that big.

"Talk to him," I said.

My aunt shook her head. "Can't. Not at this late date. He'd be so hurt. I can't do that to him."

Really? Over a kitchen? "He's a grown man," I said. "I'm pretty sure he'll be okay. And you know he wants you to be happy more than anything else. If a renovated kitchen is what it takes, he'll be ripping cabinets out tomorrow morning."

She shook her head again. "I can't do that to him. I don't know what to do, I really don't." And the rest of the evening, nothing I said budged her from that viewpoint.

"What do you think, Eddie?"

My furry pal and I were snuggled in bed. He was in the crook of my right elbow, hindering my ability to read to the point that I'd given up. The book was on the nightstand, the light was off, and I was starting the drift down to sleep.

"Is Aunt Frances having wedding jitters? Is that what the whole kitchen thing is about?"

Eddie yawned and rolled over.

"Or is she having second thoughts about marrying Otto?" The idea was a horrible one, and I was sorry I'd thought it, but now that it was in my head, I wasn't sure it would go away. "What do you think?"

Eddie, however, didn't reply.

Julia began the bookmobile day with a remarkable rendition of the theme song to *Mister Rogers' Neighborhood*, which meant the day could only get better from there on out.

When she'd finished (with open arms and upraised face), I nodded at the cat carrier. "Eddie has his paws over his ears."

"He does not," she said, then leaned forward. "Okay, so he does, but that's because he's tired and it's bright out."

I peered up at the cloudy sky. "If this is bright, I don't want to know what gloomy looks like."

"Bright for a cat," Julia said oh-so-patiently. "Their sense of light is different from ours.

Especially Eddie's. He's not a normal cat, you know."

Though this was undoubtedly true—I'd long ago decided he was his own unique species, the singular *Felis Eddicus*—I was also pretty sure that light sensitivity wasn't on Eddie's long list of unique traits.

"And what makes you perky enough to sing this morning?" I asked.

"Just woke up happy," she said. "Don't you love days when that happens?"

"These days I typically wake up with cat hair on my lips."

"And isn't it wonderful to have a furry companion who loves you so much that he sacrifices his very own fur in the name of keeping you warm on cold winter nights?"

Now that was an idea I hadn't once considered. "Then what's the explanation for morning cat hair after a summer night so miserably humid that the only thing keeping me alive is the knowledge that I get to work in air-conditioning?"

"Insulation is insulation," Julia said. "I can't believe you're not more appreciative of his efforts."

"No?" A stop sign loomed. I braked and glanced down at my pants. One, two, three . . . I got to eleven Eddie hairs before losing track. "I'd appreciate them a lot more if his former fur matched my clothing."

Julia spent much of the rest of the morning trying to convince me that Eddie and I had such a deep bond that he was trying to cover me with his hair so we'd look the same.

She failed spectacularly, of course, but Eddie and I both enjoyed her attempts, especially during the stop when he sneezed and half a hundred Eddie hairs catapulted off his body in every direction, some of them landing on me, some on Julia, and a large percentage on bookmobile patron Leon Clohessy.

"Sorry about that," I said. "We have a lint roller."

"No worries." Leon, who was sitting on the bookmobile's carpeted step, gazed at his pant legs with a remarkable lack of concern. "He has interesting hairs. So many are variegated. I had no idea cat fur came like that."

I had limited experience with other cats, since my dad had been extremely allergic, and so as far as I knew, Eddie was the only one, but that seemed unlikely.

Julia tidied some books that had been jostled by a big bookmobile thump into an unavoidable pothole. "Where have you been lately, Leon? We haven't seen you in a few weeks."

Leon was an intermittent regular, if you could say that without spontaneously combusting from the sheer absurdity of the phrase. When he was home, he visited the bookmobile every time we showed up, but he and his nonreading wife traveled frequently. A couple of years ago they'd retired Up North from downstate attorney jobs, and Leon quoted his wife as saying that she didn't care if she read another word again the rest of her life.

I didn't understand that attitude at all—surely she didn't mean fiction, did she?—but it clearly existed, and if Leon couldn't shift his wife to be a reader after forty years of marriage, odds weren't good that the bookmobile's presence could do it, either.

"Hawaii," he said. "Just got back yesterday. And I'm not sure it was a good idea. Nice to not be cold and to get some sun, but now . . ." He glanced outside and shook his head. "Now it seems like winter is going to last forever."

"How long were you gone?" Julia asked.

"A month, almost exactly." Leon went on to describe the Airbnb they had rented on the ocean. He was waxing lyrical about the scents of the blooming flowers, and when he took a breath, I interrupted him.

"Did you hear about Rowan Bennethum? She doesn't live that far from you, right?" If my math was correct, Leon and his wife had left town the day before Rowan had been killed, and this was the stop both Rowan and Leon usually visited, so their houses couldn't be too far apart.

The lines in Leon's face, which were already deep with age, went even deeper. "Yes," he said heavily. "I did. Out here someone who lives a mile away is a neighbor, especially if they're full-time folks. Is it true she was poisoned?" At our nods, he sighed. "Such a cowardly way to kill. And delayed death can make finding the killer much more difficult. I don't suppose they've arrested anyone?"

"Not yet." I hesitated, then asked, "Did you happen to see anything out of the ordinary that last day before your trip?"

"Such as?"

"Anything," I said. "The sheriff's office is investigating, but if you were out of town and your driveway wasn't plowed, they might have assumed you were gone for winter."

"Hmm." Leon put down the copy of Jonathan Franzen's *Freedom* he'd been reading. "Well, let me think. Martha was packing our bags and I was taking care of everything else, so we were busy. I certainly didn't hear anything because we'd put on Hawaiian luau music to get us in the mood. And I don't recall seeing anything . . ." He got a faraway look.

"What?" I asked, my voice almost sharp. "You remember something."

"A car," he said slowly. "We get so few cars down our road, and in winter we almost always recognize the vehicles, even in the dark. Speed, height, you'd be surprised how little it takes to pinpoint a familiar vehicle."

"You saw something unfamiliar?"

He nodded. "An SUV. With only one head-light."

The next morning, as I brushed fresh snow off the car, I waved at Eddie. He'd crowded himself onto a narrow living room windowsill and was giving me the evil eye through the glass.

"Sorry, pal," I called. "It's a library day, not a bookmobile day, and I have errands to run. See you tonight!"

I blew him a kiss—which he ignored—and got into the car, thinking about yesterday afternoon. After Leon had remembered the missing head-light, I'd immediately asked him to call Detective Hal Inwood and tell him about it. He'd pro-tested, saying how could a missing headlight mean anything and telling Hal would only result in adding extra work for the already overworked sheriff's office.

While I was glad people recognized how hard law enforcement officers worked, I was insistent that Leon make the call. "You probably won't even have to talk to him directly. He hardly ever answers his phone and you'll end up leaving a voice mail message. It'll take thirty seconds. Let him decide what's important and what's not." Leon kept demurring until I stood tall, put my hands on my hips, and stared him down.

"In just about every suspense movie ever filmed, there's a piece of evidence that, at first, seems unimportant but ends up as the turning point of the entire plot. Right now, no one knows what's important and what isn't. Do you want the end of Rowan's movie to peter out to a stupid ending?"

Once I'd finished my little outburst, I was pretty sure I'd made the stupidest analogy ever, but Leon looked thoughtful.

"Just like that Poe story," he said. " 'The Purloined Letter.' It was right in front of them all the time. You're right. I'll call that detective as soon as I get home."

Now I was itching to know if he had remembered to call, and what Hal Inwood was doing about it. If anything.

"Probably nothing," I muttered.

"I'm sorry?"

The question was a good one, because I was now standing at the front counter of Chilson's urgent care clinic. During the hours I'd spent in Petoskey's emergency room after Kristen's post-skiing adventure, I'd looked around and thought that what they could really use was a healthy pile of fiction to read. The Petoskey emergency room was outside the Chilson district, but last year a 24/7 clinic had opened up in Chilson and it was past time I talked to someone.

"Hi," I said, and introduced myself. "I have an eight o'clock appointment with Dave Landis."

The twenty-something receptionist, whose name tag said RONNIE, gave me a closer look. "You're the bookmobile librarian, right? With the cat, Eddie. What's your name again?"

Five minutes later, I was in the office of Director Dave Landis, explaining what I had in mind. "So do you think this would be helpful?" I asked. "I'd choose the books carefully, nothing bloody or gory, nothing that deals with horrible diseases. A lot of short stories, so people could finish up. And a fair amount of nonfiction, too. Essays, probably. But they'd all be donated books, so it would be fine if people took them home."

Dave, about forty and with zero hair on his head, had started nodding about halfway through the spiel I'd put together, but since I'd spent so much time preparing for this meeting, I was determined to get the whole thing out.

"Plus we're doing more and more programming at the library for all age levels, and the participation is doing nothing but going up. If you have information you'd like to get out into the community, this could be a great opportunity."

"Drug abuse," he said, jumping in when I paused to take a breath. "Opioids and heroin. I moved here from downstate last year, and I had no idea how much addiction was going on Up North."

My eyes had been opened to the problem when Ash and I were dating. As a sheriff's deputy, he saw more than his share of tragic tales with roots in addiction. "Done," I said. "It's a huge problem and I'd love to help even in a small way." And if the library board took issue with bringing an addiction discussion into the library, well, I'd just convince them they were wrong.

Dave smiled. "You're dating Rafe Niswander, aren't you? That's too bad. I don't suppose you have a sister?"

I didn't ask how he knew Rafe. Even though he'd been in town less than a year, with his job he would have met more people in that one year than I did in five. "Sorry, no sister," I said. Then, trying to learn more, I asked, "If I did have a sister, and if she had a serious addiction, could I bring her here?"

He nodded. "You bet. Matter of fact, that exact thing happened about a month ago. It was the day we got hardly any snow here, but there was six inches on the other side of the county? A woman who lives halfway to Charlevoix brought her sister here." His gaze drifted to a business card on the corner of his desk. I hadn't paid attention to them until just now, but I sat up a bit straighter when I recognized the colorful and cheery logo on the card. The Red House Café.

"We don't have beds for long-term addiction care," Dave said, "but we can treat overdoses and we have contacts with substance abuse facilities in the region. Though we do our absolute best to find beds for those in need, there are only so many out there. I tell people we'll call as soon as we find something"—absently, Dave picked up Sunny's card and tapped it on his desktop—"and we do, but sometimes it takes weeks."

"That must be hard," I said. "Telling people you can't help them."

Sighing, he nodded. "Worst part of the job." He brightened. "But when you can help people, when you know that someone has turned their life around, that makes it all worthwhile."

I thanked him for his time, told him I'd be in touch, and as I scraped my iced-over windshield, I thought about what I was pretty sure I'd learned.

Yes, sometimes I jumped to conclusions, but it wasn't much of a leap to think that Sunny Scoles had been at the urgent care clinic the day Rowan had died. If she'd taken the poison the day it had arrived at her house, and it seemed to make sense that she would have, then Sunny had an alibi. So why did the sheriff's office still consider her a viable suspect? Why on earth hadn't she told them about her alibi?

I split the rest of the morning between working on the March work schedule and rewriting position descriptions. For weeks I'd been dodging the description task, but decided that today was the day to take care of the part-time positions. And like many tasks, once I got going, it became clear that the job wasn't going to take nearly as long as I'd thought it might.

"Not half as long," I said out loud as I finished the first draft of the clerk's description. Clearly, a celebration was in order.

I spun around in my chair and made for the coffeepot. The break room was empty, so I filled my Association of Bookmobile and Outreach Services mug with the stuff of life and wandered out to the front desk, where Donna was frowning at a computer.

"Problems?" I asked.

She grimaced, but didn't look away from the screen. "Operator ones, I'm afraid, not electronic ones."

"Want me to call Josh?"

"And have him lord his knowledge over me? Let him make me feel like an imbecile? Be forced to admit that I'm incompetent and incapable of anything different?"

I eyed her over the top of my mug. "Are you feeling okay?" Because though I was well aware that there were some IT people in the world who had an unfortunate tendency to treat the people they were supposed to help with sneering condescension, Josh wasn't one of them.

"Bugger." Donna pushed herself back from the

computer and folded her arms across her chest. If she'd been seventy years younger, I would have said she was pouting, but since she was seventy-two, she couldn't have been.

"Please don't tell Josh I was slandering him," she said to her knees. "I'm just in a rotten mood."

"Um, you're not getting sick, are you?" I started to back away, but stopped when she shook her head. So far, I hadn't been sick at all that winter, and I was dearly hoping to keep it that way. "Is there anything you want to talk about? Can I help with anything?"

She perked up. "You're good at persuading. How about you come over to my house tonight and convince my husband that our next vacation should be in Antarctica. I've always wanted to go and there's this expedition next month that just had a cancellation from two volunteer research assistants. He said no so fast that he couldn't possibly have really thought about it. If you could just talk to him . . ." She sighed. "You're not going to, are you?"

Laughing, I said, "No, but I'll okay your time off if you find someone else to go with you. Or if you decide to go alone."

"Not as much fun by myself," she said. "But if it's that or not go at all . . . hmm. I suppose I could, couldn't I?"

"If it's that important to you, absolutely." How that would play out with her husband, I wasn't sure, but they'd been married for almost fifty years, so there was a good chance an agreeable resolution could be reached.

"How did it go at the township hall the other day?" Donna asked.

For a moment I had no idea what she was talking about. Then I remembered. "Bookmobile stop is all set. It was so easy to get permission, I wish I'd gone to them in the first place."

"Well, there's been some changes there in the last year or so," Donna said. "It's probably best you waited."

Once again, I didn't understand. "You live in Chilson Township, not Wicklow."

"I do. But my sister lives over there, and Bill, that's her husband, used to be on their planning commission, so I hear more than I want to about their goings-on."

And once again, I had underestimated how easy it was to obtain information when you knew the person to ask. "So what's the story with the new township hall?"

Donna laughed. "That's been an issue for ten years, ever since the township bought that property on the highway for far too much money. That's what Bill says anyway."

I remembered what Charlotte, the township clerk, had said, that the board was divided on the topic. "The previous township board didn't want to build?"

"No, they absolutely did, and half of them got voted out last election because of it. The new board is more approachable and more transparent about their decision-making process—the township even updates their website now, if you can believe it—but the word on the street is now that Rowan Bennethum's gone, the board will vote to build."

"She had that much influence?" I asked.

Donna shrugged. "All I know is that Hugh Novak and his buddies have been at every meeting the last six months, trying to get this approved, and now that Rowan isn't there, no one else is speaking up against it. Not everyone liked her, but she was smart and she was respected. Her opinion carried weight with the board." She smiled faintly. "From the way Bill tells it, there were some heated public comment periods."

Interesting. I encouraged Donna to apply for the Antarctica trip and headed back to my office, thinking about what she'd said and wondering why Neil had never called me back.

And then I moved Hugh Novak to the top of my suspect list.

Chapter 14

The hardware store's bells jingled. I shut the door behind me and stomped the snow off my boots and onto the winter entrance mat. From behind the counter, Jared said, "Morning, Minnie."

Well, some of him was behind the counter. His top half was leaning over it as he paged through a newspaper. The *Petoskey News-Review*, it looked like. Which must have been an old newspaper, since I was pretty sure there wasn't a morning newspaper within two hundred miles.

"No, hang on, I'm wrong. It's afternoon," he said, glancing up at the wall clock, which had probably hung on the wall for fifty years but was going strong, still advertising Syncro power tools.

"Just barely, though," I said, smiling. "I won't mark you down." Librarians didn't do that, of course, but many people seemed to blend the roles of teacher and librarian, so I tended to play along. "How are you doing, Jared?"

"Like most days, could be better, could be worse."

"Most things are relative," I said. "Even gravity."

"Gravity?" He narrowed his eyes and thought a minute, then nodded. "It is, isn't it? Gravity may be constant when we're down here with our feet on the ground, but if you're on the moon or Mars or whatever, it's completely different."

"Exactly," I said, beaming at my prize student. "The physical properties that produce gravity are the same no matter where you go—and please don't ask me what they are because I have no clue—but its strength varies depending on where you are." I was pretty sure I'd read there was a detectable difference in the strength of gravity between sea level and the tops of mountains, but I couldn't remember the source, so I kept quiet since I didn't want to spread science misinformation.

Jared flopped the newspaper shut. "What can I do for you, Minnie? Ready to order your cabinet hardware?"

"Yes, I am." Rafe had promised if I made a final decision this week that he would read one fiction book of my choosing from cover to cover in less than a month. I put up my chin and squared my shoulders. "Lead me to the catalogs. I'm ready." Sort of. I'd done some of the hardware homework Jared had assigned, but what I mostly knew was what I didn't like.

He studied me. "You look like you're about to

face a firing squad. This kind of thing is fun for most people."

I slumped a bit. "Once again I'm different from everybody else," I said gloomily.

"No, I get it. The problem is information overload. Too many choices. How about this? We'll work it like a flow chart, making one decision at a time, and at the end you'll have exactly what you want."

"But that's the problem. I don't know what I want." I was horrified to hear my voice shake. "Sorry, I just . . ."

"Don't worry," Jared said. "You're just nervous about making the wrong decision. It happens a lot in the construction business." He laughed. "One of the reasons I got out of it. Loved the work, but it got so I couldn't deal with the customers."

"And now you're saddled with me." I tried to smile, to make a joke out of it. Didn't work.

"Hah. You're nothing compared to some of those folks. Maybe someday I'll tell you about Crazy Larry." Jared tossed the newspaper under the counter. "Come on back. This will be fun."

And despite my trepidations, it actually was. Jared held my figurative hand all the way through the process, and at the end I was almost giddy with happiness over the final choice: brushed nickel, with oval knobs for the doors and drawer pulls that looked like what had been on the old card catalog drawers in my elementary school library. I'd toyed with the idea of Petoskey stones for the knobs, but figured those would be better in a bathroom.

"Take some pictures," Jared suggested, "and send them to Rafe."

I did so and an instant later got a return text: *What book?*

Smiling, I texted back: *Moby Dick*

Rafe, after a long pause, sent: *Kidding?*

I texted back with: *Yes. You'll enjoy War and Peace far more,* and quickly put away my phone. It was tempting to send a text to Kristen, telling her I'd finally triumphed over the hardware conundrum, but at this time of day she was probably in the middle of a run through the Key West heat and I didn't want to distract her. "Thanks so much for all your help, Jared. I couldn't have done it without you." I smiled. "Maybe you should get into kitchen design."

"Not a chance. I'd rather pull off my fingernails with a pair of needle-nose pliers," he said, but then looked off into the distance, as if he might be considering it.

I started to get up, then sat down again. There had been two reasons I'd stopped by the store. "Last time I was in, a couple of weeks ago, we talked a little about Bax Tousely and the account with the City of Chilson. Is that . . . did that turn out okay for you?"

It was an awkward question, awkwardly

phrased, but I hadn't been able to figure out a better way to ask. Luckily, Jared either didn't feel the awkwardness or paid no attention to it.

"Sure," he said. "I remember. And it had been weird, the way Bax came in, no joke or anything, then left without saying a word. Turns out it was no big deal."

"Oh?" I asked, tipping my head, silently imploring him to go on.

"Yeah. Bax stopped by last week for something else and explained. He'd been feeling like crap with the flu or something, and on top of that, he'd been up at three to start plowing. He was practically sleepwalking, sounded like. And when he was in the back here, he got a phone call from his boss saying he'd found the part they needed in the city's shop, and that he, that's Bax, should get his butt down to the job site five minutes ago or he, that's Bax again, would be busted back to low man on the totem pole."

"That's bad?"

Jared smiled. "Means you're the first to go down into a manhole or a trench to fix whatever needs fixing. Means you're the one who gets cold, wet, and dirty first and longest."

"That would get old after a while," I said, now understanding the city's pecking order a little better. And I now understood that Bax's odd behavior on the day Rowan died had nothing to do with Rowan. But there was one question remaining: Why had Leese seen Bax driving past the Bennethums' house?

"Hi, can I help you?"

The young woman in the toy store looked bright-eyed and bushy-tailed, as my father might have said. Her long blond hair was tucked behind her ears, her smile was wide, and her name tag read TAYLOR.

In my backpack was the list Mitchell had e-mailed me of the significant dates in the Bianca-Mitchell relationship. I'd stopped by to go over it with him. "Is Mitchell around?"

Taylor shook her head. "He's off today. Is there anything I can help you with?"

"Thanks, but I'm just looking around to get ideas for . . . for my nieces' and nephews' birthdays. They aren't anytime soon," I added quickly. "I just want to be, um, prepared."

It was my day for awkward statements, but just as Jared hadn't seemed to notice, neither did Taylor.

"That's a great idea," she said, nodding. "I wish more people would do that. This gives you time to learn what's available, what's in your price range, what the kids really want, and"—she grinned—"what the parents want you to get."

"It's complicated, isn't it?" I asked the question a bit slowly, because I was beginning to see that giving a great gift truly was. Mitchell had been a big help to me with the last cycle of young relative gifts, and odds were good that he'd trained Taylor to use that same approach.

"All part of the fun." Taylor smiled.

I thanked her and said I'd flag her down if I needed anything.

"Perfect," she said cheerfully. "Just give me a yell." She walked behind the counter and started tapping away on the checkout computer's keyboard.

My phone, which until now had been blessedly quiet, beeped with an incoming text. It was from Anya. *Collier just failed a big test. Any chance of finding Mom's killer soon?*

I read the message over and over again until I heard Taylor's footsteps approaching.

"Find any good ideas?" she asked.

"Not fast enough," I muttered.

"Sorry?" Taylor's face was open and questioning.

"This is a great store," I said, mustering up a smile as I shoved the phone back into my coat pocket. The girl was trying to help and I needed to be nicer to her. "How long have you been working here? I stop in fairly often, that's all, and I'm surprised we haven't met before now."

"I started right after Thanksgiving. But my schedule is all jumbled because I'm taking classes at the college and working at Fat Boys. Mitchell works it out for me, though."

"Mitchell's a good boss?" A question that, a year ago, I would have bet all the money in the world I'd never, ever ask.

"The best," she said, with small earnest nods. "Not that I've had that many jobs, but he's really nice and really patient with me. I mean, like you said, this stuff is complicated and it takes a while to figure things out."

"It does, doesn't it?" I asked.

And maybe that was my problem. Maybe I'd been thinking too simply about Rowan's death. Maybe instead of my usual method of trying to break things down into bits to make it easier to get at the truth, maybe the truth was that it was complicated, that it couldn't be broken down because it all hung together in one big tangled lump.

Still thinking, I sketched a vague wave at Taylor and headed back out into the cold.

The next day I was still troubled about Anya's text message. Since I'd fallen asleep early, I hadn't been able to talk to either Rafe (at a middle school basketball game) or Aunt Frances (evening woodworking class), so I told Julia about it on the way out to the first bookmobile stop, the township farthest south and east in the county.

"Did you text her back?" Julia asked.

"As soon as I got out on the street." I tried to

remember the exact message, but since I tended to have the memory of a plush blanket, I had to paraphrase. "I told her we were all working hard to help and that I hoped to give her good news soon."

"Bet that wasn't much comfort."

Her words were like a physical blow. *Don't cry,* I told myself. *Do not cry.* After a deep and raggy breath, I said, "I'm sure it wasn't."

"Hey, you're not blaming yourself, are you?" Julia asked. "Oh, bugger, you are. I'm sorry, honey, I didn't mean any of this is your fault. You're doing all you can, and the sheriff's office is doing all they can. But even still, Anya and Collier and Neil are suffering. And they will continue to grieve, even when the murderer is slapped into prison, because no matter what, Rowan will be dead and nothing anyone does will bring her back."

Which, of course, was the one thing they all wanted and the one thing that wouldn't happen. Then a quiet whisper wandered through my brain—*did* Neil want Rowan back? He hadn't returned any of my calls, which seemed like something a grief-stricken husband would do straightaway.

Then again, there were probably good reasons for his silence. I couldn't come up with any, but there had to be at least one out there.

The first stop of the day was one of my favorites,

primarily because of Lawrence Zonne. The octogenarian Mr. Zonne had lived in Tonedagana County most of his life, retired early to Florida with his wife, then moved back to be closer to children and grandchildren after his wife passed away. He was smart, funny, and had a memory far better than mine had ever been. Plus, he and Eddie were great pals.

"Good morning, bookmobile ladies!" Mr. Zonne said as he bounded up the steps. He pulled off a colorful knit hat and his thick white hair sprung out in all directions. "How are you this fine morning? And Mr. Edward, you are looking very handsome."

"Mrr."

"Likewise, likewise." He patted the top of Eddie's head, then after pulling off his gloves, he rubbed his hands together. I couldn't tell if it was to warm them or if he was making a gesture of anticipation, but it could well have been both.

"What do you have for me today?" he asked. "I'm in the mood for medieval adventure and derring-do."

Julia pondered the question. "Wars and battles?"

"I'd prefer more of the white knight rescuing the young maiden who is perfectly capable of saving herself, but allows herself to be rescued in order to maintain the illusion of male ego and thereby assists with the propagation of the human species." He brandished an imaginary sword and slashed at an imaginary foe.

"Mrr!" Eddie batted at Mr. Zonne's left foot.

"Are you for me or against?" Mr. Zonne thundered. "One 'Mrr' if you're a friend, two if you're an enemy!"

I laughed as Eddie chose that particular moment to lick one of his back feet. "Sounds like you should be writing romances, not reading them. Sure you don't want a second career?"

"Too much work. Especially the research." He shuddered. "Having to get the historical details right is too complicated. I would inevitably do something horrendous like having Britons eat tomatoes before they were available in that country, and I wouldn't be able to live with the scathing reviews."

Again with the complications. "Do you know the Bennethums?" I asked. "East of Chilson."

"You mean Rowan? That poor girl. She was a Funston, yes? Or was she a Raferty?" Neither Julia nor I happened to know her maiden name, but it didn't seem to matter much. "That group was all in the generation between," he said. "Tenish years younger than our offspring. I don't know them at all."

So even more complications.

At the end of the stop, Mr. Zonne went away happy with a sack full of novels by Edward

Rutherfurd and Robert Graves, with one by Michener, just in case.

"Another satisfied customer," Julia said. "In you go, Mr. Ed." She opened the door to the cat carrier, tossed a treat inside, and shut the door behind Eddie, who bounded inside after the food.

We buckled ourselves in and I started us down the road to the next stop. "Someday he's going to stop liking those treats," I said, "and my life will never be the same."

"All you have to do is find a treat he does like." Julia tapped the carrier with the toes of her boots. "How hard could that be? I mean he eats bread, for crying out loud, so you'd think any cat treat would be—"

"Mrr!"

Julia instantly stopped tapping. "Sorry, Master Edward. You usually don't mind."

"MRR!!"

The insides of my ears cringed. "Geez, Eddie, quit it already, will you? This is an enclosed space and—"

"MRRR!!!"

I braked to as quick a stop as I could, because that last howl had sounded so horrible that I was sure he was being drawn and quartered by the unseen foes Mr. Zonne had been battling. Julia opened the carrier door and I laid myself across the console, putting my head at cat level.

"Are you all right, pal?" I asked, peering in.

Eddie was sitting smack in the middle of the carrier's floor, staring at me with that look he was so good at giving, the one that conveyed contempt, irritation, annoyance, and a teeny bit of tolerance for the antics of his staff.

He didn't say anything, so I reached in. A deep purr started almost immediately.

"You are a rotten cat." I gave him a pat and latched the door.

"He's really okay?" Julia asked, frowning.

"As okay as he'll ever be." I pushed myself back upright and reached over for the seat belt. In doing so, I noticed the house on the opposite side of the road.

Around us, the land was wide and rolling. The trees had been clear-cut for lumber a hundred years ago and, due to poor soil, they hadn't fully regrown. Properties out here tended to be multiple acres, and neighbors were often barely within shouting distance. As a result of low density and disinclination for governmental interference, many of the townships on this side of the county had few regulations, a situation that could allow circumstances that would draw neighborly ire in more populated areas.

Like the house over there. Even in February, its huge front yard was occupied by a row of cars facing the street. They were, of course, snow-covered, but I'd seen them often enough in warmer times to know they were all for sale at Low, Low Prices!

"Hmm," I said.

"What's that?" Julia asked.

I drummed my fingers on the steering wheel, then pulled out my cell phone. "Listen in," I told her, and dialed the phone number for Deputy Ash Wolverson.

"Hey," he said, answering straightaway. "You guys okay?"

I looked down at my arms and legs. Looked over at Julia and Eddie. All safe and sound. "Sure. Why wouldn't we be?"

He blew out a sigh. "Lots of accidents today. The direction of the wind yesterday drifted shut most of the back roads, and you drive that bookmobile all over, and . . . well, anyway, what's up?"

A warm and fuzzy feeling curled up around my heart. Though Ash and I hadn't worked out as a couple, our new friendship was turning into something solid, something I hoped would last for years. "Did Leon Clohessy call you?" I asked. "About that SUV with a missing headlight he saw leaving Rowan's house?"

"He did." I heard the tapping of a keyboard. "Anything else?"

It occurred to me that friends could be as annoying as cats. "Yes. I assume you're going to be checking car part stores."

"On my list," he said. "But I have to be honest, it's not high up there. Hal says—"

Since I was pretty sure I didn't want to hear what Detective Inwood had to say, I talked over him. "I was just thinking that if it was the killer in that SUV, he might have bought a new headlight from a junkyard for cash, so there'd be no money trail."

I heard a sigh on the other end of the line.

"Yeah," Ash said. "He or she might have."

I felt a pang of guilt for the extra work I was tossing into his lap. He was starting to sound as tired as Hal. "Tell you what. The bookmobile route eventually goes past most of the junkyards in the county. How about if I stop and ask about headlights? If I learn anything, I'll pass it on."

"Knock yourself out," Ash said. "I have to run. See you later."

"Okay. Stay safe—"

But he was already gone.

That evening, I mulled over the events of the day. "The complications of the day, more like," I murmured.

"Sorry?" Aunt Frances asked.

We were in the kitchen, cleaning up after dinner. Rather, I was cleaning up because my aunt had (luckily for all involved) done the cooking, and she was sitting at the kitchen table sorting through the last few days of newspapers, getting ready to read the 911 reports out loud to me.

I hesitated, then blurted out pretty much everything, starting with Mitchell's list. By the time I was telling her about my junkyard call to Ash, I was putting away the last of the silverware. "So maybe it's just . . . complicated," I summed up. "What do you think?"

Aunt Frances looked at me over the top of her reading glasses. "I think you should call Anya Bennethum. And by call, I mean an actual call, not a text. The poor girl is trying to be a mother to Collier and she's floundering."

"I don't know anything about being a mother," I protested.

"No, but you're the one she's reaching out to."

It took me roughly two and a half seconds to grasp the obvious. "You're right," I said.

"Of course I am." She tapped the stack of newspapers. "And as soon as you finish talking to Anya, we can get back to the evening's entertainment." My aunt was a big believer in the carrot and stick approach, at least when it came to managing Minnie's behavior, primarily because it worked.

"Back in a few," I said, and headed upstairs to my room to make the call, pausing briefly to pat Eddie, who was curled up in a corner of the couch, snoring loud enough to rattle china.

"Hey, Minnie," Anya answered a little breathlessly. "Have they arrested someone?"

"Not yet," I said. Then, since I was still hearing panting breaths, I asked, "Um, what are you doing?"

"Oh. Sorry. I can stop." Her breathing returned to normal. "I don't like elevators much and my apartment is on the building's fourth floor. Mom always said it would be good for me either way, that I'd get used to elevators or I'd get lots of exercise."

"Your mom was a wise woman," I said.

"She—" Anya stopped. Breathed deep. Then, "I miss her," she said in a small voice.

What could I say to this young woman who was dealing with a kind of grief I'd never suffered, but almost inevitably would someday? I thought about my own mother, about the hole that would be left in my life if she died. "You'll probably always miss her," I said. "But I think it'll get easier."

"That's what everybody says." Anya sniffed.

"Since there's no way everybody can be wrong," I said, "it must be true."

She sniffed again. "I want to believe that. And I almost do, but . . . how long will it be? To get to the easier part, I mean?"

I had no answer for that, of course, so I murmured something banal and trite about being patient with herself and to make sure she got plenty of rest and to eat right.

"Okay," she said. "I'll try." After a beat, she asked, "So there's nothing new, about Mom, I mean, to tell Collier?"

"Not anything substantial." I told her about the SUV with the broken headlight and she seemed to take it as seriously as Ash had.

"Anything else?"

"Well," I said slowly. "There's one thing." I girded up my courage and dove in. "I ran into your dad two or three weeks ago and he said something about your mom and Land Aprelle getting into a big argument soon before she died. I know we talked about this at the library the other day, and—" I stopped, because Anya was doing the last thing I would have guessed she'd do.

She was laughing.

"Mom and Land had these huge arguments all the time. Like once a week, practically."

"They . . . did?"

"Sure," Anya said. "I was going to tell you about this, but you had someone you had to talk to."

Out of the vague recesses of my brain, a memory surfaced. That had been the day Graydon came back from training. "I said I'd call you, and I didn't. I am so sorry."

"That's all right. Anyway, Mom said the fights

with Land were her weekly therapy sessions. Land called them catharsis. Every time, Mom would end up firing Land. He'd ignore her and keep on doing whatever he was doing, and five minutes later they were best buddies."

I laughed. "Sounds entertaining."

"Oh, it was," Anya said, and I could hear the smile in her voice. "They had some knock-down, drag-out fights. You know," she said, "I don't think Dad understood their relationship at all. But then he never liked Land in the first place."

We chatted for a few minutes longer. I told her I'd let her know the second I learned anything from the sheriff's office, but when I hung up, I sat on the edge of the bed, staring at the phone, wondering about the possibility of the worst complication of all.

What if Neil suspected Rowan and Land had been having an affair? What if Neil himself was the killer?

Chapter 15

My dark thoughts about Neil stayed with me through the night and into the morning. Eddie, who'd slept in the exact middle of the foot of the bed, forcing me to have my feet in every place except the place I most wanted them, was of no help whatsoever when I asked him about Neil as I got dressed.

"Do you think I should tell Ash?"

No response.

"Don't tell me you think I should talk to the slightly scary Detective Hal Inwood instead of the friendly Deputy Ash Wolverson?"

No response again. Yay. "Do you think I should stay home today and tend to your every need?"

"Mrr," he said sleepily, and rolled over so I could rub his belly.

"Thanks for your help," I said.

"Mrr," he said, or almost said, because I was pretty sure he fell asleep in the middle of it.

With no guidance from Eddie, I decided to make my decision the old-fashioned way—with a coin toss. When the quarter I dug out of the bottom of my purse landed heads up, I nodded at it and called Ash. It went to voice mail, and though I tried to be straightforward and concise, there was a good chance my message was long and rambling and lacked any focus whatsoever, just like most of the voice mail messages I'd left in my entire life.

"That went well," I said after pressing the Off button. Still no response from Eddie. "Sarcasm, my furry friend. That was pure and unadulterated sarcasm. Do you think I'll sound as stupid to Ash as I did to myself? Never mind," I said quickly, because Eddie's eyes had started to open and I didn't want to hear his answer.

I kissed the top of his fuzzy head and headed downstairs to get the day rolling.

It was a library day, and it rolled along reasonably well from breakfast to noon, when I walked downtown for a prearranged lunch with Rafe.

"This could work out well," I said, sliding into a booth at Shomin's Deli.

"What's that?" Rafe reached across the table for my hands. "Crikey, what have you been doing with those? Packing snowballs barehanded?"

" 'Crikey'? I'm not sure anyone has said that out loud for seventy-five years."

"About time to bring it back."

I eyed my beloved, who was smiling at me in a way that made me want to throw myself into his arms and hold him tight, forever and ever.

Two things kept me from doing so. One, the table between us would have made the throwing part logistically difficult. Two, if he kept using the word "crikey," my undying love for him might take a hard turn.

"Hey, you two." Ash slid into the booth next to me.

Rafe bumped knuckles with him. "Have a seat, why don't you?"

"Just here to pick up the man's lunch," Ash said. "Well, mine, too, but Hal was the one who made me come here because he wants that weird Swiss cheese and olive sandwich." He made a face. "Bet Hal's the only one in the world who eats it. Wait, really?" Because Rafe was pointing at me.

"You should try it sometime," I said.

The fact that Hal Inwood and I shared a taste for anything was a little disconcerting, so I pushed that nugget of information to a back corner of my brain where it could keep company with Avogadro's number, the laws of thermodynamics, and the Krebs cycle.

"Say, Minnie, you know that message you left this morning?" Ash asked. "I'm looking into it. Just wanted you to know." He nodded at me, did the knuckle thing again with Rafe, and went to the cash register to pick up his order.

"Message about what?" Rafe asked.

I studied him, but couldn't detect the least

amount of jealousy. Excellent. "It's about Rowan's murder," I said in a low voice.

"Hey." Rafe frowned. "I thought we were partners in that, just like in everything else."

"Partners? Does that mean we're going to play doubles tennis?"

"Not a chance. You play the worst tennis in the history of the game." Our order was called and Rafe slid out of the booth to fetch and carry. In seconds he was back and we were unwrapping our food: crispy chicken wrap for him, Swiss cheese and olive on sourdough for me. "But in everything else," Rafe went on as if there hadn't been any interruption, "we're a matched set. So spill about what you told my man Ash."

As I did, I realized there were other things that had gone untold, from Anya and Collier to Bax Tousely. By the end of the telling, our lunches were gone and the ice cubes in our drinks were the size of small peas.

Rafe put his elbows on the table. "Let me get this right. You think Rowan was killed for some complicated reason and that the killer will be revealed because of the combination of an empty sugar packet and a damaged headlight."

When he put it like that, it sounded weak. More than weak; it sounded stupid. "Well, yes."

He looked at me long enough for me to decide that what was taking him so long to say anything was that he was trying to figure out how to tell me I was completely bonkers. Finally, he said, "I think you're right."

"You . . . do?"

"Absolutely. What you've picked up on are the anomalies, and Rowan lived by rules. I bet she had a certain day of the week to do laundry, instead of doing it when the hamper was full."

I always did laundry on Saturdays, but I was too happy with his approval of my theories to argue about that small life choice.

"So now what?" he asked.

There was only one thing to do. "It's time to make a list."

All I meant was a simple list of murder suspects, but Rafe wanted to make it a lot harder than it needed to be, saying that it should be a spreadsheet with columns of suspect names and rows listing dates, times, possibilities, and scenarios.

I showed him my cell phone, which I'd opened to the notes application. "I'm done. How about you?"

"That's what I'd call a good start." He pulled out his cell and snapped a photo. "And you were the one saying how complicated this was. How many complications can you get from a list of five names?"

We parted ways; he drove back to the middle school and I made my way to the library through two inches of new snow. It was, I thought, the perfect amount of snowfall. Not enough to mess up driving in any significant way, but enough to blanket the landscape with a fresh layer of white.

I was still thinking about snow and its powers when I arrived back at the library, and almost ran into a forty-ish woman in the entryway.

"Sorry," I said. "My thoughts were wandering, and . . . oh. Hey, Debbie. Here to check out the new releases?"

Debbie Ottavino smiled as she buttoned her black velvet cape and pulled on bright pink mittens. "Not today."

I widened my eyes dramatically. "Don't tell me your husband has convinced you to start reading science fiction."

She laughed. "Not yet. And no trying to convince me that *The Martian* was science fiction. That was a survival story from start to finish."

"You've almost changed my mind on that one. What did you check out?" I asked, nodding at her leather messenger bag. "Anything fun?"

Debbie lived in Chilson, worked for an accounting firm in Petoskey, and was the library's auditor. In some ways she was the stereotypical accountant—just the facts and nothing but the facts, please—but she also shattered that stereotype by having a tremendous sense of humor and a flamboyant sense of style.

"Well, I think it's fun," she said, "but I'm an

accountant, and you know how skewed our world-views are. Then again, Graydon and Trent were all smiles just now, so maybe it's contagious."

I watched her push out through the double doors. The annual audit was done, so why would our auditor be meeting with the library director and the library board president now? And what could possibly be making all of them happy?

While the library's finances were stable, we could always use more revenue. Josh wanted a new server, it would be great to expand our programming, and I'd love to be open more hours, but we couldn't afford the staff time. And then there was that nagging need to start saving for a new bookmobile. Sure, this one was only a couple of years old, but they didn't last forever and it would be better to start stashing money away now.

The whole thing was making me nervous, a feeling I hated. Add the weird questions that Graydon and Trent had been asking and you have a recipe for Minnie anxiety that rivaled driving over the Mackinac Bridge in the dark during a howling snowstorm.

I divested myself of outer clothing in my office and headed upstairs. "Knock, knock," I said, poking my head in Graydon's office. "Do you have a minute?"

"Hey, Minnie." He smiled and clicked his computer's mouse. "What's up?"

"I just wondered why Debbie was here. Is everything okay?"

"Oh. Sure," he said. "I mean, they're fine. It's just . . . Trent and I wanted to go over a few things with her, is all. Trying to get more familiar with the library's financials, not just now but the past, too, if you see what I mean."

Sort of, but not really. That was another reason I'd decided against applying for the library director's job; to me, financial statements were a mystery, and not the fun kind with a plot and characters and snappy dialogue.

"Okay," I said. "Because you'd tell me if something was wrong, right?"

He smiled. "You're my assistant. I'll always need help."

I nodded and left him to his work, but it wasn't until I was halfway down the stairs that I realized he hadn't answered my question. Frowning, I considered my options. Should I ask Trent? Or the board's vice president?

No, and no. Reason number one against stepping over my boss to satisfy my curiosity was that it would be a rotten way to treat Graydon. Number two against was I barely knew Trent and hadn't known the vice president very long, so asking a semi-sneaky question was a poor foundation for what I hoped would be long and productive relationships.

Which meant I was stuck. Being glued in

place without any way to get to my objective was frustrating. Which meant a crappy mood for Minnie until I pulled out of it.

I took a deep breath, tried to summon a happier frame of mind, and felt myself failing. Rats. What was it Aunt Frances said? "This, too, shall pass," I said out loud as the stairwell door shut behind me.

"True words," Stewart Funston said. He was standing in front of the drinking fountain, wiping his mouth with the back of his hand. "But you can make time pass faster by having as much fun as possible."

I tried not to glare at him, but that's how my look probably came across, because I was still cranky. "Sounds like what people say to justify the dumb things they do. Like that time you vandalized the principal's office." As soon as the words left my mouth, I wanted to grab them back. "Stewart, I am so sorry. I'm in a bad mood and I'm taking it out on you."

Smiling ruefully, he waved away my apology. "One of the worst things about living in the town where you grew up is that your youthful escapades never go away."

"Makes me glad I moved north."

Stewart laughed. "I find it hard to believe you've ever strayed from the straight and narrow."

Now why did that annoy me? I was, in fact, pretty much a Goody Two-shoes, but somehow

I didn't like people knowing. "Well, sorry again for dredging up your past," I said, and went back to my office, thinking that I wouldn't classify the damage that Aunt Frances had described ("furniture reduced to kindling") as a mere escapade.

Just as I was finishing the bookmobile's April calendar—well done, Minnie; this is the earliest you've ever sent out a schedule!—my cell phone made its incoming call noise. At lunch, Rafe, thinking he was funny, had downloaded the bleats of a herd of goats as my ringtone, and since it was actually pretty funny, I hadn't yet changed it.

I flipped my phone over and saw it was Barb McCade. "Hey, Barb. What's up?"

"We will be, or at least we will in a few minutes."

"Should I act as if I know what you're talking about, or should I admit that I'm clueless?"

Barb laughed. "We're at the Traverse City airport, waiting for our row to be called."

"Heading back to the sun and sand?"

"More rock than sand," she said. "Have you ever been to Arizona? No? You have to come visit us someday."

"Sounds great," I said, although I wasn't being completely sincere as I was not a fan of snakes, big spiders, scorpions, or anything remotely

300

similar. While I understood that Arizona was outstandingly beautiful, I wasn't certain that I'd fit in well with all of its creatures. "Did Cade finish his new series?"

"Close enough," Barb said. "He's going to let them sit until we get back here in April. The time lag will do him good. I think they might be his best work ever, but you know Cade."

I laughed. "Right now he thinks they're so horrible that he's on the verge of whitewashing them all."

"With a big fat brush," Barb said. "Anyway, I just wanted to hear how Kristen was doing."

"She's fine. Already back at work." She'd actually returned to tending bar less than a week after her fall. When I'd questioned the wisdom of that decision via text, she'd texted back: *Being bored makes me think about starting a new restaurant.*

Me: *In New York? Scruffy would like that.*

Kristen: *Not in winter. Brr.*

Me: *Their winters aren't like Chilson winters.*

Kristen: *Colder than Key West.*

There was no point in arguing with that, so I didn't. How Kristen and her fiancé were going to work out their geographical separation once they were married was still a big question mark, but I'd long ago put that on the list of things I wasn't going to worry about.

Barb said, "Good to hear. I wouldn't want my

301

favorite chef to have a permanent injury. The world would be a lesser place without her crème brûlée. And now we really have to go. See you in April, Minnie!"

"Have a good—" But she was already gone.

I clicked the phone off, flipped it around in my hands a few times, then stood up.

Something in my conversation with Barb had tweaked my sense of urgency about finding Rowan's killer. Yes, I could call the sheriff's office to ask about progress, but I was tired of leaving messages that might or might not be taken seriously. Sure, Ash had appeared to be paying attention to my suggestion regarding Neil, but there was more to discuss, and if there was something I could do to push the investigation forward, to help Anya and Collier, well, I was going to do it.

I slid off my shoes and put on my boots. It was time to beard the lion in his den.

I stopped at the front desk and told Kelsey I had to run an errand, that I'd be back in half an hour, then zipped my coat and headed out. At which point I discovered that the friendly two inches of snow I'd been so fond of a couple of hours earlier had turned into a sloppy layer of mushy slush.

My boots made a squishy *splash! splash!* noise as I walked downtown, which amused me to no end. I was enjoying the sound and the sight of the spurting snow so much, and enjoying the fact that my earlier bad mood was gone, that I jumped when someone spoke to me.

"Having fun, Minnie?"

Tom Abinaw, or Cookie Tom, as most people called him, was standing on the sidewalk outside his bakery, shovel in hand, smiling at me.

I spent half a second hoping my face was already red with cold, which meant he wouldn't see the slightly embarrassed flush creeping over my face. "Absolutely," I said. "You should try it. It's fun." For a three-year-old, but did that really matter?

He laughed, shaking his head. "Snow and I are not good friends. Besides, baking is enough fun for me. Speaking of which, you haven't stopped by lately."

Tom gave me a deal on the cookies I bought for the bookmobile patrons. However, there was nowhere in the library budget for expenditures like that, and I paid for them out of my own pocket.

"Christmas," I said, by roundabout way of explanation. "Every year I set a budget and every year I zip past it at light speed. One more cycle of credit card bills and I'll be paid off, so expect me soon."

"I'll be waiting," he said, nodding, and went back to his slush-shoveling.

Once again I wondered how a baker, a person

surrounded by cookies and cakes and doughnuts, could stay as thin as Tom did. Maybe he was an ultra-long-distance runner, one of those people who regularly ran twenty or thirty or fifty miles at a time. Or maybe he was allergic to almost everything, and subsisted solely on oatmeal and carrots. But you'd think that would make him grumpy, and Tom was one of the most contented people I'd ever met in my life.

"You look happy," Carl, the deputy at the front desk, said after sliding open the glass window. "So you can't possibly want to talk to Hal."

I laughed. "He can be a fun-killer, can't he? But yes, I would like to talk to him if he's around. Or Ash."

"You might be in luck," Carl said. "Or unluck, if that's a word. I think they just came back in. Hang on."

While I waited, I checked my phone and saw a new text from Anya.

Anya: *Anything new?*

Me: *At the sheriff's office right now.*

Anya: *Hope so Collier isn't going to classes*

Me: *Tell your dad.*

Anya: *Tried but nothing in days*

My jaw firmed. Something had to be done to help that boy. I started typing. *Get Collier to a doctor. I'm—*

"Ms. Hamilton? When you're ready." Detective Hal Inwood held the door open.

—I'm going to light a fire under someone's you-know-what.

Smiling, I pushed the Send button and slid the phone into my coat pocket as I walked into the interview room. "Thanks for seeing me."

"Is it too much to hope for that someday you'll call and make an appointment?" Hal sat in one of the plastic chairs.

"Not too much, no," I said. "But if the past is indicative of the future, it's not going to happen anytime soon."

"That's what I was afraid of," he said, sighing. "Ash, have a seat."

Ash, who had just come into the room, sat across from me. "Hey, Minnie."

"Have you been in contact with Rowan's family?" I asked. "Keeping them up to date with the investigation?"

There was a quick exchange of glances on the other side of the table. "When there's something to report, Mr. Bennethum is called," Hal said.

"Not the kids?" I heard the tone of demand in my voice and didn't back away from it. "Not Anya and Collier?"

"Ms. Hamilton," Hal said, "there are only so many hours in the day. Mr. Bennethum is our primary contact with the family. If he isn't communicating with his children, they should take it up with him."

"But they are!" I hopped my chair closer and

leaned forward. "They're trying, anyway, and he's not responding. I'm not sure they know where he is." I caught another silent exchange. "Do you?"

"Our information is confidential," Hal said.

I wanted to bang my fist on the table, but could hear my mother's voice in my head, admonishing me. Instead, I took a deep breath. "Fine," I said. "But you should know that Collier Bennethum is probably sliding into clinical depression. His sister says he's not going to classes and is sleeping all the time and the only thing he talks about is their mom's killer is alive when their mom is dead. I told her to tell Neil, but she says her dad hasn't answered a text in days."

Hal stirred. "I'm sorry for young Mr. Bennethum, but we're doing all we can."

"What about the broken headlight? What about the sugar packet? Stop shaking your head," I snapped, because my anger was now well and truly stoked. "That packet matters. Ask your wife. Ask Sheriff Richardson, if you don't believe me."

"Ms. Hamilton," Hal began, but I stood up abruptly. It was a waste of my time and theirs to sit any longer.

I whirled and left the room. Somewhere behind me I heard someone call my name, but what was there to say? I nodded to Carl and walked straight out into the cold.

Chapter 16

I spent the night in fitful sleep, rolling from one side to the other in a vain attempt at finding a position that would send me into slumber. Eddie gave up on me about two in the morning and did a loud *thump-thump!* to the floor. When I got up, bleary eyed and still tired, I found him curled up on the big living room couch.

"And here I thought you loved me," I told him.

"Mrr."

"Well, sure, I was moving around a lot last night, but that doesn't mean—"

"Mrr!" he said, then shut his eyes firmly.

Smiling, I kissed the top of his fuzzy head. "See you tonight, okay?"

He didn't move a muscle as I pulled on boots and the rest of my winter gear, but when I paused at the front door and looked back, his eyes were open the tiniest of slits.

"Love you, too, buddy!" As I closed the door, I could have sworn I heard one more "Mrr," which wasn't surprising since cats have an innate need to have the last word.

"Well, Eddie does, anyway," I said to myself as

I started the car. One of these days I was going to have to compare notes with other people who lived with cats. Maybe Eddie wasn't so unusual. Maybe all cats ate bread, dropped toys in their water dishes, and held complete conversations with their human companions.

I was still thinking about it when I pulled into the Red House Café's parking lot. My aunt had spent the night at Otto's house, and upon waking, I'd decided that a big breakfast was what I needed to fuel me for the rest of what was going to be a long day. And since I obviously wasn't going to cook my own food, what better place to go than Sunny's?

There were no other cars in the parking lot, but that almost made sense. It was half past eight, a little late for the early Sunday morning breakfast crowd and too early for folks who liked to sleep in.

Still, it was eerie walking into a completely empty restaurant. Really, really empty. No one was at the front counter; no one was in the dining area. "Hello?" I called. "Is anyone here? Sunny?"

The front door had been unlocked and the lights were on; it was all a little too much *Mary Celeste*. "Someone's here, right?" I asked, primarily to hear a human voice. "Anyone?" Back behind the swinging kitchen door, I heard . . . something. Relieved to get a sign of life, I headed back, but when I raised my hand to knock on the door to the inner sanctum, I stopped.

The noise was someone crying. The kind of deep sobbing that racks your insides, the kind that makes you feel as if you'll be weeping the rest of your life, the kind that comes from despair.

I pushed the door open.

Sunny was on a stool, her face in her hands, shoulders heaving. She looked up and wiped her face with her fingers. "Minnie," she managed to say. "Sorry, I'm just—" A sob overtook her and she put her face back in her hands.

I hurried to put my arms around her. "It'll be all right," I said. "Whatever it is, it'll be all right."

She shook her head against my shoulder and talked through her sobs. "No, it won't . . . It hasn't been right in years, but I didn't know . . . I can't believe I didn't . . . I've tried so hard, but there's nothing . . . nothing I can do."

I hugged her tight as she continued to cry. Her sobs eventually subsided and I released her, rubbing her back gently. "If you want to talk about whatever this was about," I said, "I'm here to listen. If you don't, that's fine, too."

Sunny gulped down a final sob and looked at me. "Come to the Red House Café, where you come in for breakfast and end up with a front full of tears."

I looked my coat, which was indeed a bit damp. "It'll dry." Eventually.

"Sorry you had to see this." Sunny pulled in a deep breath and let it out shakily. "Breakfast on the house."

"You don't have to do that," I said.

"Of course I do." She stood, expertly tore a single paper towel off a handy roll, and blew her nose. "Let me wash my hands and I'll make you whatever you want."

A few minutes later a plate heaped with chocolate chip pancakes was placed in front of me, with a jug of real Michigan maple syrup alongside. I took a bite and moaned with pleasure. "This is amazing. Better than Kristen's, and I can't wait to tell her so."

"Kristen?" Sunny's eyebrows went up. "You're not talking about Kristen Jurek, are you?"

I chewed and swallowed, and said, "She's my best friend. Do you know her?"

"She's my idol," Sunny said reverently. "I want to be her when I grow up."

That, I would not pass on to Kristen. "Well, you make better pancakes than she does, so I'd stick with who you are."

Sunny looked into the dining area. She'd propped the kitchen door open while she cooked for me, but it was still empty of life. "Not sure that's a very good choice." She pulled a stool over. "And not just because I don't know if my restaurant will make it to summer. I owe you an explanation for my crying jag."

"Not if you're uncomfortable with talking about it," I said.

"Tell you the truth, it might be a relief." Sunny stared at the counter. "Do you have siblings? Are you close?"

"A brother." Were we close? Matt was nine years older and he lived in Florida with his wife and three children. "Middling close, I guess."

"Then maybe you'll understand and maybe you won't." She sighed. "My sister and I are only eleven months apart. We grew up almost like twins. Together all the time, hardly ever fighting. We finished each other's sentences, traded clothes, all that."

Her smile faded. "Three years ago, she was in a car accident and hurt her back. To make a long story short, she got addicted to opioids and we're afraid she's going to start on heroin." Sunny's voice wobbled. "We're trying to find the money to get her into rehab. The only places with beds open are private facilities, and they're so expensive. I tried getting a loan, but that didn't work, so now we're scraping together what we can. I mean, even a week has to help, right?" Her expression begged me to agree.

"Absolutely. And no matter what, it can't hurt," I said.

"That's what I say." Sunny nodded. "Mom isn't so sure, but the rest of the family is on board. We're trying to keep my sister's addiction quiet.

She works for a big company, she's in line for a big promotion, and if this gets out . . ." She pounded one fist on top of the other. "We can't let it get out, we just can't. It would ruin her reputation."

The front door opened and closed and the voices of prospective customers trickled into the kitchen.

"Looks like I get to cook some more," Sunny said, attempting a smile. "Thanks for listening."

With my fork I speared another small wedge of pancakes, thinking that I'd finally found an answer to the question of why she hadn't admitted to having an alibi, an answer that I wouldn't have guessed in a thousand years.

Which led me directly to another question: What else hadn't I guessed?

The man sitting at the center of the long curved table banged a small wooden hammer. "The regular meeting of the Wicklow Township Board is now called to order." He laid the gavel down. "We will now recite the Pledge of Allegiance."

As one unit, the audience of about thirty people stood, me along with them, hands on our hearts. When the pledge was done, we all sat down. I settled into my hard plastic seat, trying to find a comfortable position and failing completely, and looked forward to an interesting evening. Up front were the five members of the township board. I recognized two: Charlotte, the clerk who'd given the bookmobile permission to stop in their parking lot, and the supervisor, who'd walked out with Hugh Novak.

The board's names were spelled out in nameplates sitting in front of them, so I could see that the supervisor's name was Ralph Keshwas. The nameplates of the other board members were hidden by the heads of the many people sitting in front of me, so I mentally gave them names of Young Man (he looked about my age, which made him about thirty years younger than all of his fellow board members), Serious Lady (she was reading the pile of papers in front of her with great concentration), and Eyebrow Guy (his were remarkably bushy).

"Next is approval of the agenda," Ralph Keshwas said, dropping his reading glasses from the top of his head onto his nose. "Are there any additions to the agenda?"

It turned out there were. Charlotte requested the addition of a budget amendment, Eyebrow Guy asked to add a grant application, and I started to get the feeling this was going to be a long meeting. To my left, a woman was using her purse as a clipboard as she wrote on a piece of paper. I peered at it surreptitiously, and I realized it was a copy of the meeting's agenda.

Huh.

I turned in my chair and saw, right next to the

doorway into the meeting room, a small table with a stack of papers atop. Could it be that I'd walked past the agendas without even noticing? I stood as quietly and unobtrusively as I could, tiptoed to the back, picked one up, and started to read as I went back to my chair. Next would be—

"Public comment," Ralph said. "Young lady, please state your name and address."

Dead silence.

I looked up. Every face in the room was turned to me. "Um," I said. "None, thanks." The faces stayed stuck in my direction, so I did what I did best in times of stress: babbled. "Public comment, I mean. I got up to get a copy of the agenda, that's all, I don't have anything to say, really." And since that was very clearly true, I sat down as fast as I could.

"Thank you," Ralph said, so straight-faced that I suspected an underlying foundation of irony. "Next? Okay, I think your hand was first. Step up to the podium."

"Hugh Novak, 2978 Maple Lane."

I'd been reading over the agenda, but my head snapped up.

"Tonight," Hugh said, "you have an action item of 'New Township Hall,' and I'd like to cite the reasons you should go ahead with that."

"Besides it being next to your property?" someone in the audience called out.

Hugh whirled and pointed directly at his

heckler. "You've lived here two years and now you want everything to stay the same for, what, the rest of your life? If you don't like the way things are run here, then move back downstate!"

The audience murmured, with some people nodding, others shaking their heads. A sharp rap up front quieted them all. Ralph laid down the gavel. "This is the board's public comment period," he said calmly. "Everyone will have their turn to speak, but your comments must be directed to the board and the board only."

I was sitting in the back corner, so my view of Hugh Novak was from the rear, and I could clearly see his clenched fists.

"As I was trying to say," Hugh growled out, "here are the reasons you should go ahead with a new township hall." He listed a number of items, ranging from easier voting access for the elderly to new revenue that would result from rentals of the new meeting space for high school open houses, family reunions, and wedding receptions.

When Hugh had finished his list, he gave the board a long look. "Building a new hall is clearly in the best interest of the township as a whole. Do the right thing."

He sat, arms crossed, and spent the rest of the meeting staring forward. Even when the board voted to postpone their decision on a new township hall until the next meeting, Hugh continued to stare them down, his face blank and eyes barely blinking.

"It was weird," I told Eddie as I climbed into bed. "And not a good weird. More a creepy weird, like how your tummy feels after eating that fourth cookie."

"Mrr?"

"That was what you call an analogy. I didn't actually eat four cookies, I was just comparing that feeling to how I felt at tonight's meeting." My only purpose for going to the meeting had been to learn what I could about Hugh Novak, and I'd been more than successful.

"Point to Minnie," I murmured, pulling the sheets and comforter to my chin. I patted the space next to me. Eddie jumped up, completely ignored the space I'd indicated, walked across my legs, and settled down on top of my stomach.

"Okay, then," I said. "Let's review the progress to date. There were originally five suspects, and two have been eliminated." At least by me. I had no idea if the sheriff's office had the same point of view and wasn't about to ask.

I looked down at Eddie, waiting for a response. "Right. First is Land Aprelle. It appears that Land and Rowan had a siblinglike relationship and yelled at each other on a regular basis with no lasting effects."

In addition, I'd discovered nothing that indicated their final argument had been any different, and Land's oddly furtive behavior was a result of his reluctance to tell the world that he wanted to be a wood sculpture artist. Ergo, there was absolutely no reason for him to kill Rowan.

"Second," I said. "Sunny Scoles was denied a loan that would have helped her sister, but her family is looking for other ways to raise the money, so why would she kill Rowan? Besides, Sunny had an alibi."

"Mrr," Eddie said sleepily.

"Right. That leaves three suspects. Well, four if you count Neil." I thought a minute. "No, let's cross Bax Tousely off the list. Now that we know the hardware store thing was work related, the only real reason we have to suspect him is that he was seen driving past the Bennethums' house over Christmas break."

I stopped. Could it be that I wanted to cross him off just because he volunteered at Lakeview? That I couldn't believe a guy who found homes for stray cats could be a killer? That I felt sorry for him because he'd looked so sad?

Eddie purred, making my insides vibrate.

"Not sure your opinion should count on that one," I said. "I'll leave him on the list. That gives us four possibles. Going from the least likely to the most, there's Bax, who might have killed Rowan because he was trying to kill Anya because he thought she was the one who got engaged and he was crazy with jealousy and . . . *ow!*"

Eddie had extended his claws and managed to drive them through the layers of flannel, goose down, and more flannel all the way to my very tender skin.

"Okay, okay, you're right. That's so far-fetched it's beyond the realm of possibility. Way beyond," I hastened to add as I saw the paw begin to flex again. "Three suspects, again going up from the bottom. Suspect number three is Neil Bennethum. He certainly resented the relationship between Land and Rowan and could have dreamed up an affair between them, killing Rowan because he was jealous. Plus there's the fact that he seems to have vanished off the face of the earth."

The disappearance alone didn't look good, and it made me think less of the man. His children needed him. Sure, they were nearly college graduates, but they'd lost their mother in a horrible way and Neil's absence was making everything worse.

I shook my head and moved on. "Suspect number two . . . you know, I don't know who to put at the top of the list. Stewart Funston, as much as I like him, seems to penalize people heavily for what he considers mistakes. That vandalism in the high school principal's office, and now divorcing his wife for hiding money? Who knows what happened in the years between?" Sighing,

I said, "Of course, I have no earthly clue what Rowan could have done to Stewart that might have made him want to kill her."

Eddie grunted and got up, using my solar plexus as a base for his efforts.

"Go ahead, use me for leverage anytime you'd like. Tied for suspect number one is Hugh Novak." I saw again those crossed arms and that intimidating stare. "He kind of scared me," I said quietly. "He's a big guy and I felt really small with him in the room. Not that he was mad at me, but if he was . . ."

My voice trailed off. Though I owned a concealed pistol license, I'd never felt the need to actually buy a weapon and carry it. But if I got on the bad side of somebody like Hugh Novak, maybe it was time to reexamine that attitude. Maybe it was—

Something bounced onto the floor, rolled across the carpet, and came to a rest under the bed.

I glanced around and saw that Eddie had jumped onto my dresser and was now looking in the direction of whatever it was he'd sent to the floor. When he realized I was looking at him, he sat up straight.

"What are you doing?" I asked.

In response, his right front paw reached out in a hook and sent another something to the floor.

"Seriously?" I flung the covers back. "Stop whatever that is and . . . oh, brother."

319

Due to a convenience-store snack on the way to the meeting, I'd ended up with coins in my pants pocket instead of in my car, where I usually put my loose change. I'd set it on the dresser, intending to move it to the car in the morning.

"Not a cat toy," I said, moving Eddie back to the bed. I picked up the dime and the penny he'd pushed to the floor, and tossed all the change into my sock drawer. "None of it is a cat toy, understand?"

"Mrr!"

I crawled back into bed and, with my cat perched on my hip staring down at me like a furry bird of prey, drifted into a sleep that was punctuated by dreams of Collier, at the altar with his bride, staring at the gaping dark space where his parents should have been.

Chapter 17

The next day, Rafe and I met for lunch again, but this time it was brown bags in his office.

"It still surprises me sometimes," I said, removing the cover from my nifty new sandwich container. My mom, who was constantly trying to get me to cook more and eat out less, had given me a nice set of storage doohickeys for Christmas. I'd used this one and a cube-shaped version, which I'd recently discovered was perfect for leftover restaurant oatmeal. The other eight containers were awaiting their opportunities for a useful life.

"What does?" Rafe was sitting in his desk chair with his feet propped on an open lower drawer. He asked the question around a mouthful of baloney sandwich and followed it with a chaser of bottled water. At some point we needed to have a chat about table manners, but since he had a meeting with the president of the school board in fifteen minutes, I decided to give him a pass. For now.

"That you're a middle school principal."

"Surprises a lot of people," he said. "Me, my

parents, my grandparents, my aunt and uncles, my cousins, all of my friends, and every teacher I ever had, including Sunday school."

"So pretty much everyone you've ever met."

"Well, there was this one girl," he said meditatively. "She told me I had a lot of potential, but if I didn't shape up, I was going to end up a complete loser and die a lonely and bitter old man."

A surge of jealousy leapt into my throat. I batted it down and, as casually as I could, asked, "Oh? Anyone I know?"

He grinned. "She runs this restaurant in town. You might know it. Three Seasons?"

I stared at him, then started laughing. "Seriously? Kristen said that? When?"

"First summer I met you."

Still laughing, I said, "When I was, what, twelve?" Kristen and Rafe were a year older than I was, but the three of us had formed a summertime trio throughout our adolescence. Our bond faded during college and the first postcollege years, but when I moved to Chilson full time about the same time Kristen chucked her fancy science job with a large pharmaceutical company, we'd slid back into the comfortable old ways.

"You were short then, too." He bit into his sandwich.

"Some people see consistency as a virtue."

Rafe shrugged. "And some people play with rattlesnakes."

The link between consistency and rattlesnakes was so thin as to be nonexistent, but when I'd started this conversation, I'd wanted to say something specific, so I pulled away from poking holes in his analogy. "Like I said, it sometimes surprises me that you're a middle school principal, and—"

He made a rolling motion with his sandwich. "Move on."

"Trying," I said. "But what I want to say is I'm not surprised you're a good one."

His sandwich stopped mid-roll. "You're . . . what?"

"I always knew that once you'd decided on what you wanted to do with your life, you'd be successful at doing it." Awkward sentence, which only proved something I'd known for years, that I should rehearse anything important I ever wanted to say to anyone, ever.

Plunging on, I said, "It's just that you have all these great qualities—some incredibly annoying ones, too, so quit smiling—and I'm not at all surprised that the teachers, kids, and parents think you're the best principal this school has ever had."

He shoved a dangling piece of lettuce back into his sandwich. "That's because people have short memories."

It wasn't. In the last few months more than one

teacher who'd reached early retirement age had stopped me on the street to tell me they were planning on continuing to teach for another few years, and it was all due to Rafe Niswander. "Who would have thunk it?" Mr. Conant had said wryly. "The kid who drove me batty in seventh grade is now my boss, and I can't imagine having a better one."

"Speaking of short memories," Rafe said.

He shoved the last of his sandwich in his mouth, then, thankfully, chewed and swallowed. That last bite had been huge, and though I'd been trained in emergency first aid, I'd never had to perform the Heimlich maneuver in a real-life situation.

"Speaking of short memories," I prompted, because he'd taken his feet off the drawer and was reaching for his computer mouse.

"Yeah. That." He clicked away. "There it is. Take a look."

I wolfed down the last of my peanut butter and jelly sandwich, came around, and looked at the screen. It was filled with a busy spreadsheet. "Is that your suspect list?"

"Columns are the suspect names, rows are the different bits of clues, evidence, and whatever other information we think might be useful." He tapped the screen. "You know, this might be better in a database than a spreadsheet. What do you think?"

What I thought was that he would have been better off spending his time finishing the drywall in the upstairs bathroom, but I kissed the back of his head. "This is great. Can you e-mail it to me?"

"Yes, I could, but no I won't, because I'm going to put it into Google Docs. That way we can both work on it at the same time, see? I'll e-mail you the link."

Um. "Sounds . . . great." I peered at the screen and saw that he'd added rows titled "Alibi," "Background," "Motive," "Movements," and "Previous Incidents."

"This could be really useful," I said, starting to warm to the idea. "Especially the 'Background' and 'Previous Incidents.' Those are things I have to find out, but for people like you who grew up around here the information is practically imprinted into your DNA."

He sat back, putting his hands behind his head. "And here you thought this was a waste of time."

"I didn't—" Well, I had, actually, so I took a deep breath and said the magic words. "You were right and I was wrong. I'm sorry."

He smacked a kiss on the side of my face. "And now I'm afraid I have to kick you out. My meeting starts in three minutes and this guy is always on time."

We exchanged a long kiss that made me want to lock his office door for an hour, but we eventually separated and I headed out. A quiet "Hey" made me stop and turn around. Rafe was fiddling with his mouse. "Thanks," he said, not looking up. "For what you said. About not being surprised that I'm successful."

Even though the clouds outside were thick and unyielding, sunshine suddenly filled me. "You're welcome," I said softly, and left him to his meeting.

Julia zipped Grant Jelen's last book through the scanner. "And there you go," she said, piling *The Historian* onto a teetering stack. "Sure you have enough to last until next time?"

Grant, gray-haired but tall and straight, started moving his books from her desktop to the empty backpack he'd brought in. "No," he said. "But I can borrow e-books if I have to. Prefer print, though."

"Ah." Julia glanced at me, and her blank face was a clear request for help. Her gift with patrons was more in the line of jollying along the slightly cranky ones; I usually took over when patrons were reluctant to communicate at all.

This was Grant's second trip to the bookmobile. We knew two things about him—that his name had never been in the library's computer, and that his driver's license, which he'd used to get a library card five weeks ago, had a downstate address.

Smiling, I said, "Looks like you're making up for lost time. Are you a new retiree?"

"End of December." He eyed the contents of his backpack, eyed the books still remaining on the counter, and reached into the backpack to rearrange its contents. "Spent thirty-five years working my hind end off, trying to make it to the top of the freaking corporate ladder, and all I ever got was vice president." He made a rude noise. "Worked so hard my wife divorced me and my kids hardly talk to me except to ask for money."

A little wildly, I looked at Julia. Now that he'd started talking, how did I get him to stop? We didn't need this much personal information. Sure, what happened on the bookmobile stayed on the bookmobile, but sometimes when people told you too much, they regretted it afterward.

Julia leaned forward. "Sounds like you didn't get what you deserve."

"True story." He shoved the last book into his pack and, with some effort, zipped it shut, book corners bulging through the nylon. "All I want to do now is read and work on my cars."

The reading I approved of wholeheartedly; it was how I'd like to spend a large share of my own far-off retirement. The cars, however . . .

I knew better than to ask what kind of cars he owned; we didn't have that kind of time left at the stop. So I just blurted out the question: "Are there any junkyards close by?" It was a non sequitur to end all non sequiturs, and I braced myself for raised eyebrows and a surprised look that a little girl would be interested in something like that.

"Sure," he said. "Buster's. On Lolly Road, a few miles out of Peebles. Model Ts to Hummers and everything in between. Buster's place is half the reason I moved here." Grant hefted his backpack onto his shoulders, nodded, and headed out.

"Buster's," I said to myself.

Julia flipped the laptop shut. "You're not still looking for that headlight, are you?"

"And what if I am?" I asked, helping her stretch the bungee cord around the rolling chair, which would wander all over the bookmobile if we forgot to strap it in place.

"Because if you were still looking," Julia said, "I'd advise you to remember the reactions of the other junkyard owners you've talked to lately."

I winced. More than one junkyard owner had laughed in my face when I'd asked the question. "You're kidding, right?" the most memorable had asked as he'd puffed a large cigar.

I'd edged out of the way of the smoke. "No, I'm very serious. It's important."

He'd puffed out another smoke signal. "I keep records as good as anyone, but tracking down to the headlight level isn't how I want to spend my time."

Looking around the small, poorly lit office, I'd wondered how he whiled away his hours. "Do you walk around the yard a lot? To keep thieves away, I mean?"

He'd hacked out a laugh. "You're from down-state, aren't you?"

Soon after, I'd fled, and it had taken me two days to gather up the courage to step into another junkyard. That owner didn't smoke, but the end result had been the same.

Now, I pulled out my cell phone and opened a mapping application to find Buster's. "This will work just fine," I said, nodding.

Julia rolled her eyes dramatically and said, "Let me guess. Since I wanted to get dropped off in Peebles, you driving to Lolly Road is the handiest thing ever."

"Mrr," said Eddie, who'd been perched on the driver's seat headrest. "Mrr!"

"Exactly." I beamed at them both. "Sometimes things just work out."

The weather, however, wasn't cooperating with my new plan. What had been a mild thaw—two degrees above freezing for almost eight hours—was quickly dropping to a more season-able temperature. In general, this was fine with me, but any of the side roads that hadn't been scraped free of snow (and that was most of them) were now developing the kind of conditions that made people move away from northern Michigan.

"Not us, though," I said to Eddie, soon after I'd left Julia at the out-of-the-way restaurant where she was meeting her husband for dinner. "We're brave and intrepid."

"Mrr!"

"Exactly. We're ready for anything"—I paused to navigate the bookmobile through a nasty stretch of rapidly freezing slush—"for anything Mother Nature dishes out."

The daylight, which had never been all that bright in the first place, was inching toward dusk by the time I saw the sign for the junkyard. BUSTER'S, just like Grant had said. The sign was simple—black paint on a piece of framed plywood—but it did the job well enough, and I was pleased to see that Buster's parking lot was not only big enough for the bookmobile, but also plowed.

"I'll be back in a few minutes," I told Eddie. He eyed me, but didn't say anything. "Thanks for the encouragement," I said. "It's just what I needed."

"Mrr."

As the door of the junkyard's office closed behind me, I blinked in surprise. "Wow," I said. "This isn't . . ." I trailed off, pretty sure I was about to say something offensive.

The man behind the desk, who was about my age and wearing a sleek zipped black sweater with a Buster's logo, looked up. "Let me guess.

330

You expected dark paneling, a clutter of car parts and paper, calendars with scantily clad women sitting on vehicle hoods, and cigarette smoke sticking to everything."

He was right, I had expected that. These office walls, however, were painted a warm blue gray and decorated with huge framed photos of antique cars on the streets of what could have been Chilson. His desk was piled with a single stack of papers, and the only car parts to be seen were in a glass display case.

"Well, precedent counts," I said, smiling. "And that's what the offices of the other five junkyards in the area looked like. How was I to know you'd be the single solitary exception to the rule?"

The guy laughed. "Point taken. Sorry about that; you're the first person I've seen today and I'm told that I can forget to be polite." He stood and held out a hand. "Rob Caldwell."

I introduced myself and said, "Nice to meet you. Um, if you're Rob, who's Buster?"

"No idea. I bought this place a couple of years ago and never changed the name. It's been Buster's for decades. So what can I do for you? I hope you don't want parts for that," he said, nodding at the office window, through which the bookmobile was visible. "I specialize in unusual parts, but all I have for that is a recommendation to contact a yard in Ohio."

"I'm looking for an SUV headlight."

"That I can do." Rob sat down and tapped his computer to life. "Make, model, year?"

"No idea," I said, then jumped ahead of his protest. "What I'm wondering is, has anyone else bought a headlight in the last few weeks?" Rob frowned, but his fingers were still on the keyboard, so I kept talking.

"There was a . . . crime committed just over a month ago, and someone saw a car with a broken headlight driving away. The sheriff's office is following up, they're checking auto parts stores, but they're pretty much convinced that whoever it was ordered a new one online and they'll never be able to track that." I took a deep breath. "So I'm talking to the junkyards, figuring that maybe that's where the guy bought a replacement."

Rob leaned back. "I don't have to look that up. No one has bought a headlight from me since before Christmas."

"Oh." My shoulders slumped. "Well, it was worth a try. Thanks for your time."

"Hang on," Rob said, and I turned back. "I said no one bought a headlight, and that's true." He half smiled. "But someone did steal one. And before you ask, no, I never reported it to the police, because who's going to arrest anyone for stealing a ten-dollar headlight from a junkyard?"

The insides of my wrists tingled. "From an SUV?"

"Don't remember, but I could tell you if—"

The telephone sitting on his desk rang. "Buster's Junkyard, we have exactly what your wife hopes you won't find. How can I—oh, hey, honey. What's up?" His gaze flicked to me. "I have a customer here, but—okay. I'll be there as soon as I can. Love you, too."

He hung up the phone. "Sorry, but I have to get going. My husband's family is coming up for a long weekend and half of them showed up early to beat the weather."

"You started to say something, that you could tell me it was an SUV if . . . what?"

Rob clicked his mouse, making the familiar motions of tidying up his computer desktop before leaving for the day. "Not without looking at the security video. I can do that for you on Monday. Just give me a call."

"Could you please take a minute and do it now?" I asked.

"I really have to go. Sorry." He stood.

"Please?" How could I convince him? How could I communicate how important this was? "This isn't about the headlight. That crime I mentioned? It was a murder," I said flatly. "And your headlight thief could be the killer."

Rob sat down slowly. "Murder? I heard something about a woman who was poisoned. Is that what this is about?"

"If you could just look at the security video," I said. "Please."

He glanced at the wall clock. Hesitated, then said, "Sure. I'll have to do some explaining, but sure." He started clicking away on the keyboard and chatting about the security measures he'd put in place since he'd bought Buster's. He talked about fencing and lights and how a fresh coat of paint could deter thieves and, still clicking, talked about how he'd decided to buy cameras after he'd noticed an absence of hood ornaments. "The system I installed out there is a glorified trail cam. The cameras cover the entire yard and only turn on when there's motion. I get raccoons mostly." He smiled as he clicked. "Cute little buggers, unless you're trying to keep them out of your garden. Last year Tony was at his wit's end with—ah, here it is."

Rob angled the monitor so I could see. "Yeah, that's an SUV he's pulling it out of. I meant to get out there and take a look so I could revise my inventory, but haven't got around to it yet."

I leaned forward. On the screen was the fuzzy image of a man who looked to be about six feet tall, in a dark coat wearing dark gloves and a hat. A very distinctive hat.

"Thanks," I said quietly. "One more thing. Could you please e-mail that video clip to the sheriff's office?"

Chapter 18

Mrr."

I buckled my seat belt and started the engine, talking to Eddie as I did so. "How was I supposed to know that video clip was too big to e-mail? If I have tech questions, I ask Josh, and he's not here, now is he?" Luckily, because I was sure he would have made fun of me for my lack of knowledge.

"Mrr!"

"Sure, I could have called him, but it's a little late now, isn't it? And anyway, until we get out of this valley, there's no cell service."

"Mrr!"

I slid a glance over at Eddie, turned on the headlights, and dropped the transmission into gear. "If you're asking about what I saw on Rob's video, you'll be glad to know there's no way it was Neil." Neil wasn't that tall, and he was far bigger around.

But my sigh of relief had frozen when I'd studied the image more closely. The man had been wearing a dark winter coat resembling coats worn by Hugh Novak and Stewart Funston. Far more telling was the hat, that unusual earflap fedora I'd seen both men wearing, a kind I'd never seen on anyone else's head.

"It was either Hugh or Stewart," I said out loud, easing my foot onto the accelerator and exhaling with relief when the bookmobile's tires found traction and inched us forward. Yes, we had great tires and the weight made winter driving reasonably easy, but the current road conditions were less than stellar. "Let's think about motive."

"Mrrr!"

"Exactly." I steered us out of the gravel parking lot. "We haven't the foggiest idea why Stewart might have killed Rowan, but we know what Hugh's motive probably is. At the township meeting, Hugh was furious at that guy in the audience. And if you're that angry in a public meeting, what would it take to tip you into murder?"

I thought about it as I looked both ways—no traffic, such a surprise!—and pulled onto Lolly Road. "Whoa, speaking of tipping . . ."

The time I'd been in Buster's had been long enough to turn the dusk into complete darkness and, unhappily, to freeze the road's slush to ice. The bookmobile, usually the epitome of driving stability, seesawed left and right on the slick surface. "Don't, don't, don't," I murmured in a sort of a prayer as adrenaline shot through me. "Please don't . . ."

After a few more slips back and forth, we hit a patch of actual asphalt and straightened out.

I blew out a breath and tried to release the tension in my neck. "Anyway, it was either Hugh or Stewart. Thanks to Rob, I have the video clip on a flash drive, and as soon as we get into cell phone range—and find a place to pull over because, as you know, I don't use my cell while driving the bookmobile, per library policy—I'll call Ash." Or Hal, but I'd rather talk to Ash.

"Mrr!"

"What's that? Hugh's exact motive? Huh. I thought I told you. Rowan had been organizing people to speak up against the new township hall. After the meeting, I talked to a few people, and they said she'd gone door to door, handing out information about building costs and advising folks to make up their own minds. Apparently she told everyone that if they felt strongly one way or the other to show up at the board meetings for public comment."

Even over the noise of the bookmobile, I heard the unmistakable sound of Eddie's body as he flopped against the wire door of the cat carrier. "Well, I agree with you, a new township hall doesn't seem worth murdering over, but if it's built, Hugh could make a lot more money from a business on his property if a new hall goes in."

Eddie's head clunked against the door.

"Why do you do that?" I asked. "One of these

days you're going to give yourself a concussion."

"Mrr," he said, then, from the sounds of it—I didn't dare look away from the road, so sounds were all I had to go on—he started chewing the door.

"You are so weird. But back to murder motives. I've read that domestic disputes are the number one reason for murder, with money number two, but it sure seems to me that there's a lot of overlap. I mean, aren't most fights between couples about money? And if a fight gets bad, isn't . . . oh, geez."

I eased my foot off the accelerator and said in a voice even I could hear was tight with tension, "Okay, this could be bad. Really bad."

"Mrr?"

I ignored Eddie's question. Not intentionally, really, it was just my brain was too busy trying to figure out what I was going to do in the next three seconds. Because up ahead, gusting toward us furiously, was a nearly solid wall of white. Snow. Snow coming down thick and fast. So thick and so fast that all I could do was hold tight and pray that we'd make it through.

The snow hit the windshield and we were instantly inside the whitest whiteout I'd ever endured. All the other whiteouts I'd driven through and thought were the worst had nothing on this.

"Oh, geez," I heard myself murmuring again.

"Oh, geez, oh, geez." I also heard a low growl that must have been coming from Eddie, but either the snow and wind were transforming his sounds, or he was making a noise I'd never heard.

"We'll be okay," I said, almost shouting to make sure he could hear me over the noise of the snow and wind and road. "All we have to do is get through the next few miles." I wasn't exactly sure where we were, but my guess was we were halfway between Rob/Buster's place and a highway that was bound to be in better condition than Lolly Road.

"Sure to be," I murmured. "Has to be." Because if it wasn't, we might spend the rest of the winter out here, encased in a snowbank, waiting for the spring thaw.

"Rrrrrr," Eddie said, his growl growing louder.

"Doing all I can, pal." I peered through the windshield and saw what I'd been seeing—white. "We're still on the road. Down on the right, there, I can see the edge of the asphalt." Not the actual asphalt, since everything was covered in snow, but I could make out the change in elevation from roadway to ditch. As long as I could keep that in sight, we'd be fine. At least that was my plan.

"Rrrrr!"

Once again, I ignored my cat. "You know, I used to complain about not having a white line on the edge of these roads, like on highways, but maybe it's better on these roads. What good would it do, really, and—"

"RRR!!" Eddie's growl turned into a spitting hiss, sounding like he was in a fight for his life.

"Chill, buddy," I said. "We're okay. Honest. We just have to—what in the—"

Out of nowhere, an SUV had appeared, pulling up alongside the bookmobile.

Seriously? Someone was trying to *pass* in these conditions?

I shook my head and inched the bookmobile as far to the right as I dared, but the SUV didn't go around. Instead, it moved closer.

"You have got to be kidding." Trying to give the driver the benefit of the doubt—maybe it was a guy with a wife in labor and he was trying to rush her to the hospital but she was terrified of passing the bookmobile in the snow so he was trying to get more space to go around—I steered us a teensy bit farther right and instantly felt the tires ride over the outside edge of the asphalt.

The SUV moved closer.

I did about the last thing I wanted to do—took one hand off the steering wheel. I jammed the heel of my hand into the middle of the steering column and laid on the horn.

It did no good; the SUV moved even closer, its headlights merging with ours. If it moved any closer, it would hit us and there was nowhere to go. Except . . .

I took my foot off the accelerator and started a gentle brake. Let him go around if he wanted to drive that much faster. Eddie and I weren't in a hurry. Getting back safely was far more important than getting back on time.

But the SUV slowed, too.

And moved closer.

Frightened that it was going to hit us and furious at the driver's stupidity, I did an equally stupid thing. I slammed on the brakes.

This, of course, violated a vitally important rule of winter driving, which is: *Never, ever slam on your brakes*. If you're on an icy road, all it's likely to do is put your vehicle into a slide in a direction over which you have no control.

Which was exactly what happened.

It was a long, slow slide and I had plenty of time to review all the mistakes I'd made, not only that day, but throughout my life, starting with the time I'd cut my own hair at age four and ending with not checking the weather forecast before driving out to Rob/Buster's.

"Hang on, Eddie!" I called, because there was nothing else to do. I felt a bump, and the bookmobile slid off the road, onto the narrow shoulder, and thumped into the ditch.

Hundreds of books, CDs, and DVDs tumbled to the floor, Eddie howled, I yelled, and a thousand years later we came to a stop.

I unbuckled my seat belt and scrambled over

the tilting console. The strap holding down the cat carrier had done its job; the carrier was still in place and Eddie looked up at me, unblinking.

"Are you okay?" I opened the wire door. "Please tell me you're okay."

Eddie leapt out of the carrier and onto the console, purring and rubbing his chin against my shoulder.

"Thank heavens," I said, snuggling him close. "I never would have forgiven myself if anything had happened to you."

"Mrr," he said, still rubbing.

I kissed the top of his head and looked out the windows to see what I could see. "Uh-oh." Though I was mostly seeing the white of blowing and gusting snow, I could also make out the headlights of the SUV that had run us off the road. One of the bumps we'd felt while sliding must have been it hitting the bookmobile's bumper. It had spun around and was in the opposite ditch. Facing us. With a broken windshield.

My hand automatically reached for my cell phone. It usually lived on the console, but the Ditch Episode had moved it elsewhere. I scrabbled around on the floor, found it on the far side of Eddie's carrier, and turned it on.

There was, of course, no service. At all. I'd figured as much, but I'd had to try.

"First things first," I said. "Yes, it's best to stay with your vehicle in a situation like this—

because it's way easier to find a bookmobile in a snowstorm than it is finding an efficiently sized human like me—but I have to go see if that driver is okay."

"Mrr?"

"Well, no, I don't particularly want to," I said, pulling my hat down and tugging on my mittens, "but it's the right thing to do. I'll be back in a minute."

At least I hoped I would. If the driver was hurt, I'd do what I could to help, but if he or she was hurt badly, I'd have to run back to Rob's place. And if he was gone, because his house could be in the opposite direction, I'd break in and use his landline to call for help. Then again, it might be Rob over there in the ditch. He had been in a hurry to leave, hadn't he?

I walked a zigzag path around the fallen library materials, and opened the door. This was harder than normal, because the floor was tilted at a ditch-defined angle and I had to push the door open over a snowbank. My brain was doing another type of pushing, that of pushing away thoughts about damage to the poor bookmobile. I would think about that later.

Outside, away from the headlights, I realized how dark it had become. And how much the temperature had dropped. And how hard the snow was coming down. And how hard the wind was blowing.

I shivered and sincerely hoped I wouldn't have to run to Rob's. "Hello?" I called as I walked across the road. The SUV had stopped at a steeper angle than the bookmobile, and even from the road, I could see that the passenger-side fender was a crumpled mess.

"Hello?" I approached the driver's door. "Um, are you okay?" I peered in through the tinted window. The front seats were filled with released air bags . . . and nothing else.

No one else.

What on earth had happened to the driver?

I frowned and looked down, hoping to see tracks I could follow. Maybe he or she had been dazed by the crash and wandered off into the snow. I couldn't let that happen. Without shelter, in this weather you wouldn't last overnight, maybe not even a few hours, depending on how you were dressed.

The tracks were there, but they were already filling with snow. I followed them, head down, to the back of the SUV, around the back bumper, and—

"There you are," said Stewart Funston. "Took you long enough."

"Stewart! What are you doing out here? You were driving that SUV? What were you thinking? But you're okay, right? Eddie and I are shaken up, but we're fine, and—"

My slightly anxious babble came to an abrupt

stop when Stewart stepped closer. By the red of his taillights, I could see he was holding up his right hand in an oddly familiar position.

He was pointing a handgun at me.

Since I was Minnie and didn't always think before I spoke, I said the first thing that came into my head. "You're kidding, right?" Because maybe he had one of those weird brain tumors that was making him act out of character. Or maybe he'd banged his head when his SUV had spun into the ditch and thought I was an enemy.

"I've been watching you," Stewart said, his voice sounding just like it had when we were chatting in the library about books. "Ever since you asked about that damage to the principal's office, I've been watching you."

"You . . . have?" I goggled at him. Not once had I noticed anything unusual. Either I was the worst ever for paying attention to what was going on around me, or Stewart had amazing stealth powers.

"Mostly by proxy," he said. "Chilson is a small town and it's easy to find things out if you ask the right people the right questions."

I desperately wanted to know who'd been blabbing, but it could have been anyone. It could even have been me. I'd been resisting the idea of Stewart as Rowan's killer, so I'd been cutting him slack all along. During one of our casual talks, could I have given him information he'd been slyly trying to obtain? Yup. No question about it.

"Everybody in town knows you've been helping Inwood and Wolverson with the murder investigation," he said, shifting his grip on the gun.

I knew from my self-defense classes that handguns were heavier than they looked and it took a lot of strength to hold them up for any length of time, especially with one hand. Though there was a possibility I could take advantage of that, the possibility was too slim. He was at least six feet away and the odds were far better that, if he were to pause to readjust his grip, he'd see me coming and simply whack me upside the head with the gun, no shooting needed.

"Oh?" I asked vaguely, trying desperately to form a plan, but not getting any further than . . . well, not getting anywhere, really. "Does everyone know *who* we were investigating?"

"No, but I do."

He sounded proud of himself, and I realized he was one of those people who thought he was smarter than everyone else, which always carried with it an accompanying truth: that he must be an incredibly boring dinner companion.

Stewart didn't wait for a response—another indication of an overly healthy ego—but continued on. "It was easy for me to see," he said comfortably. "All that time you spent at that restaurant the Scoles kid opened up, when you'd never gone there before? Oh, don't worry, I haven't been following you very long. But it's easy to ask someone questions when you're the only one in their otherwise very empty restaurant."

So Sunny had blabbed. No surprise there. I probably would have done the same thing if I'd been stuck by myself for hours on end.

"And Hugh Novak," Stewart said. "Almost too obvious, with that property he owns, and the fuss Rowan was putting up to a new township hall. I almost suspected him myself, and I'm the one who killed her." Stewart laughed. "Talk about bullies. He's a classic, isn't he?"

How was it I'd never noticed Stewart's self-absorption? Had his support of the bookmobile been enough for me to forgive deep personality flaws? I hoped not, but what other explanation was there? Well, maybe that he'd been able to hide his true self until he'd committed murder, and that had opened his personal Pandora's box. Something to talk over with an experienced psychologist, next time I ran into one.

"Anyone else?" I asked, inching away oh-so-slowly. It was so dark, maybe I could run off into the night and make it to Buster's before Stewart found me.

"What I don't understand is why you suspected Mitchell Koyne. He didn't even know Rowan."

No, Stewart wasn't nearly as smart as he

thought he was. And if there was a way I could use that to my advantage, I would. If only I could think of a way to do that.

"For a while it looked like you suspected Bax Tousely," Stewart mused. "But that's ridiculous. The kid can hardly kill a fly, let alone a human being. Tousely's about the least likely person in the world to kill the woman he keeps hoping will be his mother-in-law."

Interesting. So he'd missed my suspicions of Land and Neil. Not very useful, but interesting.

Stewart stepped forward, closing the gap between us to an arm's length and eliminating any possibility of my escape.

I risked a quick glance over my shoulder. The bookmobile looked stable enough, in a tilted fashion, but it was going to take a great big tow truck to get it out of the ditch. Squinting into the dark, I could just make out the fuzzy shape of my cat, who had tucked himself into the corner of the dashboard and was plastering his furry face against the inside of the windshield. Eddie . . . Stewart started talking again and I faced him with my chin up.

"It was only a matter of time," he said, "before you started pointing your stubby little finger at me. And I can't have that, so it's time for you to have an accident. Sorry," he said, not sounding the least bit apologetic, "but there's no alternative."

My first reaction was to shout that my fingers were not stubby. They were perfectly proportional to my compact frame, and if he couldn't see that, he needed to pay more attention.

That thought faded as I realized something about Stewart's basic nature. He punished people he felt had wronged him. Divorced his wife, who'd done little more than save money. Destroyed the office of his high school principal for kicking him off the football team. Was trying to kill me for finding out about Rowan. And had killed Rowan because . . . because why?

I looked past the gun because I couldn't stand to look at it any longer, and past Stewart's face, because I certainly didn't want to see his expression, and fastened my gaze on his hat.

And then I suddenly knew why he'd killed Rowan. Or at least had a good idea.

"Rowan had something you wanted," I said. "A family heirloom. You couldn't take it before your divorce, because then you would have had to split its value with your wife. And you had to kill Rowan because . . . because she was the only one who knew what it was worth."

Stewart shook his head. "You have it all wrong."

Well, I'd been wrong before. And I'd undoubtedly be wrong again, if I lived through this.

"She never should have had it," he said. "I only

took what was mine by right." His voice grew increasingly dark and threatening. "And if you hadn't come along, no one would have known the difference."

I had no clue what he was talking about, but at this point that didn't seem particularly relevant, because the direness of my situation was finally sinking into my tiny little brain. Until now, I'd been half convinced that if I could keep Stewart talking long enough, he'd back off with the threats, maybe even laugh about being in a bad mood, and we'd go our separate ways. That merry little scenario, however, was looking less and less likely.

It was time for me to make a move. Unfortunately, I had no idea what that should be.

"You talked about an accident." I was pleased that my voice was relatively clear and almost free of wobbly fear. "What kind? Because if you're planning an accident with a gun, that'll never work. Everybody knows I don't own one."

"Everybody? That's one of the worst things about you millennials." Stewart snorted. "You exaggerate all the time."

It seemed to me that what he'd just said was itself an exaggeration, but I managed to keep my mouth shut.

"But no, there won't be a gun accident," he said. "Well, not unless there's an accident." He laughed. Actually laughed out loud. I did not.

"What I have planned for you is far more realistic, with the benefit of being seasonal."

I glanced around at the blowing snow. Which suddenly felt even colder. A shiver roiled up my back, and I had to grit my teeth to keep them from chattering. "Stewart, let's talk about this," I said as pleasantly as I could. "You don't want to kill me, I'm sure you don't. Surely the two of us can find a compromise."

"Not possible," Stewart said flatly. "You're never going to keep quiet that I killed Rowan. And if I run, where am I going to go? What am I going to do? Anyway, I'm not about to leave everything I've worked for. It's bad enough giving half of it to my ex-wife." He half smiled. "Well, not quite half of it. But since you're the only one who knows, that doesn't count."

I had no idea what he was talking about, but I was far happier with him talking than with him threatening me, so I said, "You're a smart guy. I bet with a little head start you could get some money together, get a fake identity, and make a new life somewhere. There will be details to work out, but—"

"Take your hat off," he said suddenly.

"Um." I reached up and touched my nice warm hat. "It's maybe twenty degrees out here, and getting even colder. Plus the windchill is—"

Stewart reached out and roughly yanked the hat from my head. "Take off your mittens."

Real fear coursed through me. "Stewart, please . . ."

"Off," he said, and even in the dim light cast by the bookmobile headlights, I could see the emotionless expression on his face. "Your coat, too."

Without a word, I shed all of my outer gear and in seconds started shivering. I stood there, hugging my arms to my chest in a pointless attempt to keep my body warmth where it should be. In my body.

He gestured at my feet. "Boots."

"Stewart . . ."

"Boots!" he roared, pointing the gun at my chest.

Quickly, I toed them off and put my stocking feet, one by one, into the accumulating snow.

"Now walk," he ordered. "Not on the road. Into that swamp over there and no turning back." He sounded way too satisfied with himself. "In this cold, dressed like that, you'll lose all feeling in your fingers and toes in five minutes. Fifteen minutes and you won't feel your arms and legs. Twenty minutes from now you'll stumble and fall to the ground and never get up." He smiled. "Half an hour from now I'll be safe, so get going. There's a hockey game tonight I don't want to miss."

I stared at him. He was sending me to my death, but what mattered most was hockey? The man was a lunatic. But he was a lunatic with a gun.

He loomed over me. "Get. Going," he commanded, then reached out and pushed at my shoulder. I staggered, back across the road, and in front of the bookmobile that I longed to retreat into, but with Stewart and his gun so close, it wouldn't be anywhere near safe, even if I could manage to get in the door.

Truly the last thing in the world I wanted to do was walk into that flat and frozen swamp, dark and thick with cedar trees. I glanced up at the bookmobile as I passed and saw Eddie's face peering down at me.

Eddie, I'm so sorry.

I waded through the deep snow in the ditch, looking back only once.

"Keep going," Stewart said, waving the gun around. "Twenty minutes from now you won't feel a thing."

I turned back around and faced the forest. Every step I took, the sound of the wind increased. Snow pelted my face. I was so cold I could hardly breathe.

The last thing I heard before the sounds of the storm closed around me were the plaintive howls of my cat.

Chapter 19

Snow and darkness swirled around me. Every step I took felt like a journey of a thousand miles. Every step took me farther away from the road, from the bookmobile, from Eddie.

I made my way through the drifted thigh-high snow and clambered up the far side of the ditch. There, I paused to catch my breath. "Get moving," Stewart's voice called through the wind. A sharp gunshot rang out. I ducked. Which wouldn't have helped me escape a bullet, of course, but you can't help your instincts.

"Next time I'll be aiming for you," Stewart shouted. "Keep going."

"Jerk," I muttered. And kept going.

The sun was long gone, but the moon must have been rising somewhere, because even through the snow, I could detect the vague shape of the line of cedar trees. When we'd been driving past at forty miles an hour, the thicket of cedar trees had seemed to be an impenetrable wall of green. Now that I was up close and personal, even in the almost-dark I could see that wasn't quite the case. There were gaps and holes where bigger trees gave way to baby trees. I slid in through a gap and immediately learned two things. One, the snow wasn't nearly as deep inside the cedar forest, and two, and an even better thing, the wind barely penetrated.

Not that I was going to do a jig about my situation. I had no hat, no mittens, no coat, and no boots, and I was stranded in the middle of nowhere during a blizzard. But I was youngish and healthy and at least Stewart had only taken all my outerwear. If he'd taken all my clothes, I'd be truly desperate instead of just desperate.

"Right," I said out loud. It was time to make a plan. And it needed to be a good one.

I risked a glance over my shoulder. If I couldn't see Stewart, there was no way he could see me, especially since my eyes were now adjusted to the dark and he was trying to see through the bookmobile's headlights. I could make out everything in front of me, which at this point was exclusively snow-laden cedar trees and the occasional vine.

Ignoring the very real possibility that I'd been walking through a thicket of poison ivy, I hugged myself tight, holding in as much body warmth as I could, and through my shivers, tried to think.

What was the biggest problem? That I was cold and rapidly getting colder. I wasn't sure Stewart had his facts right about how quickly I'd succumb, but he probably wasn't far off. We were five miles from anything and I wasn't at all certain I'd be able to walk that kind of distance.

The only solution? Get back to the vehicles and, once there, figure a way out of this mess.

What was the problem with that solution? Stewart was standing there, waiting for me to come back. What had he said, in half an hour he'd be safe? All I had to do was wait for thirty minutes.

"Rats," I said out loud. For the first time in my life, I regretted not wearing a watch. My cell phone was back in my coat pocket and I had no way to tell time. How long was half an hour? If you were reading a wonderful book, it went by in a flash. If you were standing in line to get your driver's license renewed, it was forever.

How long had I been standing in the cedar trees already? I had no idea. Five minutes? Probably not even that.

I counted out the seconds the way my dad had taught me to count the time between flashes of lightning and thunder—one, one thousand; two, one thousand—but that was so boring I stopped at thirty.

"Be conservative," I said out loud. At the sound of my own voice, I hunched down, making myself a smaller target, I suppose, for a bullet from Stewart's gun. But that was silly since the storm was so loud I'd barely heard my own footsteps. Then again, with stocking feet, maybe my footsteps were somehow noisier in the snow than booted feet and—

"Stop that," I muttered.

Now wasn't the time to worry about what I couldn't change. Well, technically, I shouldn't ever worry about that kind of thing, but now was what mattered. I needed to summon everything I could remember about cold weather survival from every book I'd ever read and from every person who'd ever mentioned a trick about staying warm during ice fishing.

Rafe . . .

Through chattering teeth, I said, "Stop that," a second time. I needed to focus. If I was going to get out of this, I needed to be more than smart; I needed to be . . . savvy. Not a term that typically applied to me—and never had, I was pretty sure—but if there was a time to marshal my inner resources, it was now.

I nodded to myself. Good. Inner pep talks were an excellent idea. Next I needed to capitalize on that, and to stop wondering if the cold was already impacting my brain because a word like "capitalize" was running through my head when on the edge of survival.

I had library and information science degrees, not business, though none of those would be any use in this particular situation. What I should have majored in was outdoor recreation. Or maybe I should have joined the military. Then again, if

I'd done either of those things, I wouldn't be out here in the cold in the first place.

And I was cold. So very, very cold.

How long had it been? It seemed like forever that I'd been standing here, doing nothing but thinking in circles, but how long had it been really? Ten minutes? Could it have been fifteen? Probably not.

I shoved my hands into the pockets of my sweater . . . and found a pair of gloves. Glory hallelujah, the last time I'd worn this sweater had been during the mild thaw and I'd done the books-to-library hauling without my outer coat. A huge smile spread over my face. Sure, they were thin gloves and might not do much good, but they were far better than nothing.

It took a minute to fumble the gloves onto my hands. Once they were on, though, confidence surged through me. I could do this. I would do this. Stewart not-so-fun Funston wouldn't be the cause of my death. He would not get off scot-free for killing Rowan. He would not win.

I stomped my feet, left, right, left, right, trying to keep the blood flowing, trying to keep frostbite out of my toes, because I liked wearing summer sandals, and if my toes fell off, none of my sandals would fit for beans.

"Okay," I said. "It's time to get going."

All the books I'd read about surviving in the wilderness noted how easy it was to get lost, wandering about in circles for hours without a clue where you'd really been going.

That wasn't going to happen to me, mainly because I knew that a river curved around to the east, north, and south, and the road was behind me to the west. Then again, I might freeze to death before I got anywhere.

With that not-so-comforting thought, I started walking, one foot in front of the other.

Time and distance. I didn't want to walk far, but for at least the next fifteen minutes, I needed to keep moving or I'd turn into a Minnie-cicle. Assuming my back was to the road, if I turned to the right ninety degrees, I'd be walking parallel to the road, heading back toward Buster's and the closest likely human contact.

"Keep going," I said, mimicking Stewart's voice.

Stewart. The muscles in my jaw bunched at the thought of him. He had a lot to answer for, and it was up to me to make sure that happened.

"Just go," I told myself, and went, counting steps and using my fingers as an abacus of sorts. Every step used up roughly a second. Ten steps and I extended one finger. Another ten steps and I extended a second finger. Six fingers out and I'd walked for one minute. How far? Sixty feet maybe, since I was tramping through snow and stepping over branches and downed trees.

So not very far and not for very long.

I took a deep breath, coughed as the cold seared my lungs, and walked for sixty feet. Did it again. And again.

When I'd reached ten minutes—with my right hand now full of the twigs I'd picked up to track the time since I'd run out of fingers—I started veering back toward the road.

Or where I thought the road was. Fifty steps later I wasn't so sure. Another fifty and I was sure I was completely lost and doomed to die a frozen death. Then, through the trees and their wind-whipped tops, came the most beautiful noise I'd ever heard, faint yet indubitably distinct.

"Mrr!"

I shifted direction immediately, turning a bit to the right, and twenty paces later I could see, ahead and high up, a lightening in the darkness. The road, a wide swatch cut out of the cedar forest, lay directly ahead of me.

"Thanks, Eddie," I whispered.

As I edged out of the tree line, I heard another unexpected noise—the bookmobile's engine starting up.

"No, no, no . . ." I hopped into a run.

Stewart was trying to get the bookmobile out of the ditch. He wanted to drive it somewhere else to throw the suspicion in another direction. But Eddie was in there. Alone with Stewart.

I couldn't let it happen, couldn't let anything happen to my cat, my fuzzy friend, my pal.

Panting, I hurtled through the blizzard, running toward the man who'd just tried to kill me, running toward the cat who'd saved me in so many ways. "Eddie . . ." I gasped out. "Hang on, bud, I'll get you. Just hang on."

Large taillights appeared through the snowy murk, rocking back and forth, back and forth.

Perfect.

I slowed and, with an eye on the bookmobile, jogged over to Stewart's SUV. He'd slid it into the ditch, but it wasn't in all that deep, and I bet he'd left his keys in the ignition. With his four-wheel drive, I'd be out of there in no time. Less than ten minutes of frantic driving and I'd be at Buster's, where I'd break in if I had to and use his phone to summon help. Ten minutes from that point and help would arrive. Twenty minutes and Eddie would be safe. Twenty minutes were all I needed.

It was an excellent plan and I was almost smiling as I reached the SUV and took hold of the door handle.

"No . . ." I whispered, staring. "He didn't. He couldn't have."

But he had. The SUV's door was locked.

Bad words circulated in my head as I frantically tried the other doors. Rear driver's side door, back door, both passenger side doors—all locked. What kind of person locked his vehicle before setting off to commit murder? Who did that?

I thumped the heel of my hand against the front passenger door, the door most hidden from the bookmobile—I didn't want the gun-holding Stewart to have any inkling where I was—hoping against hope that the thing was just frozen shut, not locked, but it didn't budge.

More bad words trickled into my brain. But saying them out loud wouldn't help anything, so I let them go and tried to think. Was there another way in? Maybe I could smash a window . . . I knelt on the snow and scrabbled around for a rock.

The third time I grabbed an icy chunk of snow, I gave up. There were rocks down there, but I didn't have time—Eddie didn't have time—for me to find something suitable. Besides, if he'd locked his vehicle, he'd probably taken the keys. There had to be a different way. And if there wasn't a different way, I had to make one.

A shiver roiled through me, from bottom to top, a shiver so strong that I almost fell to my knees. I'd been doing my best to ignore my shivering body, but I wouldn't be able to do so much longer. Maybe Stewart had been closer than I'd thought with his half-hour estimate.

The bookmobile's engine revved up and down as Stewart did his best to move it forward and backward. After one look at how deep the tires were ground into the snow, I could have told him it would be no use, but I wasn't about to tell him, and even if I had, he wouldn't have listened to me. He was that kind of guy.

I stood there, on my tiptoes to peer over the top of the SUV, trying to think through the numbness of every body part I owned. With escape in Stewart's vehicle out of the picture, the number of possible options had been cut in half. The only thing left was to sneak aboard the bookmobile, incapacitate Stewart, and figure out some way to summon help.

Piece of cake.

"Keep going," I said, and forced myself to smile at my own inside joke. Not that it was funny, but poking fun at Stewart made me feel a little better, and at this point, that was enough.

I hunched down low enough to be fairly sure the top of my head was out of sight of the bookmobile's side mirror and crab-walked across the road to the bookmobile's rear bumper. If I tried to get in the side door, the door we used ninety-nine percent of the time, odds were good that the motion of opening the door would catch Stewart's attention, which was pretty much the last thing I wanted to do since he was bigger, stronger, and almost certainly still had that gun.

That left the door in the rear of the bookmobile, the door that provided access to the handicapped lift. Most people didn't even know it was there, and I prayed Stewart was one of them.

I reached up with shaking fingers and flipped open the tiny door, revealing the keypad, and also revealing my complete inadequacy as a human being. Because I couldn't remember the code. Couldn't remember the last time I'd used the code. Couldn't remember when I'd last used this entrance. I couldn't remember anything, I was going to freeze to death out here, Eddie was going to freeze and—

"Stop that," I whispered.

And then remembered the four-digit code. It was the day I'd started working at the library, June 14, better known to the keypad as 0614. How could I have forgotten? I tapped out the numbers and waited for the quiet *chunk* of an unlocking door.

Nothing happened.

"Don't do this," I muttered and tapped the numbers again.

Still nothing.

On my third time through, it occurred to me that my fingers were too freaking cold to make the thing work. It seemed like I was pushing hard enough, but I'd lost most of the feeling in my fingers long ago and it was hard to tell. I considered and discarded the idea that the cold was a problem for the mechanism, because I had no way around that. But if it was just me . . .

Still hunched down, I inched backward into the dark. When I was convinced that Stewart wouldn't be able to catch my movements through any of the mirrors, I skittered across the ditch and into the cedar trees, where fallen branches were strewn across the snow.

I picked up a stick that was a half inch in diameter, stepped on it to break off a foot-long length, and hurried back to the bookmobile. With one end of the stick positioned against my shoulder, I aimed the other end at the keypad and pushed 0.

A glorious beep filled my ears. This was going to work; it was really going to work! Grinning, I punched the rest of the code and heard the sweet sound of the lock unsnicking. "I'm coming, Eddie," I breathed softly. "Just hang on."

My fingers still weren't working for beans, so I pushed at the door handle with the side of my palm, lifting it up. It clicked open so noisily that I crouched down even smaller.

All I heard was a string of curse words coming from the front, words that sounded a lot like what had gone through my head when I'd found Stewart's SUV locked. His dealt more with the uselessness of snow tires and the weight of books, but the gist was the same.

He shifted the transmission back and forth, back and forth, but there was nothing for the tires to grip except icy snow, a substance notorious for being gripless.

I slowly cracked open the back door, waited

until he was in the middle of a shift, and slithered inside, or with as close to a slither as I could do being nowhere near the skinniness of a snake and half frozen to boot.

The mechanism of the wheelchair lift provided some visual shelter from Stewart's view, but as soon as all of me was on board, I clicked the door shut and scurried behind the rear desk. For a moment I hunched back there, panting as quietly as I could while a semblance of warmth crept back into my limbs. It wasn't exactly toasty back there, but at least it was out of the wind. I tried to flex my hands and was cheered to see my fingers obey my mental command by moving all of an inch.

Excellent. Though it would take more time for my fingers and toes to warm up than I had to spare, at least I had some control.

"Mrr?"

I heard the double thump of Eddie's feet as he jumped up onto the desk and looked up to see him looking down at me. With an index finger that I couldn't completely straighten, I made the universal *Shhh!* gesture. Of course, since I was making it to a cat, there was a large chance the gesture wasn't nearly as universal as I'd like, but there wasn't much else I could do.

"Mrr," Eddie said softly.

We'll get out of this, I promised him silently. *Don't know how exactly, but we'll be fine.*

Up front, Stewart was still focused on shifting back and forth. I tried not to think about the damage he could be doing to the transmission and unhooked the bungee cord that held the desk chair in place. The warmer I got, the more my brain was starting to work. If I was lucky, soon I'd be able to do simple addition. And since that was the only kind of addition at which I was competent, that would clearly mean my mental ability was at full capacity.

Two plus two is four, I thought to myself. *Four plus four is eight.* A plan was starting to gel, but what if it was a horrible plan conjured up by a panicking librarian? If I waited a little longer, would I come up with a better plan?

Eddie oozed down to the floor. His mouth opened in a silent "Mrr" as he whacked my ankle with the side of his head.

I let my hand rest on his back for a short moment, thinking how sorry I was to have gotten him into this mess, but at the same time I was grateful for his presence. His warmth seeped into my palm, and my fingers started to tingle with what would be a painful coming-back-to-life process.

But there was no time to think about that. At some point Stewart would abandon his pointless efforts, and when he turned, he would see me. I had to make my move and I had to make it now.

Taking a deep breath, I rolled the chair in front of me and, on my knees, started the long journey forward.

Since Stewart was taller than I was, I couldn't be sure what he could see in the rearview mirror. Would he see more floor or more ceiling? If it was ceiling, I was fine. If it was floor . . . well, if he glanced up, it would take him a moment to register why the chair was there and why it was moving, and I'd have to take advantage of that pause.

I tried to work out the mirror angles in my head but didn't like the conclusion, so I stopped thinking about it.

Inch by slow inch, I moved ahead, around all the fallen items, past the children's books and puppets, past the magazines and DVDs, past the young adult books, and into the nonfiction and adult fiction. The plastic runner we put down on the carpet in winter was blessedly quiet under my knees and I moved as fast as I could.

Questions kept popping into my head, questions for which I desperately wanted answers but had no way of getting:

Where was the gun?

What was Eddie doing?

How long was Stewart going to keep trying to rock the bookmobile?

What would he do next?

And back to, *Where was the gun?*

The bookmobile lurched backward. "Hah!" Stewart shouted. "I knew I'd get it!"

My mouth went dry. This was not part of the plan. The plan could not be carried out if the bookmobile was moving. If that happened, I'd have to come up with another idea and this one was already on the outside edge of possible. What could—

There was another lurch. The bookmobile rolled back to where it had been and settled in for a long winter's nap.

Stewart cursed a long colorful streak, then growled out, "If I did it once, I can do it again," and dropped the transmission into Drive.

It was now or never.

I shoved the chair away from me, spinning the seat so that it would make as much noise as possible. I was still on my knees, trying to stay out of his line of sight. This was the first tricky part. I needed a few seconds, just a few seconds was all, but wasn't sure I'd get them. If Stewart kept turning around, he'd see me. If he had the gun handy, it was all over. If, if, if . . .

Stewart's head snapped around. "What the—" His gaze fastened on the chair. It zoomed toward the passenger's seat, thumped against it, and toppled to the floor.

I was already moving, but Eddie was faster.

"MRR!!" He jumped on top of the passenger's

seat headrest and faced Stewart. "MRR!!" He spat and hissed and growled.

"Shut up," Stewart said. "Why do people have cats anyway? Dogs are the only pets people should have. Cats are useless, all they do is— *urk!!*"

I tightened the bungee cord I'd slid around his neck. "Oh, I don't know about that," I said breathlessly, hauling hard. "I'd say he was quite useful in distracting you while I snuck up from behind."

"You . . . can't . . . do . . . this," Stewart gasped.

"Pretty sure you're wrong about that. Oh, look, your face is turning a lovely shade of red. Do you think it'll turn blue soon? How about I take your gun and then I'll think about not choking you to death."

"It's . . . in the . . . SUV."

I *tsk*'d at him. "Try again," I said, pulling a teensy bit harder, which made me feel queasy.

"Pocket," he said in a . . . well, in a choked voice. "Right pocket."

I put both ends of the bungee cord in one hand and reached for the gun with the other. "Oh, my favorite, a Beretta. Is that the PX4 Compact? How handy that you have the same kind of gun I always use on the gun range. Now we'll—"

Stewart jabbed out with his elbow and knocked the gun out of my hand.

I dropped the bungee cord and lunged for the

gun. Stewart was doing the same thing, but I was ahead of him, reaching. He grabbed my ankle and hauled me backward. "No little girl is going to get the best of me," he snarled, and elbowed me in the ribs so hard that I cried out in pain.

"*MRR!!!*"

"*Oww!* Get off me, cat!!"

Stewart's grip on my ankle released and I scrabbled the last few feet for the gun. When I had it in my hands, I kept moving away from Stewart, farther out of his reach, but I needn't have gone to the effort, because when I turned around, Stewart was still wiping the blood out of his eyes, proof that Mom was right when she'd told me that scalp wounds bleed a lot.

Eddie, for his part, was already sitting on the console licking his front paws.

"Here." I tossed Stewart the roll of fishing line I'd picked up from the floor, very pleased that we'd started lending ice fishing equipment that winter. "Tie your ankles together."

"I will not." He rubbed his sleeve over his face and started to get to his feet. "Because you're not going to use that gun. Even if you know how to use it, you wouldn't be able to shoot a human being. The pain you'd inflict? The mess you'd make?" He shook his head. "Just don't see it happening."

The gun's barrel wavered as I thought about it. Maybe he was right. But then I thought about what he'd done to Rowan. What he'd done to Neil and Collier and Anya. What he'd tried to do to me. What he almost certainly would have done to Eddie.

I clicked off the safety and pointed the gun at his chest. "Are you willing to take that chance?" My voice was calm. Measured. Confident. "Sit down and tie your ankles."

For the merest fraction of a second, he hesitated. And then he did what I'd told him to do.

Ten minutes later, I'd bound his hands together, taken his phone and car keys out of his coat pockets, and was starting his SUV with Eddie at my side. It didn't take much to get out of the ditch and then we were up and away.

At the top of the next hill, I called 911 and did my best to tell them where I was and what had happened. As soon as the dispatcher said deputies were on their way, I thanked her and said I needed to call someone else.

"Please stay on the line, ma'am," she said. "I'd like to make sure you're okay until the deputies arrive."

"Thanks, but I have to go." I ended the call, started the next, and reached out to pet Eddie, his purrs filling my ears and heart.

"Minnie?" Rafe asked. "Where are you? I thought we were meeting at six. Are you okay?"

"I'm fine," I said. "We're fine." And then, suddenly and unexpectedly, I began to cry.

Chapter 20

My aunt looked at me across the kitchen table, which was practically groaning under the weight of the food she'd piled onto it. Scrambled eggs, bacon, and waffles. Hash browns, sausage, and biscuits. And then there was the sourdough toast and fresh-squeezed orange juice. The four of us sitting at the table hadn't a chance of eating it all, but I was going to do my best to do justice to my aunt's post-traumatic cooking. "So would you have done it?" she asked. "Shot him, I mean?"

The evening before, Rafe, Aunt Frances, and Otto had gathered together in the boardinghouse living room while I'd huddled on the hearth in front of a roaring fire with my hands around a mug of hot chocolate and Eddie on my lap. I'd stayed awake long enough to outline what had happened on Lolly Road, but now it was morning, the same group was gathered, and my aunt wanted details. So, being the kind and generous niece that I was, I did my best to oblige.

"I'm not sure." Anticipating the expression she was about to assemble her face into, I kept going before she wasted all that energy. "If he was going to hurt Eddie, absolutely. If he was going to hurt me . . . probably. But I might have kept wondering if he'd really do it, might have kept thinking about a different way out. So . . . I just don't know."

Just at that moment, the jar of orange marmalade called to me, so I busied myself with toast and knife as the trio exchanged looks.

"You're nuts," my loving aunt said.

I kept slathering on the marmalade. Eddie, who I'd left on my bed, snoring, wandered into the kitchen and flopped on the floor next to me. I angled my foot to touch him and felt his breaths going in and out.

Rafe was next. "You could have," he said confidently. "In some part of that quick-moving brain, you would have figured out there wasn't any other option and done it."

The marmalade was getting thick, but I kept laying it on.

Otto stirred. "There's no point second-guessing. Minnie did an outstanding job in a difficult and frightening situation."

"Mrr!"

"And it goes without saying," Otto continued, almost without a break, "that we're grateful she had Eddie with her yesterday. Without his critical assistance, she might not be here this morning."

"Mrr," Eddie said, apparently mollified.

Aunt Frances handed around a bowl of

scrambled eggs. "But what I don't understand is the why. Why did Stewart kill Rowan?"

Last night I'd been too tired to explain. Had actually fallen asleep while describing how the responding sheriff's deputies had found Stewart, with hands and ankles still bound, hunting for a hidden spare set of bookmobile keys so he could start the engine. He was getting cold, he'd said.

My sympathies had not been with him, and I was very glad that two different law enforcement vehicles had arrived because I would not have been happy to share a backseat with the man who'd tried to kill me.

Once we arrived at the sheriff's office, the story eventually came out. It had taken a while, but the combined questioning of Hal and Ash and Sheriff Richardson, with perhaps a bit of pressure from the glowering presence of myself and Eddie (in his carrier), got results.

"It was a cover-up," I said, forking off a piece of sausage. "He was covering up that he'd stolen something from Rowan."

"You mean something valuable?" Rafe asked.

After chewing and swallowing the yummy maple-flavored sausage, I said, "That's the thing. She didn't know it was worth more than a penny. Only Stewart did."

My aunt sighed. "The cold has addled her brain. We can only hope that someday she'll recover completely."

Rafe pushed a stack of blueberry pancakes in my direction. "Have some carbs. They can't hurt and might help."

Otto smiled and added coffee into my mug. "Tell us more," he said.

I added a pancake to my plate, ladled a generous dollop of maple syrup over it, and told the rest of what I knew.

"When Stewart and Rowan's grandparents died, Rowan, as the oldest grandchild, inherited their grandmother's coin collection, a collection all the cousins had played with as kids."

The trio was nodding, so I went on.

"Collier and his girlfriend got engaged at Thanksgiving, remember? And the big family dinner was at the Bennethums', so there was a lot of talk about family and heirlooms and Rowan remembered the coin collection, which she'd almost forgotten about."

Ash had corroborated this by calling Neil (who hadn't answered) and Anya and Collier (who had). I took in one bite of pancake and another of eggs. "When it came time for dessert, along with the pumpkin and apple pies, Rowan put Grandma's coin collection on the table for everyone to see."

"What kind of collection was it?" Otto asked. "From a certain time period? Civil War? Or gold coins?"

I shook my head and smiled as I picked up a

piece of bacon. "It was the most romantic coin collection ever. Grandpa had given Grandma a brand-new uncirculated coin as an anniversary present for every year they'd been married, starting in 1936."

"What kind of coin?" Aunt Frances asked. "Half-dollars?"

I paused for coffee. "What he gave her were pennies."

"Pennies?" Otto laughed. "Not much of an anniversary present."

"Family lore says it started as a joke and just kind of continued on."

Rafe took my coffee mug and topped it off. "Bet I know how it started. That movie *Pennies from Heaven* came out in 1936."

I blinked. He'd said it with such assurance that I believed him implicitly. It could have been a ruse, but since I'd almost died less than twenty-four hours ago, I didn't think he'd be trying to scam me for at least another day. "How do you know that?"

Looking serious, he tapped his head. "Steel trap. Never forget a thing that's unimportant."

"Good to know," I said, toasting him with my mug. "Anyway, with all the pennies out on the table, there was plenty of opportunity to take a close look at them, and Stewart did."

"That boy was always looking for get-rich-quick schemes," Aunt Frances mused. "A few years after he graduated from college, back in the late nineties, he quit the company he was working for and started one of those dot-com companies. And don't ask me what they were supposed to be doing, because I have no idea."

Otto chuckled. "Exactly. I still find it hard to believe so much money was invested in dot-coms. A classic speculation bubble. We can all be fooled some of the time."

"The pennies," Rafe said, dragging the conversation back to center. "What was with the pennies?"

I held up two fingers. "It wasn't all of them. Just a couple of very special ones."

Aunt Frances cut into her waffle. "How special can pennies be? I've heard of silver dollars worth a couple of hundred dollars, and you see those special offers in magazines for commemorative coins, but I don't remember anything about a penny."

"In Grandma's collection," I said slowly, because I was trying to remember the details and didn't want to get any of it wrong, "were a mint condition 1944 steel wheat penny and a mint 1943 copper Lincoln penny."

I waited a beat because Otto was getting a faraway look on his face. But he didn't say anything and I carried on.

"Together, the two of them are worth more than three hundred thousand dollars."

Coffee spewed across the table as my aunt started choking. Otto patted her on the back until her spasms eased and Rafe got up for paper towels.

I cut and ate my sausage and, when the fuss died down, started talking again.

"That's just the amount of money Stewart needed for the boat he'd been dreaming about for years, the boat his now ex-wife would never let him buy. He thought he could sneak the pennies out of the collection, replace them with garden-variety 1943 and 1944 pennies, and no one would ever know."

"So what happened?" Rafe asked. I'd paused, because the next part was the hardest to tell.

I sighed. "At the family Christmas party, Rowan told Stewart she'd decided to hand over the coin collection to Collier as an engagement present, and that she'd do so when he and his fiancée came up during Martin Luther King, Jr. weekend. Stewart . . ." I stared at my plate.

"That was when," I said quietly, "Stewart realized time was running out. Up until then, he thought he'd have time to find replacement coins. But now that he only had three weeks, he decided it was easier to just kill Rowan. He knew she had heart issues, so he put together a cocktail of medications he'd accumulated, crushed the pills, stopped by her house, and dropped the powder into her coffee, hoping that the stimulants would give her a heart attack." Which it did. "With Rowan dead, Stewart had all sorts of time to replace the pennies since the coin collection was pretty much the last thing on anyone's mind."

There was a long pause, at the end of which Aunt Frances said, "In the back of the shop, there's a stack of cherry that came out of the orchard down the road from the Bennethums' house. What do you think about me making Collier and his fiancée a clock out of it for a wedding present? A grandfather . . . no, a grand-*mother* clock."

"Sounds like a grand idea," Otto said. "Let me know when it's time to sand. That seems to be my forte in the woodworking area."

Rafe nodded. "Great idea. I can take a few days off from the house if you need some help."

I almost couldn't breathe. The sensations rushing through me were a tangled mess. I was sad, but joyful. Unhappy and happy at the same time. Tired, yet energized. But I knew one thing for certain. I was lucky to have these people in my life. So very, very lucky.

My aunt looked at me. "What do you think, Minnie?"

And all I could do was smile.

Otto and Rafe headed out after breakfast, Otto to an appointment with a nonprofit agency that would undoubtedly land him some volunteer work as their bookkeeper, Rafe to the school, because somehow it was Friday and the world was continuing as it normally did.

Aunt Frances told me to sit and drink coffee while she finished the dishes, but I felt an urge to move. Last night, Ash had driven me to the hospital, where they'd pronounced me fit to continue life. Rafe had arrived just as I was checking out, sweeping me into a huge hug that had warmed my heart, but my body racked with the occasional shiver all the way home.

"I'm fine," I'd told the three of them last night as I'd sat close to the fire. My aunt had paid no attention to me, and as soon as I'd told the bare bones of what had happened, she'd shooed me upstairs and tucked me into bed, taking my e-reader out of my hands and putting Eddie on my chest.

This time I wasn't about to let her coddle me, so I ignored what I assumed was a suggestion and started to dry the dishes as she washed.

Aunt Frances rolled her eyes, but didn't actually force me back to the table and put the coffee mug in my hands. "When did Darren say they were going to get out there?" she asked.

Darren was the bookmobile's mechanic and he'd been the first number I'd called after dialing 911 and Rafe. I'd called Darren even before I'd called Aunt Frances, a tiny little fact that she had no reason ever to learn.

I glanced at the wall clock. "The tow truck should be on its way. I'll know after lunch what Darren thinks the damage will be." And then I'd be on the phone with the insurance people. My afternoon would be nothing but fun.

Aunt Frances dropped a handful of silverware into the strainer. "Sometimes I wonder if I should have gone into the car repair business instead of woodworking." She grinned. "But then I remember I can't stand the feel of grease under my fingernails."

Before I could acknowledge that could be an occupational difficulty, she said, "Forgot to tell you. Celeste must have read about your bookmobile escapade on Facebook. She sent me an e-mail this morning and her exact words—her only words—were, 'Tell Minnie to keep her feet warm.'"

I smiled and wiggled my toasty-warm toes. Cousin Celeste understood priorities. It was entirely possible we'd get along just fine.

My phone, sitting in the middle of the table, dinged with an incoming text. I wandered over to look. It was from Trock: *Had my scout look at Red House Café, like you said. Will fit in perfect for a spring episode since we need a replacement restaurant for one that closed. (Off to buy a tux for the wedding. Always wanted one, couldn't justify until now. Life is good.)*

I texted him a quick thanks with lots of

exclamation points, and hummed a happy tune. It was good to have friends, and every once in a while it was great to have a friend who was the star of a popular television restaurant show.

Aunt Frances, still washing, said, "Forgot to tell you. Yesterday I met up with Land Aprelle."

My ears perked up. "You did? How did that go?"

"Seems odd he's only a year younger than I am," she said. "But age is a funny thing. Anyway, I did what you suggested, stopped at his house and didn't go away until he showed me some of his pieces."

I waited, but she didn't say anything. She'd fallen into a fast and sudden silence, and it was clear from the way she was missing half the soapsuds as she plied the spray nozzle that her mind wasn't on what she was doing.

"And?" I prompted. "What did you think of Land's work?"

"What?" She blinked out of her trance. "Oh. It's outstanding. Truly amazing stuff. I'm still trying to figure out how he did the interior hinge work on that box. He said he didn't use a biscuit joiner or a hand chisel, so how on earth . . ."

She went quiet again, but before she went to a mental dimension where I couldn't follow, I asked, "The big summer art show. Is his stuff good enough?"

My aunt gave a very unladylike snort. "Are

you kidding me? He'll be the star of the show and I'm going to make sure he prices his pieces right. He has a dining table inlaid with the state of Michigan, showing inland lakes, for crying out loud, that he had priced for a few hundred dollars. He's an idiot if he doesn't sell that one for thousands."

Smiling, I dried and put things away as she talked. After last night, hearing some good news was soothing. "You're still my favorite woodworker," I said. "Especially since you're making that wedding present for Collier."

"Ah, he's a decent kid," she said. "By the way, I hear Anya and Bax Tousely are talking again."

"Really? Where did you hear that?" Social media wasn't her thing.

"I have my sources," she said airily. She glanced at me and relented. "Emily Tousely, one of my students, is Bax's younger sister. Before class started, I heard her chatting with a friend. She was all excited that her brother was talking to Anya again. He'd been worrying about it for days, trying to get up the courage to call, and he finally did."

Then that day at Lakeview, the look on his face probably hadn't been sadness or guilt, but anxiety. So much for my powers of observation.

But at least a few things were starting to right themselves for the Bennethums. Rowan's killer was behind bars, which should help Collier come to grips with his mother's death; Anya and Bax might get back together; and the mystery of Neil's absence had also resolved itself.

Last night at the sheriff's office, just as I was getting ready to leave, he'd returned Ash's call and apologized for his recent noncommunication, saying that he wasn't dealing well with Rowan's death and had checked into a personal retreat center, and one of the conditions of staying there was to leave all electronics behind. He'd told Anya and Collier where he was going, but being one of those guys who felt therapy wasn't manly, he'd asked them to keep quiet about it.

I almost felt guilty about briefly suspecting him of his wife's murder, but not quite, since I still thought he'd let down his children by leaving when they needed him most.

"Speaking of weddings," I said, "we should talk about yours."

My aunt scrunched up her face. "Do we have to? Because I'd really rather not."

"Yes, because I have the answers to all your problems."

"How nice," Aunt Frances muttered. "I can hardly wait."

"Oh, ye of little faith," I said, and I was probably smirking a bit, because I really did have all the answers. They'd come to me as I was tromping about in the cedar forest, fully formed solutions to problems that, compared to freezing to death while running from a guy with a gun, were easily solved.

"Problem number one," I said, "is the wedding and honeymoon venue. You wanted it to be in Bermuda, but that just isn't possible. The solution is to have the wedding here—and I'll offer the library's community room as a location—and have the honeymoon in Bermuda. You don't get to have a destination wedding, but you still get to go to Bermuda, and isn't that what you really wanted?"

I knew it was, because she'd talked about visiting Bermuda for years. The destination wedding angle had been a spark of an idea that had managed to find enough fuel to grow, but it was time to toss a final bucket of water on it and move on.

"Hmm." Aunt Frances slowly slipped the plates into the sink. "You know, you could be right."

"The other real problem," I said with confidence, "isn't directly a wedding problem, but is more of a post-wedding problem. You hate Otto's kitchen and can't stand the idea of cooking in it."

"I'll get used to it," she said stoically. Then she completely undercut the stiff-upper-lip attitude by sighing and adding, "Eventually."

"Or not."

Aunt Frances frowned. "Don't toy with me, young lady. What are you talking about?"

"Last night when you were making hot chocolate, Otto and I had a little chat. No, don't look like that. He said he always suspected you hated the kitchen and was already planning a renovation. He's just going to move it up a little, is all. Give him the name of your favorite kitchen designer and he'll get an appointment as soon as possible."

My aunt stared at me, slack jawed. "You didn't. He didn't. He's not."

"He is," I said. "And if the timing works out— and if you make decisions as fast as you normally do, it should—the work can happen while the two of you are in Bermuda."

Though her jaw moved up and down a couple of times, no words came out. Since I didn't know what else to do, I kept going.

"And if you want, I'll do the project supervision as a wedding present, and send you photos every day." Her expression was unreadable. A funny feeling started forming in the bottom of my stomach, so I quickly added, "Only if you trust me, of course. I mean, you know how I feel about cooking and kitchens and hardware, but supervising your project would be different. All I have to do is pretend to be you, and— *ooff!*"

The air whooshed out of me as my aunt grabbed me and gave me a massive hug. And it was possible, although it was almost too hard to believe, that she was crying.

• • •

Whistling a happy tune, or at least doing something relatively close to whistling, I walked downtown. The sky had cleared, the sun was out, and it was a beautiful winter day in northwest lower Michigan, specifically in Chilson, and there was no place else on earth I'd rather be.

"Hey, Minnie!" Mitchell's head popped out of the toy store. "Come in a minute. Coffee? No? Well . . ." He peered down at me. "You look okay, but I just wanted to make sure. I mean, I heard that . . . that . . ."

"I'm fine," I said. "No frostbite for me or Eddie, and the bad guy is in jail." I gave a few more details and hoped he wouldn't ask any more questions, because I'd have to tell the story at the library and there were only so many times I wanted to talk about it.

"Good to hear. So . . ." He rubbed his face with his hands. "I probably shouldn't bother you with this right now, but have you figured out anything else about Bianca and me? Because I really think she's going to break up with me."

"Mitchell, you've been worried about that since you started dating. What's changed between now and last week?"

He shuffled his feet. "Well, nothing that I know of, but that doesn't mean there's not something."

"Talk to her," I said. "Talking is the only thing that's going to clear this up. The sooner the better."

"Sure, but—"

"Talk!" I said in my Librarian Voice, hardening my heart to his protest. "Do it today," I added in a softer tone, then murmured some words of encouragement, which didn't seem to make a dent in his unhappiness, but he sighed and said he would.

Outside on the sidewalk, I saw that the blue sky had managed to grow even bluer. Smiling up at the boundless infinity, I decided to take the gorgeous morning as a sign that Mitchell's troubles were transitory.

"Morning, Minnie!" A blond woman waved at me energetically. "How are you this fine morning?"

"Hey, Bianca." I smiled. "How's business?"

"Horrible, but I don't care. I'm going to get engaged today," she said cheerfully.

"Um, congratulations." I almost winced, because I was pretty sure I'd sounded like I was asking a question.

Luckily, she didn't seem to notice. "My Mitchell is such a lovable lug," she said, laughing. "I am *so* tired of waiting for him to ask me to marry him. I thought he might pop the question at Christmas, but nothing happened. This morning I woke up and saw this blue sky and decided today was the day. I'm going to propose to him!"

She pulled a small box out of her pocket and opened it, right there on the sidewalk. "These are my great-aunt's rings, the aunt I'm named after. Mitchell might want to buy me something new, but I'd rather wear these than anything from a store. What do you think?"

The question was asked almost shyly. "I think they're wonderful," I said. And they were. The engagement ring's largish diamond sparkled, glinting with the colors of the rainbow, and the tiny diamonds in the wedding band twinkled cheerily in the sunlight. "Mitchell's a lucky man."

"Hah." She snapped the box shut and put it back in her pocket. "I'm the lucky one." She grinned and headed off to her future.

I watched her go, tempted to follow along and watch the fun through the window, but I strongmindedly pushed aside the temptation and went on my way. My coworkers had been texting me all morning and I'd only kept my cell phone from wearing out by telling them I'd be in before noon and would explain everything.

So that's what I did. As soon as I walked in, I pulled Donna aside and promised her a special telling if she'd man the front desk solo for fifteen minutes, then assembled the rest of the interested staff—which was everyone except Graydon, who was closeted upstairs with Trent—in the break room.

After I'd finished, there was a moment of stunned silence. Then the questions began.

Holly came in first by half a syllable. "Is Eddie okay? You would have said if he wasn't, but you didn't say for sure, so I need to hear you say it."

"Have you heard from Darren?" Josh asked. "About the bookmobile, I mean?"

"And how about you?" Kelsey asked, handing me a mug of coffee. "Don't worry, I didn't make this pot. How are you doing? Being cold like that . . ." She shook her head.

Smiling, I answered all their questions. "Eddie is indeed okay. He slept on my feet through the night, and when I left the house, he was still sleeping."

I turned to Josh. "Darren says there is some minor body damage, but the engine and transmission are fine." Which was a huge relief as big expensive repairs were not part of the bookmobile's budget. They should have been, but I'd decided to push what extra bookmobile money there was into a fund for the eventual purchase of a replacement vehicle.

After taking a deep sip of the dark life-giving liquid, I said, "And I'm fine. Really." This was essentially true, but I had briefly considered driving downtown instead of walking.

"What did you tell Graydon?" Holly asked.

When I didn't respond, she asked a bit hesitantly, "Um, Minnie? You did tell him, didn't you?"

I had. But last night's conversation had been odd, filled with hints and undertones I hadn't understood, though at the time I'd put it down to mild hypothermia and fatigue. However, in the bright light of the break room, surrounded by friends, I realized I still didn't understand what he'd been getting at when he'd told me things would be changing. I'd been too tired to ask what he meant, but now I was itching to find out.

First, what would be changing? He couldn't be talking about ending the bookmobile, could he? Or letting staff go? What was so horrible here that he and Trent needed to change anything? Had we done such a terrible job that the board was going to reorganize everything? Sure, there was always room for improvement, but to talk about a need for massive changes was ridiculous!

It had taken all of two seconds for me to stoke my irritation and anger up from embers to a steady flame.

"There you are."

All heads turned. Graydon was in the doorway. "The board is asking for you," he said, nodding at me.

"Right now?" I asked. Technically, I wasn't supposed to be at work for another half hour.

"They've called a special meeting." He sounded almost apologetic, which made the insides of my palms tingle. Why would Graydon need to apologize for anything? There was only one possibility: The board wanted to fire me. I'd crashed the bookmobile too many times, gotten involved in murder too many times, dragged the library's name into the mud . . . it had all added up and now they wanted me out.

I nodded, since my suddenly-dry mouth made it impossible to use actual words, and accompanied by the sympathetic glances of my coworkers, I went up to meet my doom.

I let myself into Rafe's house—*our* house, I reminded myself—and set Eddie's carrier onto the entry mat I'd bought a few weeks ago. "We're here!" I called out, unlatching the wire door.

As I divested myself of outerwear, I watched the feline progress. First, Eddie's nose came out, then his head, ears twitching. One front paw reached out to rest gently on the mat, then the other came out to meet it. Then, in a sudden leap to the floor, all of Eddie was out of the carrier.

"In the kitchen," Rafe called back. "Hope you're hungry."

"How odd," I said to Eddie. "This particular kitchen is the last place I'd expect to find food." But Eddie was too busy sniffing his new environment to pay any attention to anything I said.

I put my coat in the front closet, slipped into moccasins I'd bought last month, and picked

Eddie up, using my legs to lift because he really was a pretty big cat. "Come on, buddy. Let's go see what Rafe hunted and gathered for our sustenance tonight. I wonder if—"

My words came to a halt, just like I did. Eddie and I had walked through the living room and the dining room, and now an amazing sight greeted us.

The last time I'd seen the kitchen, it had been a mostly empty room, empty because the cabinets were still somewhere else, nowhere near completion. There still weren't any cabinets, but in the middle of the room stood a square table and two dining chairs. On top of the table was a white tablecloth, china, and flowers, all lit by the soft glow of candlelight.

Rafe, dressed in paint-splattered jeans and sweatshirt, stood behind one chair. "Would you like to be seated, miss?" He pulled out the chair smoothly.

I grinned and let a squirming Eddie drop to the floor. "Why, yes, I would." Now that my eyes had adjusted to the dim light, I saw that the tablecloth was actually a drop cloth, that the china was made of paper, that the flowers were silk poinsettias that looked suspiciously like the ones from the Christmas wreath we'd bought, and that the candles were stuck into the bottoms of cut-off tubes of caulk. Still, he'd gone to a fair amount of effort, and knowing that he'd done it just for me was making me a little wobbly.

"Dinner will be served momentarily," he said as I sat and hitched forward to the card table. "I hope sandwiches from Fat Boys will be to your liking?"

"How could they not?"

He turned, reached into a white bag that was sitting on a pile of paint cans, pulled out two foam boxes, and uncrated our dinner.

"Mrr."

"Don't worry, young lad," Rafe said. "Yours is next. Hope you're okay without a plate." Out of the white bag came a smaller foam box.

I couldn't quite see the box's contents, although from the sound of it, Eddie was plenty happy with whatever it was. "What did you get him?"

"Piece of fried fish with all the breading taken off."

I rolled my eyes. "You'll probably be his favorite from now on."

"Thought I already was." Rafe sat. "So what happened at the meeting?"

After I'd come back downstairs from my board summons, I'd texted him that there'd been a special meeting and I'd tell him about it over dinner. "It's kind of a long story," I said slowly.

"They're not firing anyone, right?" he asked. "And not getting rid of the bookmobile?"

"No," I said, shaking my head. "That wasn't it at all. It's just . . ." I paused, because old emotions, ones I'd thought had long since faded, were coming back to life. I swallowed. "Remember Stan Larabee?"

"Well, sure." Rafe nodded. "His donation to the library paid for the bookmobile. And he's the . . ." His voice trailed off, because he'd come to the sad part.

"And he's the one," I said, "that I found in that farmhouse almost two years ago, just before he died." It had been a difficult time, but Stan's killer had eventually been brought to justice. And soon after, it turned out that Stan had willed the bulk of his substantial estate to the library. However, the relatives had come out of the woodwork to contest the will, and it had been in the hands of lawyers ever since.

"The estate has finally been settled," I said. "That's why the board had a special meeting. Graydon and Trent have been handling the settlement details, and they were announcing it to the board."

"And they invited you, too?"

I nodded. "Because the bookmobile was mentioned specifically in the will. Stan . . ." A knot in my throat caught my words and I had to cough it out. "Stan wanted to create a foundation with enough capital to buy a new bookmobile every ten years."

And that was why, when I'd first met Trent, he'd been asking so many questions about the bookmobile. Otis, the outgoing president, had handpicked Trent as the new president because Trent's attorney skills included handling large bequests. In addition to the bookmobile, Stan's wishes also included some other odd details that hadn't been explained fully to me, but I wasn't going to worry about those right now.

Rafe put his sandwich down, got up, and came around the table. He pulled me up into a massive hug and twirled me around. "I always knew I liked that Stan," he said, after putting me down and giving me a big smacking kiss.

"Yes," I said, sniffing a bit, but it was a happy sniff. "Me, too."

The board had also apologized for keeping me in the dark about Stan's will, Graydon and Trent especially.

"We know you're the soul of discretion," Trent had said, "but until the decision was final, the attorneys all insisted that the board and the director be the only ones to know."

I'd been fine with that—mostly—and had forgiven them completely when I'd seen the number of zeros on the check the library would receive even after the bookmobile foundation was set up. Soul of discretion I might be, but I wasn't sure I'd be able to keep that kind of news to myself.

Rafe gave me one more hug. "So all's well that ends well, right?" he asked, ushering me into my chair again. "But there's one thing we have to talk about," he said.

"What kind of thing?"

"You came very close to becoming Stewart's second murder victim. I know you're fine, but it was a close call and thinking about it scares me."

Rafe's face, normally full of humor and mirth, was filled with worry and concern. "You said you can't walk away from friends who ask for help. I understand that. And I love you for it. But we have to think up a different way to do this."

I frowned. "To do what?"

"To fight crime and stuff."

" 'And stuff'?"

He shrugged. "Don't want to leave out any possibilities. So here's what I'm thinking. If a friend comes to one of us with a problem, big or small, we work on the solution together. Me and you. You and me. We're a team."

I smiled, my heart full to bursting with love for this wonderful, though sometimes annoying, man. "A team. You and me."

"Mrr!"

Without missing a beat, Rafe made the necessary correction. "You and me and Eddie."

My furry friend jumped onto my lap and I hugged him tight. "The best team of all," I said. "The absolute best."

Books are produced in the United States using U.S.-based materials

Books are printed using a revolutionary new process called THINKtech™ that lowers energy usage by 70% and increases overall quality

Books are durable and flexible because of Smyth-sewing

Paper is sourced using environmentally responsible foresting methods and the paper is acid-free

Center Point Large Print
600 Brooks Road / PO Box 1
Thorndike, ME 04986-0001 USA

(207) 568-3717

US & Canada:
1 800 929-9108
www.centerpointlargeprint.com